Praise for Henning Mankell and

CHRONICLER OF THE WINDS

"Henning Mankell is an addictive writer."

—*Los Angeles Times Book Review*

"Elegant and artful. . . . [Mankell] continues to understand, and probe, the underside of everyday living. The result is writing that walks a line between ephemeral and everlasting."

—*The Washington Post*

"Mankell writes eloquently of the realities of poverty and violence without becoming sugary or didactic. . . . An expert craftsman."

—*The Observer* (London)

"Henning Mankell is a most remarkable man. . . . A talented artist who with strokes of his brush evokes the dampness and cold of Sweden and also the smoke-filled desert townships in South Africa."

—Archbishop Desmond Tutu

"Mankell uses all his stories to address the most urgent problems of civilization."

—*Newsday*

Henning Mankell

CHRONICLER OF THE WINDS

Internationally bestselling novelist and playwright Henning Mankell has received the German Tolerance Prize and the U.K.'s Golden Dagger Award and has been nominated for a *Los Angeles Times* Book Prize three times. His Kurt Wallander mysteries have been published in thirty-three countries and consistently top the bestseller lists in Europe. He divides his time between Sweden and Maputo, Mozambique, where he has worked as the director of Teatro Avenida since 1985.

www.henningmankell.com

ALSO BY HENNING MANKELL

Depths

KURT WALLANDER MYSTERIES

Faceless Killers

The Dogs of Riga

The White Lioness

Sidetracked

The Fifth Woman

One Step Behind

Firewall

The Man Who Smiled

The Return of the Dancing Master

A KURT AND LINDA WALLANDER MYSTERY

Before the Frost

CHRONICLER
OF THE WINDS

Henning Mankell

Chronicler of the Winds

TRANSLATED
FROM THE SWEDISH
BY
Tiina Nunnally

VINTAGE BOOKS
A Division of Random House, Inc.
New York

FIRST VINTAGE BOOKS EDITION, JUNE 2007

This is a work of fiction. Names, characters, places, and incidents either are the product of the author's imagination or are used fictitiously. Any resemblance to actual persons, living or dead, events, or locales is entirely coincidental.

Cataloging-in-Publication Data for *Chronicler of the Winds* is on file at the Library of Congress.

Vintage ISBN: 978-0-307-28044-2

www.vintagebooks.com

Printed in the United States of America
10 9 8 7 6 5 4 3 2 1

The human being has two eyes;
one sees only what moves in ephemeral time,
the other
what is eternal and divine.

ANGELUS SILESIUS

If this is the best of all possible worlds,
what must the others be like?

VOLTAIRE, *Candide*

When there were no depths,
I was brought forth;
when there were no fountains
abounding with water.

Proverbs 8:24

CHRONICLER
OF THE WINDS

Prologue: José Antonio Maria Vaz

On a rooftop of sun-scorched, reddish clay on a sultry, humid night beneath the starry tropical skies, I who bear the name José Antonio Maria Vaz stand waiting for the world to end. I am filthy and feverish, my clothes are hanging in tatters, as if they were in wild flight from my gaunt body. I have flour in my pockets, which for me is more precious than gold. A year ago I was still somebody, a baker; whereas now I am nobody, a beggar roaming aimlessly beneath the searing sun in the daytime and then spending the endless nights on a desolate rooftop. But even beggars possess traits that give them an identity, that distinguish them from all the others on the street corners who hold out their hands, as if they wanted to give them away or sell their fingers, one by one. José Antonio Maria Vaz is the vagrant who became known as the "Chronicler of the Winds." Day in and day out, my lips move without cease, as if I were telling a story to which no one has ever bothered to listen. As if I have finally accepted that the monsoon which sweeps in from the sea is my only listener, always attentive, like an old priest waiting patiently for the confession to come to an end.

At night I retreat to this deserted rooftop, since here I feel I gain both space and a viewpoint. The constellations are mute, they do not applaud me, but their eyes flash and I feel as if I can speak straight into the ear of eternity. And I can look down and see the city spread out before me, the city of night, where uneasy fires flicker and dance, unseen dogs laugh, and I wonder about all the people down there asleep, breathing and dreaming and making love, while I stand on my roof and talk about a person who no longer exists.

I, José Antonio Maria Vaz, am also part of this city which clings to the slopes down the wide estuary. The buildings perch like monkeys along the steep banks, and for each day that passes, the number of people living there seems to swell. They come wandering from the unplumbed interior, from the savannah and the remote, dead forests, down toward the coast where the city lies. They settle there and do not seem to notice all the malevolent glances that meet them. No one can say with certainty what they will live on or where they will find a roof over their heads. They are swallowed up by the city, become a part of it. And every day more strangers arrive, all with their parcels and baskets; the statuesque black women with enormous cloth bundles atop their noble heads, walking along the horizon like lines of small black dots. More and more children are born, more buildings clamber along the steep slopes, to be washed away when the clouds turn black and the hurricanes rage like murderous bandits. This is the way it has been for as long as anyone can remember, and there are many who lie awake at night, wondering how it will end.

When will the city crash down the slopes and be swallowed by the sea?

When will the weight of all the people finally become too great?

When will the world come to an end?

Once I too, José Antonio Maria Vaz, would lie awake at night and ask myself these questions.

But no longer. Not since I met Nelio and carried him up to the roof and watched him die.

The anxiety that I sometimes felt is now gone. Or rather, I have come to understand that there is a crucial difference between feeling afraid and feeling anxious.

That was something else that Nelio explained to me.

"If you're afraid, it's like you're suffering from an insatiable hunger," he said. "But if you're anxious, you can fight off your anxiety."

I think about his words, and I now know that he was right. I can stand here and look out over the nighttime city, the fires flickering uneasily, and I can recall everything he told me during those nine nights that I spent with him and watched him die.

This rooftop is a vital part of the story. I feel as if I were at the bottom of the sea; I have sunk down and can go no further. I am at the bottom of my own story; it was here, on this roof, that it all began and it all ended.

Sometimes I imagine my task to be this: that for all eternity I will wander at the bottom, on this roof, and direct my words to the stars. Precisely that will be my task, forever.

So here is my strange story, a story impossible to forget.

It was on that night a year ago, near the end of November, when the moon was full and the night was clear after the heavy rains, that I placed Nelio on the filthy mattress where nine days later, as dawn broke, he would die. Since he had already lost a great deal of blood, the bandages—which I did my best to fashion from strips that I tore from my own worn clothing—did little good. He knew long before I did that soon he would no longer exist.

That was also when everything started over, as if a peculiar new way of measuring time was suddenly established. I remember that quite clearly, even though more than a year has passed since then and many other things have happened in my life.

I remember the moon against the dark sky.

I remember it as a reflection of Nelio's pale face on which salty beads of sweat glittered as the life left his body slowly, almost cautiously, as if trying not to wake someone who was asleep.

Something important came to an end on that early morning, after the ninth night, when Nelio died. I have a hard time explaining what I mean. But at some moments in my life I feel as if I am surrounded by a vast emptiness. As if I were inside an enormous room made of invisible membranes from which I cannot escape.

That was how I felt on the morning when Nelio lay dying, abandoned by everyone, with me as the only witness.

Afterward, when it was over, I did as he had asked me to do.

I carried his body down the winding stairs to the bakery, where the heat was always so intense that I never got used to it.

I was the only one there at night. The huge oven was hot, awaiting the bread that would soon be baked for the hungry day to follow. I shoved his body into the oven, closed the door, and waited for exactly one hour. That's how long it would take, he had said, for his body to disappear. When I opened the door again, there was nothing left. His spirit blew past me like a cool gust from the heat of the inferno, and then there was nothing more.

*

I went back up to the roof. I stayed there until night fell again. And it was then, beneath the stars, in the faint moonlight, with the gentle breeze from the Indian Ocean brushing my face, in the midst of my grief, that I realized I was the one who had to tell Nelio's story.

Quite simply, there was no one else who could do it. No one but me. No one at all.

And the story had to be told. It could not be left lying there like some abandoned and cast-off memory in the storerooms that are housed in every human brain.

The fact is that Nelio was not merely a poor, filthy street boy. Above all else, he was an unusual person, elusive and enigmatic like a rare bird that everyone talks about but which no one has actually seen. Though he was only ten years old when he died, he possessed the experience and wisdom of someone who had lived to be a hundred. Nelio—if that was his real name, because from time to time he would surprise me by calling himself something else—wrapped himself in a magnetic field that no one could see or penetrate. Everyone treated him with respect, even the brutal policemen and the always nervous Indian shopkeepers. Many sought his advice or hovered timidly nearby in the hope that some scrap of his mysterious powers would be transferred to them.

And now Nelio was dead.

Sunk in a deep fever, he had laboriously sweated out his last breath.

A solitary wave traveled across the sea of the world, and then it was finished and the silence was terrifying in its emptiness. I stood looking up at the starry sky and thought that nothing could ever be the same.

I knew what many people thought. I had thought the same thing myself. That Nelio was not really human. That he was a god. One of the ancient, forgotten gods who had defiantly, perhaps foolishly, returned to earth and slipped inside Nelio's thin body. Or if he wasn't a god, then he was at the least a saint. A street-child saint.

And now he was dead. Gone.

The gentle breeze from the sea which had brushed my face suddenly felt cold and ominous. I gazed across the dark city that was clinging to the slopes above the sea. I saw the flickering fires and the solitary street lamps where the moths were dancing, and I thought: This is where Nelio lived for a brief time, here in our midst. And I am the only one who knows his whole story. I was the one he confided in after he was shot, and I carried him up here to the roof and laid him on the filthy mattress, from which he would never rise again.

"It's not that I'm afraid of being forgotten," he told me. "It's so that the rest of you won't forget who *you* are."

Nelio reminded us who we really are. Human beings, each of us bearing secret powers we know nothing about. Nelio was a remarkable person. His presence made all of us feel remarkable.

That was his secret.

It is night by the Indian Ocean.

Nelio is dead.

And however unlikely it may sound, it seemed to me that he died without ever being afraid.

How can that be possible? How can a ten-year-old boy die

without betraying even a glimmer of terror at not being allowed to partake of life any longer?

I don't understand it. Not at all.

I, an adult, cannot think about death without feeling an icy hand around my throat.

But Nelio only smiled. Clearly he had yet another secret that he would not share with the rest of us. It was odd, since he had been so generous with the few possessions he had, whether it was the dirty shirts made of Indian cotton that he always wore, or any of his unexpected thoughts.

The fact that he no longer exists I take as a sign that the world will soon come to an end.

Or am I mistaken?

I stand here on the roof and think about the first time I saw him lying on the filthy floor, struck down by the bullets of the demented killer.

I call on the soft night wind blowing in from the sea to help me remember.

Nelio once asked me, "Do you know what the wind tastes like?"

I didn't know what to answer. Does the wind really have a taste?

Nelio thought so.

"Mysterious spices," he said—I think it was on the seventh night. "That tell us about people and events far away. That we can't see. But that we can sense if we draw the wind deep into our mouths and then eat it."

That's how Nelio was. He thought it was possible to eat the wind.

And that the wind could dull a person's hunger.

Now when I try to recall what I heard on those nine nights I spent with Nelio, it occurs to me that my memory is neither better nor worse than anyone else's.

But I also know that I am living in a time when people are more likely to forget than to remember. For that reason I understand more clearly my own fear, and why in fact I am waiting for the world to end. Human beings exist to create and to share their good memories. But if we are to be honest with ourselves, we should recognize that these are dark times, as dark as the city beneath my feet. The stars shine reluctantly on our neglected earth, and memories of good times are so few that the vast rooms in our brains where memories are stored stand empty and locked.

It is in fact quite odd for me to be saying these things.

I am not a pessimist. I laugh much more often than I cry.

Even though I am now a beggar and a vagrant, I have retained the baker's joyful heart.

I see that I'm having trouble explaining what I mean. If you have baked bread as I have in a hot and suffocating bakery since the age of six, then words might not come so easily to you either.

I never went to school. I learned to read from scraps of old newspapers, often so old that when the city was mentioned it still bore the now discarded colonial name. I learned to read while we waited for the bread to bake in the ovens. It was the old master baker Fernando who taught me. I can still remember quite clearly all those nights when he raged and cursed at my laziness.

"Letters and words don't come to a person," he would say with a sigh. "A person has to go to *them*."

In the end I learned. I learned to deal with words, although from a distance and always with the feeling that I was not truly worthy of them. Words are still strangers to me. At least when I am trying to explain what I think or feel. But I have to try. I can't wait any longer. A year has already passed.

*

And yet I still haven't spoken of the dazzling white sand, the rustling palm trees, or the sharks that are occasionally seen just beyond the crumbling jetty in the harbor.

But I will do that later.

Right now I'm going to talk about the remarkable Nelio. The boy who came to the city from nowhere. The boy who made himself a home inside an abandoned statue in one of the city's plazas.

And this is where I'm going to start my story.

Everything begins with the wind, the mysterious and enticing wind that sweeps in over our city from the eternally wandering Indian Ocean.

I, José Antonio Maria Vaz, a lonely man on a rooftop under the starry tropical sky, have a story to tell.

The First Night

When the shots were fired on that fateful night and I found Nelio soaked in his own blood, I had been working at the bakery of the confused and half-crazed Dona Esmeralda for several years. No one had lasted there as long as I had.

Dona Esmeralda was an amazing woman; everyone in the city—and they all knew who she was—either secretly admired her or wrote her off as insane. When Nelio, without her knowledge, lay on the roof of the bakery and died, she was more than ninety years old. Some claimed that she was a hundred, but no one could say for sure. With Dona Esmeralda, nothing was certain. It was as if she had existed for all time; she was one with the city and its founding.

No one could remember her ever being young. She had always been ninety or perhaps a hundred years old. She had always driven around in her ancient car at high speed with the top down, veering from one side of the street to the other. Her clothes had always been made of voluminous silk; her hats were fastened under her wrinkled chin with broad ribbons. It was explained to strangers—who barely managed to avoid being run over by her wild careering—that even though she had always been exceedingly old, she was the youngest daughter of the infamous municipal governor Dom Joaquim Leonardo dos Santos, who during his scandal-ridden life had filled the city with innumerable equestrian statues in the various central plazas.

Countless stories circulated about Dom Joaquim, particularly about the vast number of illegitimate children he had fathered. With his wife, the birdlike Dona Celestina, he had had three daughters; Esmeralda was the one who resembled him most, in temperament if not in appearance. Dom Joaquim belonged to one of the oldest colonial families that had come from the other side of the sea in the middle of the previous century. His family had quickly become one of the most preeminent in the country. Dom Joaquim's brothers had won positions through their prospecting for gems in the remote provinces, as big-game hunters, prelates and military officers.

At a young age, Dom Joaquim had cast himself into the chaotic arena of local politics. Since the country was governed as a province from across the sea, the locally appointed governors could generally do as they pleased; no one had any opportunity to keep an eye on what they were up to. On those few occasions when suspicion grew too great, government officials would be dispatched from across the sea to find out what was actually going on within the colonial administration. Once Dom Joaquim filled their offices with snakes; another time he installed a number of wild drummers in a neighboring building, whereupon the government officials either flew into a rage or lapsed into a deep silence and then departed as soon as they could find passage to Europe. Their reports had always been reassuring: all was well in the colony. In recognition of which, Dom Joaquim would stuff little cloth bags of gemstones into their pockets as he bade them farewell at the dock.

Dom Joaquim was first elected municipal governor when he

was no more than twenty. His opponent, a kindly and credulous old colonel, withdrew from the race after Dom Joaquim cunningly spread a rumor that the man had been convicted of unspecified crimes in his youth, when he was still living on the other side of the sea. The accusations were false, but the colonel realized that he would never be able to extinguish the rumors and gave up. As in all other elections, fraud was the fundamental organizational assumption, and Dom Joaquim was the winner by a majority that far exceeded the number of registered voters. The principal element of his campaign was a promise, if he were elected, to increase dramatically the number of local holidays, which he implemented immediately after he had been sworn in and appeared for the first time on the steps of the governor's residence wearing the plumed tricorn hat, the symbol of his new, democratically achieved eminence.

Dom Joaquim's first act as newly elected governor was to order a large balcony to be built on the façade of the palace from which he could address the citizenry on appropriate occasions. Since he had been legitimately elected, he took pains to ensure that no one could challenge his position as governor, and he was reelected over the next sixty years by an ever growing majority, in spite of the fact that the population decreased drastically during this period. When at last he died, however, he had not been seen in public for a long time. He was so confused by then and had sunk so far into the haze of old age that sometimes he imagined he was dead, and at night he would sleep in a coffin standing next to his wide bed in the governor's palace. But no one had the courage to question the wisdom of his continuing as governor; everyone feared him, and when he did finally die—hanging halfway out of his coffin, as if he had wanted to crawl out to the balcony one last time and look over the city which he had transformed beyond recognition during his long years in power—no one dared do anything until several days later when, in the stifling heat, he began to smell.

He was Dona Esmeralda's father, and she was just like him. When she raced through the city in her open convertible, she would see everywhere the mighty statues crowding the plazas, and every one of them reminded her of her father. Dom Joaquim had always been on the lookout for the least sign of revolutionary discontent and unrest. In his early years he had appointed a body of secret police, a unit which everyone knew about but which officially did not exist. Their only task was to mix with the people and listen for the tiniest hints of unrest. At the same time, Dom Joaquim took quick action whenever a revolution in a neighboring country threw the current despots into prison, drove them into exile, or put them in front of a firing squad. By then he would have already offered a price for the statues that the enraged populace was toppling to the ground. He paid handsomely for them, and they were transported to the city by ship and by rail. The old inscriptions were filed off, and Dom Joaquim ordered his own family name to be engraved on the statues. Since his ancestors were of simple peasant stock from the Mediterranean plains, he felt no compunction about inventing a new family tree for himself. In this way the city became filled with statues of former generals belonging to his family. Since revolutions in the neighboring countries were a regular occurrence, the influx of statues became so overwhelming that Dom Joaquim was forced to build new plazas to make room for his purchases. At the time of his death, every conceivable space in the city was taken up with British, German, French and Portuguese monuments to individuals who were now included in the multitude of generals, philosophers and explorers with which Dom Joaquim, in his inexhaustible fancy, had endowed his lineage.

His daughter, the eternally ninety-year-old Esmeralda, would rush past all these memories of Dom Joaquim and his life in her frantic quest for a meaning to her own life. She had been married four times, never for more than a year since she would almost at once grow bored, and the men she had chosen would flee, terrified of her violent temper. She never had any children—although there were rumors that she had a son concealed somewhere who would one day make himself known and get himself elected governor as his grandfather's successor. But no son ever turned up, and Dona Esmeralda's life continued to shift course in her restless search for something that she never seemed able to define.

During this time in the life of the city, which might also be called the era of Dona Esmeralda, colonial war had finally spread to this country too, one of the last on the whole African continent to be so affected. Those young men who had decided to fulfil their inescapable historical destinies and liberate the land from the ever weakening colonial power had crossed the border to the north and entered the neighboring country, which had already overthrown its past and established its own military bases, its own university. Later, when the time seemed ripe, the men came back over the border, now fully armed with weapons and self-confidence.

The war started on a dark September evening when a local *chefe de posto* was shot in the thumb by a nineteen-year-old revolutionary, who would later become the first military commander-in-chief of the independent nation. During the first five years of the war, the country on the other side of the sea refused even to acknowledge that it was going on. In the increasingly transparent propaganda, the revolutionary army was labeled as misguided terrorists, deranged *criminosos*, and the populace was exhorted to grab them vigorously by the ears instead of listening to their malevolent talk about another time and another world in the offing. Gradually, however, the colonial power was forced to acknowledge that the young men were extremely determined and that they quite obviously had the ear of the disloyal public. A colonial army was hastily dispatched; the soldiers began haphazardly bombing the areas where the revolutionary liberators were believed to have their bases, but without fully appreciating it, they suffered one defeat after another. To the very end, those who had come to the country as colonizers refused to accept what was happening. Even when the young revolutionaries surrounded the capital and stood just a few kilometers outside the black townships, the white colonizers continued to administer and to plan for a future that would never be realized.

Only afterward, when their defeat was a fact and the country had proclaimed its independence, were the long rows of white headstones in the cemeteries discovered. There lay the young boys, often no more than eighteen or nineteen years old, who had come across the sea to take part in a war they never understood, to be killed by enemies they had never even glimpsed. Chaos erupted in the city. Many of the colonizers fled for their lives, leaving behind their homes, their cars, their gardens, their shoes and their black mistresses; trampling over one another in the departure hall at the airport and fighting for passage on the ships about to leave the harbor. Those with sufficient foresight had exchanged their money and possessions for gemstones, now hanging in little cloth bags inside their sweaty shirts. The others left everything behind and departed the country cursing the injustice of the revolutionaries, who had stripped them of all they owned.

Although Dona Esmeralda had never been interested in political matters and was at the time at least eighty years old, she understood early on, presumably from sheer instinct, that the young revolutionaries were going to win the war. A new age would arise, and she would be forced to choose which side to be on. It was not difficult for her to grasp that she belonged with the young revolutionaries. With a mixture of anger and joy she would gladly fight the heavy-footed bureaucracy, which seemed to be the only thing the colonial power had bestowed upon its distant province. She put on the darkest hat she owned, possibly meaning to camouflage her treacherous intentions, and drove her car out of the city, taking the north road. She passed through a number of military roadblocks, where the guards tried in vain to make her turn back, warning that she was now entering areas controlled by bloodthirsty revolutionaries who would confiscate her car, tear off her hat, and then slit her throat. When she continued regardless, they concluded that she was crazy, and it was there, at those roadblocks, that the rumor was born which definitively pronounced Dona Esmeralda to be mad.

It is true that she was stopped by the young revolutionaries, but they neither tore off her hat nor slit her throat. On the contrary, they treated her kindly and with respect. At one of the nearby encampments a commandant questioned her as to why she was traveling all alone in her big open car. She stated briefly that she wanted to enlist in the revolutionary army, and she pulled out of her handbag a rusty old cavalry pistol that had belonged to her father. The young commandant, whose name was Lorenzo and who would later end up in disgrace because of a ferocious lust for other men's women, sent her on to a base sixty miles farther into the bush to an officer higher up the chain of command who would be better able to determine what should be done about Dona Esmeralda.

This man, whose name was Marcelino and who was a brigadier

general in the revolutionary army, was familiar with the old governor Dom Joaquim. He welcomed Dona Esmeralda, gave her a uniform cap in exchange for her motley hat, and personally handled her briefing in the ideological doctrines of the revolution. Then he sent Dona Esmeralda to a mobile field hospital, where he thought she might do the most good. Under the direction of a team of Cuban doctors she soon learned to assist with complicated operations. That was where she stayed for the rest of the colonial war. When the new leaders at last made their jubilant entry into the city, the populace watched with astonishment as the convertible, which they recognized at once but which they had not seen on the streets for a number of years, reappeared with Dona Esmeralda driving and with one of the revolutionary leaders standing behind her, waving. In the chaos that prevailed during that intoxicating time after the liberation, she was asked by the new president what role she would like to play in the revolutionary transformation of the old society which was now being initiated.

"I want to start a theater," she replied without hesitation.

Surprised, the president tried to persuade her to assume a role of greater revolutionary moment, but she was insistent. When the president saw that he would not be able to change her mind, he issued a decree, which he later had the Minister of Culture confirm, stating that Dona Esmeralda would be in charge of the city's only theater building.

The new era had begun. Dona Esmeralda was so preoccupied with her new life that she didn't seem to notice that the statues, which her father had gone to so much trouble to acquire upon the demise of various dictators, had once again been toppled and were being transported to an old fortress, where they were either stored or melted down. The city, which up until then had been branded by her invented ancestors, was now transformed without her noticing it. She spent all her time inside the dark and decrepit theater, which had long stood abandoned. It had fallen into a sewer-like condition; the stench was horrific, and the rats, as plump as cats, ruled the stage where old sets stood and rotted.

With furious energy Dona Esmeralda declared war on the rats and the stench and then threw herself into a strenuous campaign, resolved to reconquer the theater, which sat like the wreck of a ship in the sludge. No one who saw her during this time failed to observe that Dona Esmeralda's madness had now become full-blown. With disgust and poorly concealed contempt, people decided that she was expending her energies on an absolutely useless task, the greatest sin that anyone could commit. After a while she managed to win the help of some young people who were both unemployed and ignorant of what a theater was all about. Dona Esmeralda used to say by way of explanation that it was "like film without a projector." When she held out the illusory possibility that the young people might one day try their skill on the stage—which was still half buried in the overflowing sewer—she managed to persuade them to hitch up their skirts, roll up their trouser legs, and slog around in the muck, chasing the rats with sticks and lugging out all the rotting stage sets.

After six months she had made so much headway that she had reclaimed both the stage and the hall with its rickety red plastic seats, and she was finally able to get the electrical wiring to function as well. It was a big moment when she turned on the lights for the first time. Two thirty-year-old spotlights simultaneously exploded with powerful blasts. But for Dona Esmeralda they were like saluting rockets. Now she could at last see her theater. And what she saw convinced her that she was right, although nobody else had any idea what was in her mind.

Six months more and she had gathered around her a group

of similarly inclined people, and she had written a play about a *halakawuma* who was constantly giving the king bad advice. It was a play that took more than seven hours to perform. Dona Esmeralda built the sets, sewed the costumes, directed the actors, and played those parts herself which she had not been able to find anyone else to fill.

On a December evening the theater was to be re-inaugurated. She had sent invitations to the president and the minister of culture, who was not entirely pleased that Dona Esmeralda had refused the good advice of the ministry's many bureaucrats about how the theater might best be run. A strong rainstorm shorted out the electrical circuits just as the performance was about to begin. The president had sent his regrets, but the corpulent former shoemaker, Adelinho Manjate, who was now the minister of culture by virtue of his success as a dancer during his years as a revolutionary soldier, *was* in attendance. The performance was delayed for several hours. The rain poured through the roof onto the festively clad but increasingly disgruntled audience.

It was past ten o'clock by the time Dona Esmeralda was able to switch on the spotlights again and the first actor, who had forgotten his lines, stepped onto the stage. The performance turned out to be a peculiar experience. It went on until dawn the following morning. None of those present, perhaps least of all the actors, fully understood what the play was about. On the other hand, none of those in attendance ever forgot what they had been part of. Dona Esmeralda, finally alone on the stage at first light, was filled with that singular sense of joy which only those who have achieved the impossible can feel. She thought nostalgically of her father, the old governor, who had not been there to witness this proud moment, and then she realized she was hungry. During the past year she had scarcely had time to eat.

She went out into the city. The rain had stopped and there was a fresh scent from the blooming acacia trees that lined the main streets. She regarded the people she met with curiosity, as if she were noticing for the first time that she was not alone in the city. And she discovered that all of the statues with which her father had adorned the plazas had disappeared. For a moment she felt old, sad that the new era clearly meant that nothing would remain as before. But her triumph was stronger than her sorrow, and she cast off her melancholy thoughts. She stopped at a café, sat down at a table, and ordered a glass of cognac and some bread. As she pondered how she was going to find the money to continue to operate the theater, she chewed on the bread. That was when it occurred to her that the old ticket office and the abandoned café in the foyer of the theater could be revamped as a bakery. By selling bread she could earn the money she needed. She ate the rest of the bread, stood up, and returned to the theater to start the process of cleaning up, to make room for the dough blender and the ovens. To obtain funds for the necessary investments, she sold her car to an official at the British embassy, and three months later she opened the doors to the bakery.

I, José Antonio Maria Vaz, came to Dona Esmeralda as soon as the rumor spread through the city that she was going to open a bakery. At that time I was working for the baker Felisberto in the harbor district, and I had no thoughts of quitting. And yet, one afternoon after work, I couldn't resist going over to see Dona Esmeralda, who was just then hiring bakers. A long line wound its way out of the side door of the theater. I went to the end of the line, even though I knew it was pointless. But I couldn't resist the temptation to stop and, for once in my life, come close to the strange Dona Esmeralda. When it was finally my turn, I was admitted and led into a room where the sparkling stainless-steel dough blender stood waiting to begin its work. Dona Esmeralda was sitting on a low stool in the middle of the room, wearing a long silken gown and a wide-brimmed, flower-patterned hat. She gave me a solemn look. There was something inquisitive about her glance, as if she were asking herself whether she had met me before. Then she nodded abruptly, as if she had made an important decision.

"You look like a baker," she said. "Do you have a name?"

"José Antonio Maria Vaz," I told her. "I've been baking bread since I was six years old."

I told her where I was working, but I wasn't sure whether she heard what I said.

"How much is Felisberto paying you?" she interrupted me.

"I earn 130,000," I said.

"I'll give you 129,000," she replied. "If you really want to work here, you'll make do with less than what you're getting from Felisberto."

I nodded, and so I was hired. That was more than five years ago, but I can still vividly recall the moment. Dona Esmeralda asked me to get started at once. She wanted me to help her with the plans to buy flour and sugar and yeast and butter and eggs. During those long days and nights when we worked together before the bakery opened, she told me about her life. That's how I know all that I know about her. It was through her that I began to understand something about the city in which I live, and about the country that is mine.

Whether Dona Esmeralda was crazy or not, I can't say. On the other hand, I can certainly attest that she possessed an energy and determination that I had never before encountered. The people around her could collapse with fatigue, just from watching her at work in her theater and bakery. Although she was then between eighty and ninety years old, she never rested. Many nights she didn't even bother to go home; she would simply curl up on some flour sacks, call goodnight to the bakers, and then get up again after half an hour, bursting with renewed energy, as if she had awakened from a long night's sleep. Sometimes, as we waited for the bread to rise, we would discuss when and what Dona Esmeralda actually ate. She was always scraping off the dough from around the edges of the dough blender with her fingers. No one had ever seen her eat anything else. On the other hand, she always had a bottle of cognac nearby. We suspected that it was from the bottle that she drew the strength she needed, but since we were simple people who had never had either the money or the opportunity to taste foreign distilled drinks, always celebrating instead with *tontonto,* we used to discuss whether her bottles might also contain something that kept a person young. Maybe Dona Esmeralda had a *curandeiro* who infused her drinks with magical powers.

When I, José Antonio Maria Vaz, first came to Dona Esmeralda's bakery, which she had named the Holy Bread Bakery, I had just turned eighteen. I was a trained baker, although I was still lacking my master's certificate. But I had been baking bread since I was six years old.

It was my father who took me over to my uncle, Master Fernando, who ran a bakery in the African *bairro* out past the airport. My father, who all his life long was an extremely impractical man, had one day looked at my hands and decided that they were suited for shaping croissants. I would find both my future and my livelihood as a baker. Like almost all other Africans, we were poor. I grew up during the time when no one had yet heard anything of the young revolutionaries who had already gone across the northern border. No one could possibly imagine that anyone would ever question the power of the whites who ruled our country and our lives, and even less that one day the whites would have to flee head over heels, never to return. For generations we had been forced to bow our heads in submission. Even though I now know that oppression can never become a habit, and even though back then opposition did exist in the silence leveled at all the whites who ruled over our lives, there was still no one except the young revolutionaries who seriously believed that anything could be changed. On many occasions, and when he was certain that no white person could hear what he said, my father, who spent his long life talking incessantly, would curse those who had come across the sea and forced us to work on their tea plantations and in their fruit orchards. But it was a protest that tied itself into complicated knots and never led to anything but more words.

For forty years my father sat under a tree in the open area among the sheds and hovels of the *bairro*. He sat in the shade and talked with the other unemployed men while he waited for the food to be ready which my mother prepared over an open fire. He talked without stopping for all those years; my mother listened with resignation and never with more than half an ear to what he said, and yet I think it was his beautiful voice that had once made her fall in love with him. They had eleven children; I was the eighth, and seven of us grew up and outlived both our parents. My father, Zeca Antonio, came originally to the city from one of the remote western provinces, and he always talked about how he would one day take his family back there. He met my mother, Graça, almost as soon as he arrived in the city. She was born here, and she was enchanted by all his words. They built their shabby hut in the *bairro* that had sprung up in connection with the construction of the new airport. Neither of them could read or write, and of us children, only one of my sisters and I ever learned to handle spelling and words.

It wasn't until later, after the young revolutionaries had come to the city and Dom Joaquim's equestrian statues were toppled from their pedestals, that people became truly incensed. As if they saw for the first time the centuries-old injustices to which they had been subjected; and they assumed that the liberation, the freedom that the young revolutionaries talked about, meant the freedom not to work. When they realized that freedom meant they would have to work just as hard, but now they would also have to think for themselves and plan the work that had to be carried out, there were many people who deep in their souls felt thoroughly bewildered. Several years after the whites had disappeared back across the sea, I often heard my father complain about the actions of the young revolutionaries just as quietly as he had once criticized the conditions of the colonial period. And in all seriousness he would express longings for the good old days, when there was law and order and the whites still decided what thoughts needed to be thought. It was a confusing time, when we suddenly had to stop saying *patrão* and call everyone *camarada* instead. It was a time when everything was supposed to change, but everything stayed the same, only in a different way.

That was also when the long civil war broke out. The young revolutionaries, who had become middle-aged and rode around in black Mercedes escorted by the shrill sirens of motorcycle police, called the others in the war *bandidos armados*. From what we could understand, it was the whites who had fled and now dreamed of returning who stood behind them. They had formed a bandit army of malcontent blacks. One day they would return and put Dom Joaquim's statues back in the plazas, they would retake power and decide what thoughts people should think, and the middle-aged revolutionaries would be forced once more to cross the northern border. In the name of these whites, the bandits committed terrifying acts, and we all harbored a great fear that they would win the war.

It wasn't until the year I met Nelio that the war ended. A peace agreement was signed, and the leader of the bandits came to the city and was embraced by the president. The whites had already returned. But they were different whites; they came from countries with peculiar names, and they did not come to chase us back to the tea plantations and fruit orchards. They came to help us rebuild everything that had been destroyed during the war. Many of them bought their bread from Dona Esmeralda. We knew that our bread was good. If anything ever went wrong with the bread, Dona Esmeralda would close up the bakery at once and refuse to open it again until the bread had regained its former quality.

I quickly learned to enjoy working for Dona Esmeralda, though she could be capricious and temperamental, and she seldom had money to pay our wages when the last day of the month came around. The proximity of the theater was something that gave a particular substance to my life and filled it with new and unusual experiences. A short time after the legendary premiere, Dona Esmeralda had formed an ensemble that was not supposed to do anything but perform plays. That alone, in the eyes of many, was a scandalous excess on her part. Did she really think that people should be paid for standing on the stage a few evenings each week? Could a theater be anything but a hobby? Dona Esmeralda, of course, passionately defended her efforts, and she gathered around her all those people who were regarded as the most talented actors in the country. In the daytime they rehearsed the new plays, and at night they gave their performances.

A winding staircase led from the bakery up to the theater's roof. Right under the roofing sheets we could crawl through a duct that was once used for the huge air-conditioning machines. Through a hatchway we could then slip down into a room where an old film projector stood, like some sort of prehistoric beast. Through the peepholes in the wall we could see what was happening on the lit-up stage. Dona Esmeralda knew that when we bakers had time we used to watch the rehearsals; she encouraged us to do so and to tell her what we thought about the play we had seen. And she often told us that if we were quiet she would let us sit in the upper galleries when a new play was so near completion that they were ready to do a dress rehearsal.

As a baker who only learned to read when I was fifteen—thanks to old newspapers and Master Fernando's stubborn battle with my laziness—naturally I cannot presume to judge the dramas that Dona Esmeralda and her actors staged. And yet I think I could tell that many of the young actors were talented; at least those of us who worked in the bakery believed in their performances, believed in the people or animals they played, and we often laughed. But I think I can also say that Dona Esmeralda was not a good playwright. We would often crawl through the shaft and listen to Dona Esmeralda and the actors squabbling. The actors didn't understand what she meant in her plays, and Dona Esmeralda was angry because she hadn't managed to explain to the actors what she wanted. Terrible arguments would erupt, as if the rehearsals themselves were dramatic performances. But they always ended with Dona Esmeralda getting her way. She was the one paying the actors' wages, she was the one with the greatest stamina. Those of us who worked in the bakery felt as if we were especially privileged—which partly compensated for the wages which occasionally failed to materialize altogether or were exceedingly late—because we had this opportunity to look into the worlds that were continually being created and obliterated on the stage that Dona Esmeralda had reclaimed from the stinking sewers.

There were moments of great magic on that small stage, illuminated by the ancient spotlights, which would sometimes go dark with a powerful bang. I can still see the way spirits hovered over the stage in the form of yellow cloth flowers that Dona Esmeralda herself scattered, hanging aloft among the treacherously rotten catwalks up in the flies. It gives me shivers to remember the slave ships with their groaning cargo, which glided across the stage with fluttering white sails stitched together from old sheets and flour sacks, and an anchor that looked as if it weighed a thousand kilos, even though it was only papier mâché stretched over a chicken-wire frame. The actors roamed through time and space with Dona Esmeralda's incomprehensible plays as their guides. We bakers, dressed in white, would crawl into the roof duct or sit on newspapers so we wouldn't get the seats dirty in the uppermost galleries, and whenever we laughed, it was a signal to Dona Esmeralda that a performance was ready and that it was now time to open the box office and announce a new premiere.

All of us were secretly in love with the beautiful young Eliza, Dona Esmeralda's big star. She was only sixteen, but she enchanted us with her confident ease on the stage, whether she was playing a cynical, heavily made-up *puta* in one of Dona Esmeralda's more realistic plays or a woman poetically balancing a water jug on her head beside some imaginary river whose invisible water flowed across the stage. All of us bakers loved her, and we mourned long and deep when one day she no longer appeared on the stage. An official from a foreign embassy, who had come to the theater one night and had in due course returned for twenty-three performances in a row, proposed to Eliza, and then they left for some country on the other side of the sea. I often wondered what Dona Esmeralda had felt at that moment, whether she felt betrayed and sad, or whether she was full of anger. She never said a word.

Some months later she discovered Marguerida, who before long had made the memory of Eliza fade. The world of the theater was a world which never seemed to come to an end.

For me, José Antonio Maria Vaz, it meant a whole new life when I stepped before Dona Esmeralda's eyes and found deliverance and work. Afterward I thought that even though my father had done nothing but talk his whole life, at least he had been right about my hands. I was truly a baker; I had landed in the right place in life, the place that everyone searches for but so few actually find. I made friends with the other bakers and the enticing girls who stood behind the counter and sold the fresh, fragrant bread. I got to know all the people who lived around the theater, on the broad avenue which runs straight through the city up to the old fortress where Dom Joaquim's equestrian statues stood abandoned. And I became especially good friends with the street kids who lived in cardboard boxes and rusting cars, surviving on whatever they could find in the garbage cans, whatever they could manage to steal and then sell, or sell and then steal back.

That was also the first time I heard about Nelio.

I can no longer remember who first mentioned his name. Maybe it was Sebastião, the old soldier missing one leg who lived in the stairwell of the studio belonging to the invariably mournful Indian photographer Abu Cassamo. The café next door was owned by the perpetually drunk Senhor Leopoldo—

one of the whites who did not take part in the great exodus to return to his homeland on the other side of the sea. He entertained the few customers who sought out his dingy café with incessant curses about the way everything had gone to the dogs since the young revolutionaries had entered the city and seized power.

"Everyone's laughing," he used to say. "But what are they laughing at? At everything going to hell? The blacks should be crying instead. Things were different in the old days, before . . ."

It might have been one of them. But it might also have been someone else, maybe some chance customer in the shop buying bread. But what I do remember quite clearly are the words that were spoken, the words that made me aware for the first time of the existence of a strange street kid named Nelio.

"The president ought to make him his adviser. He's the smartest person in the whole country."

Several days later one of the girls who sold bread pointed him out to me; I think it was the thin little girl called Dinoka, who was always swinging her hips so seductively whenever a man came by. She pointed at a group of street kids who had their headquarters right outside the theater. The boy she identified as Nelio was the smallest of all. He might have been nine at the time.

"He's never been beaten up," said Dinoka with awe. "Just think, a street kid who's never been beaten up."

The life of the street kids was hard. Once they ended up on the streets, there was most often no turning back. They lived in filth, sleeping in cardboard boxes and rusty cars, scavenging food wherever they could find it, drinking water from the cracked fountains that still remained from Dom Joaquim's day. When it rained they would kick mud onto the cars that were parked outside the banks and then innocently set about washing them down when the owners came out to drink their afternoon coffee at the Scala or the Continental. They stole when they had the chance, they carried sacks of flour for Dona Esmeralda in exchange for old bread, and they knew that life would never get any easier.

Each group of street kids had its own territory, and they organized their lives into small dictatorships in which the leader had unlimited power to judge and to mete our punishment. They often got into fights with each other, or with other groups that intruded on their territory, or with the police, who were always suspecting them of having stolen whatever couldn't be found. They chased the wild dogs. They caught rats in ingeniously designed traps, and then they doused them with gasoline siphoned off from cars, and they cheered as the rats were incinerated.

They came from all sorts of places, and they all had their own stories. Some had lost their parents during the long war, others had no memory of ever having had parents. Many had fled from stepparents; others had been literally thrown out of the house when there was not enough room or food for them any more.

But they were always laughing. Sometimes when the heat of the bakery was too strong and the bread wasn't yet ready to be taken out of the ovens, I would stand outside and watch them. They were always laughing even when they were hungry, tired or sick. They laughed nonstop, especially at the fury of the drunken Leopoldo. Occasionally he would come tearing out into the street from his café if he thought they were making too much ruckus and throw beer cans at them, even though he knew that the next day the cans would be neatly lined up outside his café door and cause him a lot of trouble as he was about to open.

The stories about Nelio were legion. About his slyness and cunning, about his ability to administer justice, and especially about how he managed to avoid being beaten up. I also heard rumors that he possessed magic powers, that he carried the spirit of a deceased *curandeiro* who in the beginning of time, when the city barely existed, had exercised his power over the people who lived near the wide estuary.

So I knew that he existed. I understood that he was remarkable.

But I had never talked to him. Not until that night when I was alone in the bakery and heard the loud shots from inside the theater. I raced up the winding stairs and sneaked into the uppermost gallery. To my surprise, I saw that the spotlights were on, and there was a set onstage that I had never seen before.

And in the middle of the light lay Nelio. Blood was streaming from his body; it was almost black against his white, Indian cotton shirt. I stood there in the dark with my heart pounding and tried to think. Who had shot him? Why was he lying on the stage in the middle of the night, bathed in the spotlight and blood? I listened for any sound, but everything was quiet.

Then I heard him wheezing, lying there on the stage. I fumbled my way down the dark steps, in constant fear that someone would pop up out of the dark and aim a gun at me too. When I reached the stage at last and fell to my knees at his side, I thought he was already dead. But as if he had heard me, he opened his eyes. They were still clear, even though he had lost a great deal of blood.

"I'll go and get help," I said.

He shook his head weakly. "Carry me up to the roof," he said. "All I need is fresh air."

I took off my white apron, shook off the flour dust and ripped it into strips. Then I wrapped them in a bandage around his chest where he had been shot; I lifted him and carried him up the narrow stairway to the roof. I kept a mattress there that I had found one morning next to the garbage cans outside the bakery. That's where I set him down. I bent my face close to his mouth to see if he was still breathing. When I was sure that he was alive, I raced down to the ovens, got some water and a lamp, and went back up to the roof.

"I have to get help," I repeated. "You can't stay here."

Again he shook his head. "I want to stay here," he said. "I'm not going to die. Not yet."

He sounded so determined that I couldn't make myself object, even though deep inside I knew what he needed most was a doctor.

He turned his head and looked at me. "It feels so cool up here," he said. "This is where I want to stay."

I sat down beside him. Now and then I gave him some water to moisten his lips. Since he had been shot in the chest, I didn't dare let him have anything to drink.

That was the first night.

I sat on the mattress at his side. When he seemed to be asleep, I would go down to the ovens to make sure the bread was not burning.

When it was still long before dawn, he opened his eyes again. By then he had stopped bleeding, and the bandage had grown stiff on his thin chest.

"The silence," he said. "Here I can dare to release my spirits."

I didn't know what to say. The words sounded strange coming from a boy who was only ten years old.

What did he mean?

Much later I would understand.

That was all he said.

For the rest of the night, that first night, he was silent.

The Second Night

I have sometimes wondered why the sunrise arouses such melancholy in my soul. Often I would stand on the roof after a long night in the bakery where the heat was at times so intense that I felt it was about to drive me mad. In the early dawn, when the city was just starting to wake up, I would feel the coolness of the morning breeze from the Indian Ocean, watch the sun rise out of the sea like a huge globe, and feel a heavy sadness in my weary mind.

Could this melancholy be a greeting from the spirits, those who care even about a simple baker? A reminder of the mortality that also awaits me?

But on that morning, on that second day when Nelio had already been lying on the filthy mattress for many hours, I had no time to think about the spirits. I usually washed off the steam and sweat from the long night in the bakery at a water pump behind the theater, where two carpenters would already be at work building the sets for Dona Esmeralda's productions. Then I would walk home through the city, which at that time of morning still smelled fresh, home to the place I shared with my brother Augustinho and his family in a *bairro* perched along one of the steepest slopes at the mouth of the river. But on that morning I did not leave. That wasn't entirely out of the ordinary, because sometimes I would lie down to sleep in the shade of the tree which years ago had taken root between the theater and the Indian photographer's studio.

I was also the only one who ever went up to the roof. I had kept secret the existence of the almost invisible extension of the winding staircase and the rusty sheet-metal door. I'm not sure that even Dona Esmeralda knew it was there. I don't think she has ever set foot on the roof. If there was one thing in life that didn't interest her, it was a view, no matter how spectacular it might be.

On that morning, when Nelio lay up there on the roof breathing fitfully, I couldn't go home. I had to stay. Hastily I washed up at the pump and then went to see Senhora Muwulene, who lived in a garage behind the courthouse, several blocks from the theater. Senhora Muwulene had been a famous *feticheira* back when the white colonizers, clumsily and with increasing resignation, had tried to outlaw what they scornfully regarded as our primitive superstitions. The whites had never understood the importance of the spirits in a person's life. They had never understood the necessity of staying on good terms with the souls of your ancestors; they had never grasped that a person's life involves a constant struggle to keep the spirits in a good mood. No doubt that's why the whites lost the war in the end and were forced to return to their own country. It was the offended spirits who won the war, more than it was the young revolutionaries.

But to the amazement of Senhora Muwulene and all the rest of us, the young revolutionaries were even stronger in their condemnation of our tradition of worshiping the spirits and regulating our lives in accordance with their wishes. At that time Senhora Muwulene used snakes to make pronouncements about the future and people's health. She lived outside the city, on the island which on a clear day can be seen from the bakery roof. At a huge public rally on the island, the local police inspector, who couldn't have been more than seventeen years old, had obeyed a directive issued by the young revolutionaries. All sorcerers and medicine women, including Senhora Muwulene, were to renounce immediately all their supernatural powers and to undergo extensive health-care training instead. Otherwise they would be thrown into prison. Everyone except Senhora Muwulene complied at once, since the police inspector had announced that the prison would be set up in the ice house of the fish factory, which the whites had hurriedly relinquished when the young revolutionaries seized power. Before they left, however, they destroyed the ice machines. The stench of rotten fish hovered over the island for years afterward. But Senhora Muwulene had no intention of renouncing her supernatural powers. She turned up at the public rally with a number of snakes in her basket, and the ominous snarl that rose up from the crowd when the police inspector attempted to arrest her finally made him give way.

Later, Senhora Muwulene moved to the city and established herself and her snakes in the garage behind the courthouse. Sometimes the snakes would escape and slither into the rooms where court proceedings were under way. Panic would break out and the proceedings would come to a halt as Senhora Muwulene crept about, gathering up her snakes, which were usually hiding in the dark corners behind the heavy tables of the prosecutors and attorneys. The tables were made of the black, ironlike wood that is found only in our country.

So it was Senhora Muwulene that I was on my way to see, and she smiled her toothless smile when she saw me coming. I told her right away that I needed herbs to treat a young man who had been shot in the chest and had lost a great deal of blood.

Senhora Muwulene didn't ask any questions about what had happened. But she did want to know whether Nelio was left-handed and whether he had been born on a Sunday or on a day when the wind was blowing from the north. I told her honestly that I didn't know. Senhora Muwulene sighed and complained of my ill-prepared visit. Then she mixed some crushed leaves with a thin clear liquid that she poured from a bottle which had previously contained aftershave lotion. I paid her and then hurried back to the bakery. Following Senhora Muwulene's instructions, I diluted the contents of the bottle with water and went up to the roof. Nelio hadn't moved since I left him; he was lying motionless on the mattress. But when I knelt beside him, he opened his eyes and looked up at me.

Does the face of a dying person seem more distinct? Is it only in the proximity of death that a person's features appear as they really are? I thought about this as I gave him the diluted potion to drink. Still, I was worried that if he drank anything it would seek out forbidden paths in his wounded chest. But I knew that I had to take the risk; there was no alternative as long as he refused to let me bring help or to take him on a cart to the hospital, which stood on the highest hill in the city. When he had finished drinking I lowered his head back down to the mattress. He closed his eyes after the exertion, and I looked at him and thought that even totally black people, like him and me, could turn pale. I touched his forehead and could tell that he had a fever; I hoped that Senhora Muwulene had mixed the best herbs she had.

Nelio was ten years old, maybe eleven. And yet I had the feeling that it was a very old man who lay there on the mattress. Did the hard life of a street kid induce a different kind of aging than for the rest of us ordinary people? A dog that is fifteen is already extremely old. Did the same apply to Nelio? I had no answer to my own questions, and I realized with despair that in a short time he would be dead. But soon I could tell from his breathing that he had slipped into a deep sleep again. It looked as if Senhora Muwulene's herbs had already brought down his fever; his forehead felt much cooler. I stood up and looked out over the city as I ate a piece of the bread I had baked during the night.

Since it was still early in the morning, I knew that the theater would be empty. The actors seldom arrived to start rehearsals before ten o'clock. Nelio was asleep and his breathing was steady now, so I went down the winding staircase, back to the stage where the nighttime drama had been played out. The old cleaning woman, Cashilda, was slapping the seats with a rag, making clouds of dust. She was so old that she could neither see nor hear. On several occasions she had confused morning and night; she had arrived at the theater in the middle of a performance and set about slapping at the seats while the audience was sitting in them. When the actors heard the continuous slapping sounds and the angry protests coming from the dark theater, they stopped the play. Some of them went down to explain to Cashilda that it was evening, not morning, and that she shouldn't be slapping at the seats when people who had paid for tickets were sitting in them. Then the performance continued. The theater was always dirty because Cashilda was old and tired. But Dona Esmeralda didn't have the heart to get rid of her. When I entered the theater, she didn't notice my presence. I looked at the stage and discovered that the set from the night before was gone. I stared at the stage in disbelief. Could I have been mistaken? No, I was positive. It was not my imagination or a dream. A set had definitely stood there: an endless blue sky and a landscape of rippling elephant grass. But now it was gone. A solitary door stood on the stage, intended for the new play that Dona Esmeralda had lately started to rehearse.

Why had Nelio been lying on the stage in the spotlight? What had happened in the empty theater the night before? Who had shot him? I climbed onto the stage and could see the dark patch of blood. It was real blood, not a theatrical illusion left over from some previous performance.

My thoughts were interrupted by Cashilda, whose dim eyes had caught sight of me. She thought I was one of the actors and that the rehearsals were about to begin. She always talked very loudly because she was deaf, and she started shouting her apologies because she hadn't yet finished the cleaning.

"It doesn't matter," I shouted back. "I'm not an actor. I'm a baker."

But she didn't understand what I said. To her, I was an actor who had arrived early. I left the stage and went back to the roof. Nelio was still asleep. I thought I should put a new bandage on his chest, but I didn't want to touch him; I didn't want to wake him. I sat in the shadow of one of the chimneys and gazed out over the city. From far off came the sounds of all those people who for one more day were doing their utmost to survive.

I saw before me all the thousands upon thousands of people who, with clenched teeth, were holding on to the futile dream that today, in spite of everything, things might be a little better than the day that had just passed. At the same time I wanted them to stop for a moment and think: right now up on Dona Esmeralda's roof a boy lies dying.

I must have fallen asleep sitting there in the shade of the chimney. When I woke, it was late afternoon. I sat up with a start, at first not sure where I was. I had been dreaming about my father;

he had been talking to me nonstop, but I couldn't recall a word that he said. Then I remembered what had happened, and I went over to the mattress where Nelio lay. He was asleep, his face was very pale, but his breathing was still steady and his forehead was cool. Since I was hungry, I went down to the little courtyard behind the bakery which is covered with a roof of woven palm leaves. That's where the bakers ate their meals, and the cook, Albano, still had some boiled rice and vegetables left, which he had served earlier in the day. After I filled my plate and began to eat, I realized that I was extremely hungry. In a few hours I would have to start work again; the night was going to be a long one, and I didn't know how long Senhora Muwulene's herbs would keep the fever down.

I had just finished eating and pushed my plate aside when Albano, who is big and fat and always stinks of homemade after-shave, sat down on the bench across from me, wiping the sweat from his brow with his grubby apron.

"The police have been here," he said.

I held my breath. "Why is that?"

Albano threw out his hands. "Why do the police ever come?" he said. "To ask questions, to snoop around, to kill time."

I knew what he meant. Nobody had any faith in the police. They rarely solved a crime; their percentage of solved cases must have been almost zero. On the other hand, they eagerly accepted bribes, and everyone knew that they often allied themselves with thieves and took a share of the impounded goods before regretfully informing the robbery victims that, unfortunately, nothing had been recovered.

"Questions about what?" I said.

"Somebody heard shots in the night," Albano said. "Coming from here. From the bakery or the theater. Did you hear anything?"

Albano is a friend. I like him, and not just because of the food he cooks. I could have told him the truth. I would have been grateful for somebody to share Nelio with. But I said nothing. I'm still not sure why. But I think it was because I sensed that Nelio wouldn't have wanted me to. When I carried him up to the roof, he talked about the silence and the peace, and I took that to mean that he wanted to be alone with his pain and those thoughts that only he knew.

"No, nothing," I said. "If anyone had fired a shot, I would have heard it."

"That's what we told them, too," Albano said.

"Did they believe you?"

"Who knows what the police believe? And who cares, anyway?"

To change the subject, I asked him to pack up a little of the leftover rice and vegetables in a piece of newspaper, so I would have something to eat during the night. I didn't know whether Nelio would be able to eat anything, but I thought that rice and vegetables would be better than bread. Albano did as I asked, and I left the bakery as the girls who sold bread were mopping the floor and wiping the shelves while the last customers bought the remaining loaves. I got things ready for the night and spoke to Julio, the boy who was my dough mixer, telling him how much flour to bring from the storeroom. Several hours later we were alone, and just before midnight Julio went home. I did the first baking. After I had put the baking pans into the ovens, I hurried up the winding staircase to the roof. Nelio was awake when I arrived.

It was on the second night that he began to tell his story.

Somewhere down on the street, behind a dilapidated building right next to the theater, a woman was standing outside in the dark, pounding corn for the next day. As she pounded the grain with a heavy wooden pole, she sang. I sat next to Nelio, and we listened to her song and the sound of the pole, thudding regularly and tirelessly like a heart.

"Whenever I hear a pole pounding corn, I think about my mother," Nelio said, and his voice sounded unexpectedly strong. "I think about her and I wonder whether she's still alive."

Then he told me about where he grew up and the gruesome events that had cast him out into a world he knew nothing about. He told me about the first time he ever saw the ocean, and about how he finally came to the city. He didn't tell me everything straight through. Now and then he would grow too tired, the fever would return, and he would sink down into darkness. But he always came back. It was as if he dived into the sea and vanished, eventually coming up to the surface again, but in a completely different place.

Just before dawn he managed to eat the rice and vegetables I had brought from Albano. Each time he lapsed into the fever I would go back to the ovens. Nelio seemed to have an agreement with the fire, because his periods of silence and fever always came when I needed to take out the baked bread and put new pans into the ovens.

That night he started telling me about his life—although I didn't yet realize how his story was going to change my own life.

He grew up in a village far beyond the great plains, in a long valley right below the high mountains which mark the border to the regions where the people speak different and to us incomprehensible languages, and where they also have strange customs. The village was not a big one. The huts were built of sun-dried clay with a pole in the middle to hold up the roof, which was made from woven reeds gathered in the river nearby, where crocodiles lurked below the surface and hippos bellowed in the night.

He grew up with many brothers and sisters, with his mother Solange and his father Hermenegildo. That was a happy time; he couldn't remember that he ever had to go hungry to the mat where he slept at night and shared his blanket with several of his siblings. They always had corn or sorghum, and with his brothers and sisters he had learned where the bees hid their honey.

His father was gone for long periods of time. Nelio knew that Hermenegildo worked in the mines in a country far away, but he didn't know what mines were except that they were hollow pits stretching deep into the earth. Inside were glittering stones that white people paid his father to bring up. When he came home, he brought them presents and he always bought himself a new hat. For Nelio, his father's hat was the first sign that a world outside existed in which everything was different. He tried to imagine that he would some day experience the amazing moment of putting a hat on his head, a hat with a wide brim and a leather sweatband inside the crown.

His earliest memory was of his father lifting him high into the air to let him greet the sun. Whenever Hermenegildo was home, time would stand still and the world was complete. After he had set off again on one of the paths that wound along the river, off toward the high mountains where there was a road and maybe even a bus that would take him back to the mines, life would revert to the way it was before. So Nelio remembered his first years using two different measurements of time: a time and a life when his father was home, and an entirely different time when he was alone with his mother and siblings. When Nelio was five years old, he began tending the goats with the other boys; he had learned to shoot birds with a slingshot and to handle the complex stick-fighting duels that all boys in the village had to master. One time a leopard had appeared near the village, another time a lion was heard roaring in the distance. Every morning he woke to the sound of his mother standing outside the hut pounding corn with a pole that was so heavy he couldn't lift it. And she would sing as if she were taking strength from the tones that issued from her throat.

The catastrophe came like an invisible predator in the night.

He was asleep. It was during the hottest season of the year, and he could still remember that he was lying naked on his reed mat. He had thrown off the blanket, his body was wet with sweat, and his dreams were uneasy from the stifling heat.

Suddenly the world exploded. A sharp white light yanked him awake; someone screamed—maybe it was one of his siblings, maybe his mother. In the desperate chaos that erupted he was trampled underfoot. He still didn't understand what was happening and he couldn't find his pants. He was flung naked into the catastrophe, and at last he realized that it was bandits who had come sneaking up in the dark; they had come to burn and pillage and kill. The attack kept on into the dawn, but the huts burned with such a powerful glare that no one noticed the sun coming up. Suddenly it was simply there. By then the village had been burned to the ground and many people had been killed—slashed by machetes, stabbed by sharpened steel pipes or smashed by wooden clubs.

Afterward it was so quiet. Nelio still couldn't find his pants, and he was squatting behind a basket where his mother had stored the corn they had harvested several weeks before. The scorched stench of the burned huts was overpowering; it was a smell he would never forget. That's the way the world smelled when it came to an end in smoke and fire and chaos. That was the stench that came when people were hurled out of their dreams to meet death. It arrived with the ragged bandits, drunk on *tontonto,* drugged with *soruma.* It was very quiet. The bandits had herded together those still alive—maybe half of the villagers, men, women and children—in the open area in the middle of the huts where they would dance and drum whenever they had celebrations.

Nelio fell silent, as if the words had become too difficult for him. Then he looked at me and continued his story.

"It felt as if the spirits of our ancestors had gathered there too; they hovered uneasily, as if they had been chased as brutally as we were out of their invisible resting places. I stayed squatting behind the woven basket. I understood what was happening, but I was still more afraid of being caught without my pants if one of the bandits suddenly noticed me and dragged me into the open. I tried to make myself invisible, using my terror as my cloak, and waited to see what would happen. There were maybe fifteen bandits. I didn't know how to count in those days. But there were about twice as many bandits as the goats in one of the flocks that I watched, which usually had seven or eight. The bandits were filthy and dressed in worse clothes than the ones we wore. Some of them had heavy military boots with no laces; the others were barefoot. Some of them had guns and cartridge belts; others carried long knives, axes, machetes and clubs. They were young, some of them not much older than me, and the youngest ones stood in the background, holding their weapons tight. But even the young ones had blood on their clothes; their faces were bloody too, and their hands and feet.

"There was a leader, a man who was older than the others, and he was the only one wearing a uniform jacket, which was stained, and a torn cap. When he opened his mouth I could see that he was missing a lot of teeth, maybe he had no teeth at all. He was drunk like the others, but he seemed to be drunk with the power he had over us in the village, now that all our houses had been burned, many were already dead, and those still alive were filled with terror. From time to time he would swat at the air, as if the restless spirits were bothering him. Then he began to talk, in a shrill voice, almost like one of the birds that would hover above the river where the women went to get water. He spoke the same language that we did, although he had a slight accent, which told me that he came from a region closer to the high mountains. He said they had come to liberate us. They had come to liberate us from the party and the government that now ruled us, the young revolutionaries' party. If we refused to be liberated, he would kill us all.

"They had burned our village and killed many people to show us they were serious in their struggle to liberate us and to help us have a better life. Now they wanted food and they would need help in transporting it from the village. I thought in panic about the basket that I was hiding behind. That was where the corn was. When they lifted the basket, they would find me. I tried to make myself even more invisible. With tears in my eyes, I started burrowing at the sand, as if I still had time to make a hole I could disappear into. At the same time I tried to see my father among those who had been herded like cattle in the open area, in the celebration area which was now like a graveyard, encircled by the ragged men with their bleary eyes and all those bloody weapons. I didn't see him, and I thought that he might be hiding, the same way I was, maybe behind one of the burned huts. The man who was the leader of the bandits was still talking. He said they had not only come to liberate us, but some of us would also have the opportunity to accompany them on their continuing journey, to other villages that would be liberated too. At those words, all of the people who stood anxiously huddled together began to moan and cry.

"That was when I saw my mother. She was squeezed in with the other women. On her back she was carrying my sister, who had been born a few weeks before. Her face, normally so beautiful, was contorted with the same fear as was in the faces of the other women. Her eyes were searching frantically for something that she couldn't find. I realized that it was me she was looking for. At that moment I understood, beyond anything I had ever before experienced, what it means to have a mother, and I knew I was going to lose her, just as I might have already lost my father.

"The bandits suddenly grew restless. They started lashing out, kicking aside the old men and women, hitting some of the boys who were older than me across the back of the neck and screaming at them to round up the goats. Then they began lining everyone up in a long row; their fear and moaning increased, and I had started to cry too, even though I didn't notice it at first. Several of the young women were shoved off to the side; they tore at their clothes when they saw that they were going to be forced to accompany the bandits as prisoners when they left the village.

"At that moment something horrifying happened. One of the men who saw his wife being led away was brave enough to step out of line and say that he would not allow them to take his woman. I saw who it was: Alfredo, my father's cousin, a skilled fisherman who never said an unkind word about anyone. Now he showed a courage he didn't even know he possessed, stepping out of the line as if he had stepped out of another life and taking a stand to protect his panic-stricken wife. At that moment he was defending us all, not just his own honor or his wife's. It was as if he were attacking everyone's terror with his action. The leader of the bandits stared at him, uncomprehending. Then he gave an order to one of the youngest boys who was with him. Without hesitation the boy, who was maybe thirteen, stepped forward and chopped off Alfredo's head with an axe. His head tumbled into the sand, coloring it red, and his body toppled, blood gushing from his neck. It was all so fast that at first nobody took in what had happened.

"In the midst of the silence, the boy started laughing. He wiped his axe on his jacket. And he laughed. That was when I knew that he was scared too. An invisible axe rested at all times against the back of his own neck.

"A loud howling and moaning rose up from the horrified people who were my friends, my neighbors, my relatives. I saw my mother press her hands to her eyes, and I hated myself for being so little, for being so scared, and for not being able to help her. The bandits themselves were now growing uneasy, screaming and striking out at everyone around them. They scooped up whatever food they could find, but for some reason they didn't see the basket of corn that I was hiding behind. And then they started taking away some of the younger women. To my horror I saw that they had also begun tugging at my mother; she was still young and they wanted to take her too. She screamed and called my father's name. They struck her, but she kept on resisting.

"That's when I could no longer stay hidden behind the basket of corn. I was still not wearing any pants. But I saw how they were trying to take my mother away from me, and that was something I could not let happen. I stood up, dashed naked across the sandy space where Alfredo's head was already covered by a swarm of green flies, and took a firm grip on my mother's *capulana*. The leader of the bandits, who seemed to take a special interest in my mother, looked at me in surprise. He saw that I was her son. Everyone used to say that we looked so much alike. He grabbed my little sister from my mother's back where she had been tied on in the same way I had once been. He went over to a big mortar that the women used to pound corn and stuffed my sister inside. Then he lifted up the heavy pole and handed it to my mother.

"'I'm hungry,' he said. 'Crush the corn and what's in the mortar so we can have some food.'

"My mother tried to move toward the mortar. She screamed and fought, but he held her off. Finally he hit her and she fell to the ground, and then he grabbed me by one arm.

"'You have to choose,' he shouted at my mother. When he yelled, his voice had a strange hissing sound, almost like an animal, because he didn't have any teeth in his mouth.

"'I'm going to chop off this chicken's head,' he said. 'I'm going to chop off his head if I don't get some food.'

"My mother lay on the ground screaming. She tried to crawl over to the mortar that my sister was stuffed into. I could feel myself peeing from fear; the evil that was holding onto me was so big and so incomprehensible that I wanted to die. I wanted to die, I wanted my mother to die, and I wanted my sister to live. Someone would lift her up and tie her to their back. One of my aunts, who was also mother to my sister, would lead her back to life. No one should have to die crushed by a pole in a corn mortar. Such a sacrifice could not be worthy of death.

"Suddenly the man with no teeth seemed to give up. He shouted a few brusque orders to his waiting men. They began herding together the goats and the women and the half-grown boys, who carried on their heads the food the bandits had found in the village. They also dragged along me and my mother, who at the last moment tried to tear herself away to get my sister, who had started to cry down in the mortar.

"The leader must have heard her, the faint cries from inside the mortar. Because all of a sudden he picked up the pole that was lying on the ground beside Alfredo's head. He looked at the pole, as if he didn't at first understand why he was holding it.

"Then he lifted it up—the man with no teeth, who had come with his men like beasts of prey in the night to kill us in the name of liberation—and he slammed it into the mortar until my sister stopped screaming.

"My mother heard the screams stop. She turned around and saw what had happened, how the man with no teeth pounded the pole one last time, and then everything was very still.

"At that moment it felt as if the world died. Even though many of us were still alive, we were actually dead. Even the spirits, which were fluttering restlessly all around, fell to the ground like a rain of tiny, cold dead stones.

"I remember very little of what happened after that. My mother, who had fainted, was carried and dragged along by the bandits. I was still naked and my body was slashed by the thorny bushes we passed on our way toward a destination which none of us knew. I thought that we were walking like ghosts through a landscape that was no longer alive, a group of people all dead, bandits who were dead, breathing an air that was dead too. There was no more life; it had all come to an end when my sister stopped screaming. The river, which we glimpsed now and then through the brush, was dead, the water was dead, the sun burning in the sky was dead, our weary footsteps were dead. We were a caravan of dead people who had left our lives behind us. We were on our way toward eternal nothingness. We walked when it was dark, and we walked in the early dawn. Out in front moved the scouts whom the man with no teeth had sent ahead. Whenever they saw people, we would take a long detour. In the daytime we waited for darkness in the shelter of groves of densely intertwined trees.

"By then the bandits had already begun to divide the women up among themselves. But they didn't want anything to do with my mother. She cried the whole time and wouldn't stop even when they kicked and hit her. I tried to stay near her at all times. I still had no pants, but one of the other women had torn off a scrap from her *capulana*, which I had wrapped around my waist. The bandits forced the women to make the food, which they then ate, not sharing any with us. After they had eaten they would drag the women into the bushes. When the women came back, their clothes would be torn and in disarray, and I could see that they were ashamed. The bandits were constantly drinking from their cans filled with *tontonto*. Sometimes they would fight. But most often they would go to sleep if the man with no teeth didn't send them to scout or keep watch.

"We trudged through a landscape that seemed to have been abandoned by everything alive. There weren't even any birds. Judging by the sun, I could tell that we first headed north; then one day we turned to the east. Still none of us knew where we were going. We weren't allowed to talk to each other, we were only permitted to answer the questions that some of the bandits asked us. I looked at the boys who were only a few years older than me. Although they were young, not even full grown, they behaved as if they were old men. I would often sit and sneak a glance at the boy who had chopped off Alfredo's head with his axe. I thought about the way he had laughed because of the terror that filled him. I wondered how his spirit would some day be received by the dead, by his ancestors. I thought they would probably punish him. I couldn't imagine that the spirits would fail to punish each other for the crimes they had committed when they were alive.

"Late one evening we reached a high plateau. For several days the path we had been following grew steeper and steeper. When we came to the top, other bandits were already there, along with several poorly built huts, flickering fires and lots of guns. We had arrived at one of the bases which the bandits concealed in inaccessible places and which the young revolutionaries seldom managed to find. I remember nothing from our first night there except that we were exhausted. My mother had stopped crying by then, but she had also stopped talking, and I thought that her heart was paralyzed with sorrow for all those who were left behind in the burned village. The bandits herded us into one of the huts. I lay for a long time on the hard earthen floor in the dark, listening to the bandits getting drunk on palm wine, now and then arguing or singing obscene songs or cursing the young revolutionaries. I had a hard time falling asleep because I was so hungry. It felt as though fierce animals were biting me in the stomach, making tiny holes through which all my strength was seeping out, like the last drops of water in an almost dry riverbed. But I must have fallen asleep at last.

"In the morning I woke up from a deep slumber. We were herded out of the huts, and I saw that the bandits were sitting in a circle, as if they were preparing for a council meeting. I could tell at once that the man with no teeth was no longer the one in charge. There was another man—short, with narrowed, squinty eyes—who now seemed to be the leader of the bandits. We were herded into the circle and ordered to sit down. The day was stifling; in the distance, black clouds loomed, gigantic shadows which surely contained much rain. The man with the squinty eyes was wearing a uniform that was both clean and without holes. He stood in front of us and welcomed us to this plateau, which he said was a liberated area. He explained that this was where we would be living from now on. In various ways we would take part in the war against the young revolutionaries. We should be prepared to sacrifice our lives if need be, and we should all obey the orders we received if we wanted to stay alive. Then we were given food and water. Even though we were all very hungry, no one ate more than the barest minimum. We were still overcome by such great fear that our stomachs had shrunk, as if they too had tried to make themselves invisible. Afterward all the boys, including me, were told to go with the man with the squinty eyes and several other bandits, all of whom carried guns. My mother tried to hold me back—her hand was like a claw around my arm—but I looked at her and told her it was best if I went. I would return. If I refused, they might kill me. I stood up and went with the others.

"That was the last time I saw my mother. Her hand, which had so often caressed my forehead, had gripped my arm like a claw. Her fingernails dug so deep into my skin that I had started to bleed. Her fingers had spoken to me. She was so afraid of losing me too.

"I stood up and did not look back.

"We followed a path until we reached a small ravine that ran like a crack straight through the high plateau. That was where we stopped. There were as many of us boys as I have fingers on my hands, and I was the youngest. The others were my friends, my brothers, my playmates.

"After that everything happened very fast. The man with the squinty eyes stepped up to me and handed me an extremely heavy gun. Then he told me to curl my forefinger around the trigger and to shoot the boy standing in front of me. Although I understood what he wanted, I was filled once again with great fear.

" 'If you want to live, you have to shoot him,' repeated the man with the squinty eyes. 'If you don't shoot, you're not a man. Then you'll have to die.'

" 'I can't shoot my brother,' I said. 'And I'm not a man, anyway. I'm still just a boy.'

"He didn't seem to hear what I said. 'Shoot him if you want to live,' was all he said. 'Shoot him.'

"The boy standing in front of me was named Tiko. He was the son of one of my father's brothers, and we had often played together, even though he was several years older than me. Now he stood before me and cried. I looked at him, and I knew that I would never be able to shoot him. Not even to save my own life. I also knew that the man with the squinty eyes was serious. He would kill me, maybe even with his bare hands, if I didn't do what he said.

"At that moment I grew up. I made a decision that in all probability would mean my own death. But if I didn't do what I knew I had to do, my life would lose all meaning. I could not shoot my brother.

"I thought about my sister who had been killed in the mortar. I wanted her to be in my thoughts when I died. I knew that we would soon see each other after I too had been killed.

"I gripped the trigger with my forefinger, swiftly aimed the gun at the man with the squinty eyes, and squeezed. The shot hit him in the chest, and he was flung to the ground. I can still see the look of surprise on his face before he died. Then I threw the gun away and ran as fast as I could toward the path from which we had come.

"The whole time I expected someone to shoot me in the back, the whole time I saw my sister before me in my mind, and I ran so fast that my bare feet barely touched the stony ground. It wasn't really me who was running, it was the life inside me that ran, and I knew they would soon catch up with me and then I would die. Later I learned that there are moments in life when you become whatever you are doing. In those moments I was a pair of feet and legs that were running—nothing else.

"I reached a spot where the path divided, and I ran to the left, although that was not the way we had come. I came to a steep slope and could go no further. Then I made for where there was no path, following the edge of the steep cliff until it began to slope downward and it was possible for me to slide over the edge and slip down toward the valley spread out below. They still hadn't managed to catch me. When I reached the bottom of the valley I stood up and for the first time looked back. I could not see the bandits anywhere. I kept on walking through the valley, which was quite flat and seemed to be endless. When it grew dark I stopped near a tree and climbed up into the top branches. I was very thirsty and had to use my last strength to heave myself up into that tree.

"In the early dawn I set out again. I didn't know where I was going; I thought about my mother and my sister, about my father and the burned village. But I also thought about the brother I had refused to kill and the man with the hard, squinty eyes. I was only a boy, but I had already killed a man.

"Late in the afternoon, when my lips were cracked with thirst, I came to a small stream. I drank my fill and then sat down in the shade of a clump of thick bushes. I still wasn't sure that the bandits were going to let me get away. And I didn't know what to do. I remember the terrible loneliness I felt sitting there next to the stream.

"It felt as if the world had ended, and I was the only one left alive. No matter which direction I took, I would still be alone.

"But I was wrong about that. Because while I was sitting in the shade of the bushes, I discovered that there was someone on the other bank of the narrow stream. That was where I met the white dwarf, who later led me here to the city."

It was dawn by the time Nelio stopped talking. A light rain had begun to fall and I made a canopy of flour sacks over him. I touched his forehead and noticed that the fever had returned. Before I got up to go and get more of Senhora Muwulene's herbs,

I thought for a long time about what he had told me. I still didn't know what had happened that night on the stage of the theater. What was he doing there? Who had shot him?

Nelio was asleep.

I stood up and stretched my back, which ached. Then I left him alone with the dreams I knew nothing about.

The Third Night

That night I thought Nelio was going to die, and I would never find out why he had been shot. For long periods he was submerged in the high fever raging through his body. He raved deliriously and thrashed about on the mattress, and it was like watching someone in the last stage of fatal malaria; there was nothing more that either I or anyone else could do for him. He was going to slip away from life without ending his story.

But he fought his way through that crisis too; he was still stronger than the fever caused by his wounds, and when dawn came, his forehead felt cool and he was sleeping peacefully. He had even asked for a little bread before he went to sleep. During the day I fell asleep too. I rolled out a reed mat that I had borrowed from Senhora Muwulene when I went to get more of her herbs. I told her how things stood since I believed I could rely on her. But I didn't tell her the whole truth: either that it was Nelio, a street boy, who lay on the roof of the theater, or that he was the one who had been shot. I simply said that someone had been wounded, someone who needed my help. She made no comment, she just mixed a new batch of herbs, crushing some tiny leaves that glowed a bright red, leaves I had never seen before. But I didn't ask her what they were. She wouldn't have told me anyway. She would have treated me with the same lofty contempt she had once shown the young police inspector when he tried to take her snakes away from her.

It was late that night when Nelio took up his story again. By this time I had told my dough mixer to go home, and everything was set for a lonely shift in the bakery; no one seemed to have any idea that my thoughts were far away from the ovens, up on the roof, where Nelio lay.

But there was one thing that had happened during the day which I realized had something to do with Nelio's gunshot wounds. Rosa, one of the enticing girls who sold the bread we baked, pointed out that a group of street kids who usually hung around the theater and the bakery had disappeared. I went out to the street, and saw at once that it was Nelio's group that had gone. I asked one of the other boys, who for some reason was called Nose, whether he knew where they were.

"They're gone," was all he said.

Gone. Maybe they had found a better street. With more expensive cars that would pay better if they made them dirty and then washed them clean.

I can't honestly say whether it was my curiosity or my concern for Nelio that was stronger. But as my ancestors are my witness, I hope it was my concern. That night I couldn't help asking him about what had happened. Nelio didn't seem surprised by my question. His answer was firm yet evasive.

"I haven't got as far as that yet," he said. "I haven't even arrived in the city yet."

Then he looked me right in the eye, and he spoke as if he were a wise old man, not the pale and emaciated ten-year-old who was lying before me on the filthy mattress I had found one day next to a garbage can.

"I'm telling you my story to stay alive," he said. "Just as it was my life itself that was running when I fled from the bandits, now my life is contained in the words that describe everything that happened."

I realized then that Nelio knew he was going to die. He had known it all along. He wasn't telling the story of his life to me. He was telling it to himself and to the spirits—the spirits of his ancestors, which were hovering invisibly all around him as he lay there on the roof, waiting for him to return to them and to the life that exists before and after all our lives.

I asked him nothing more. I knew he would live long enough to answer all my questions when at last, at the end of his long journey, he would come to the night when he was shot.

That night I also changed the bandage around his chest. I had bought some strips of cloth from Senhora Muwulene. To my surprise, I saw that they were pieces of a torn flag, although I couldn't say from what country. They might also have come from one of the old leftover colonial banners, maybe hidden away in some dark garret because no one knew what to do with it. She had soaked the strips of cloth in a bath of herbs and told me to wait until the breeze from the sea made the air cooler before I changed the bandage. In the flickering light of the kerosene lamp I could see that the two holes from the bullets were beginning to darken. The bullets had not gone straight through his body; there was no exit wound on his back. And there were powder burns on his shirt. Nelio must have been shot point-blank in the chest.

Nelio knew who had shot him. But that didn't necessarily mean he knew why.

Or did he? During those nights when he lay on the roof and waited for the spirits to come for him, I never once saw him upset by what had occurred. Had he been expecting it? I was burning to know the answer. But I only asked him once. Then I understood that he was telling his story the way a person lives his life. The events were not scattered about, they were happening all over again, in the same order, through his words.

One day comes before the next.

I tried to be gentle, but Nelio was in pain when I changed the sticky, stiff bandage for the strips of flag that Senhora Muwulene had dipped in the bath of red leaves. I saw the way he clenched his teeth, and once he even fainted for a few seconds when I was forced to tug on a scrap of bandage that was stuck to one of the gunshot wounds. Afterward he lay for a long time saying nothing. The woman who reminded him of his mother stood in the darkness below the roof and pounded her pole on the corn in her mortar. I shivered at the memory of what Nelio had told me the night before. I kept asking myself: Where does the evil in human beings come from? Why does barbarism always wear a human face? That's what makes barbarism so inhuman.

That night I had a lot to do downstairs in the bakery. A religious sect that was active in the city had placed an order with Dona Esmeralda for a particular type of bread which had to be baked longer than normal. I had made it many times before, so I knew that you had to be more vigilant than usual. But at last I finished the bread for the sect. When I went back up to the roof, Nelio was awake. I gave him water. The night was exceptionally clear, the stars seemed very close. We heard the sound of drums from somewhere in the night. The woman with the corn had fallen silent. Another woman laughed loudly and passionately. Then she too was silent. Dogs howled and mated in the dark; a truck with a coughing engine passed by on the street below.

*

That was when Nelio returned to the riverbank, where he had sunk down to rest after his long flight from the bandits. When he continued his story his voice was different from the night before. Then it had been meditative, at times sorrowful and hard. Now there was joy in his voice because the bandits were no longer right behind him.

Across the river he caught sight of someone. At first he had thought it was an animal, maybe one of the rare white lions he had heard the old people in the village talk about, the lions that heralded great events, although no one could foretell whether the events would be good or bad. Then he saw that it wasn't an animal but a person, a person who was both small and white, a *xidjana*. Nelio crouched down, because he wasn't sure whether bandits could also be small and white. But the dwarf on the opposite bank had seen him and called to him in a language that was almost the same as the one he spoke.

"What's a child doing all alone by the river?" His voice was squeaky and shrill. "What's a child doing all alone by the river when there's no village nearby? Have you lost your way?"

"Yes," Nelio said. "I'm lost."

"Then you're going to see things that you hadn't expected," said the dwarf. "Come over here. There's a place where you can wade across, below the tree that fell into the river."

Nelio waded across the river where a half-rotten tree trunk had sunk into the sand bar. When he reached the dwarf, he was sitting on the ground with his legs crossed and chewing on a root which he had washed clean with river water. Next to him stood a big leather suitcase with elaborate metal fastenings. Nelio had never seen a suitcase. He thought that if it had been a little bigger, it could have been the dwarf's house that he was carrying around with him.

The dwarf unwrapped a piece of cloth lying nearby, took out

another root and handed it to Nelio, who took it because he hadn't eaten in a long time. Nelio started gnawing on it. The root had a bitter taste. He had never seen that type of root before, and he thought to himself that he was already in a place where the plants that grew out of the ground were different from the ones growing in his village, which had been burned down.

"Don't eat so fast!" cried the dwarf, and Nelio was suddenly afraid that he had fallen into the hands of a bandit after all, disguised as a dwarf and albino.

Nelio began chewing more slowly. They ate in silence. Even though the dwarf, who had not yet mentioned his name, was sitting several yards away, Nelio noticed that he smelled like a flower—a sweet scent, almost like a woman getting all dressed up for a man.

It took a long time to finish the roots. The dwarf was still silent. But at last, when only the stem remained and he had used it to rub his teeth clean, he started to talk again.

"Have you a name?" he shouted, as if he couldn't speak without trying to make himself heard all over the world.

"Nelio."

The dwarf gave him an intent look. "I've never heard that name before," he said. "That's no name for a black man. That's a white man's name, short and meaningless."

"My father's oldest brother gave it to me."

"That name will never make you happy," said the dwarf, but he didn't explain what he meant. A little while later he stood up, as if to move on. Nelio stood up too. He discovered that he was taller than the dwarf standing in front of him.

"Where are you going?" the dwarf asked him.

"Nowhere," Nelio said, and he noticed that he had been infected by the dwarf's shrill voice. "Nowhere!" he shouted.

"Don't yell!" shouted the dwarf. "I'm right here. I can hear you.

My legs and arms may be short, but my ears are big and deep."

Then he was silent for a moment, pondering.

"Someone who is on his way to somewhere can hardly keep company with someone who is going nowhere," he said. "But we can try. You can come along with me if you carry my suitcase."

"Where are you going?" Nelio asked. "Do *you* have a name?"

"Yabu Bata," said the dwarf, putting his suitcase on top of Nelio's head. To his relief, Nelio discovered that it wasn't heavy.

"What do you have in the suitcase?"

"You ask too many questions," shouted the dwarf. "My suitcase is empty. I have it with me in case I find something I have to take along."

They set off. The dwarf walked fast, with his crooked legs pounding against the dry ground. They followed the river south.

After they had walked for hours and the sun was already nearing the horizon, the dwarf stopped abruptly, as if he had suddenly thought of something.

"I'm going to answer your question now, about where I'm going. I had a dream that I was supposed to set off on a journey in search of a path that would show me the way."

Nelio put down the suitcase and wiped the sweat from his face. "What path?" he asked.

"What path?" the dwarf repeated angrily. "The path I dreamed about. That will show me the way. Don't ask so many questions. We have a long way to go."

"How do you know that?"

Yabu Bata looked at him in astonishment before he replied.

"A path that you dream about and that's supposed to show you the way can't be nearby," he said at last. "Anything important is always hard to find."

*

When the evening light was glowing on the horizon, they set up camp. They had stopped near an abandoned termite mound, in the middle of a vast plain. In a solitary tree sat an eagle, regarding them with watchful eyes.

"Are we going to stop here?" Nelio said. "Shouldn't we climb up in a tree? What if the wild animals come?"

"You don't know anything," Yabu Bata said angrily. "You haven't learned a thing. You've lost your way, and you should be glad I'm letting you carry my suitcase. We're going to sleep inside the termite mound, of course. Give me a hand now, and don't ask so many questions."

With great vigor, Yabu Bata attacked the hard shell of the termite mound with a crude knife which he wore on his belt. Nelio could see that he was very strong. He helped out by shovelling away the hard clay that Yabu Bata hacked loose. At last he had cut an opening to the hollow inside the termite mound.

"Throw some grass inside," the dwarf said.

"Why?"

"You're still asking too many questions. Just do as I say."

Nelio gathered up grass until Yabu Bata told him that was enough. He took a piece of flint from his pocket and struck fire. The grass inside the termite mound began to burn. Nelio leaped backward and stumbled over Yabu Bata's suitcase. Two snakes slithered out of the termite mound and disappeared into the grass.

"Now we're alone," chuckled Yabu Bata. "Now we can crawl inside and go to sleep."

It was stuffy inside the termite mound when Yabu Bata placed his suitcase in front of the opening. Their bodies brushed against each other, and Nelio smelled the strong scent of perfume, which prickled his nose. But he didn't want to ask Yabu Bata why he smelled like a woman. A dwarf and an albino might possess many secret powers, which shouldn't be unnecessarily provoked. Instead, he ought to be grateful to be allowed to accompany Yabu Bata and carry the dwarf's empty suitcase on his head.

"You were fleeing from the bandits," Yabu Bata said suddenly in the dark. "You didn't lose your way. Why did you lie to me?"

Nelio thought that Yabu Bata must be able to read his thoughts. He couldn't keep a secret from an albino, who would never die. Everybody knew that about albinos: they lived forever. They had no spirits, they never had to cross over to the other life, they existed for all eternity, white and visible. How could he have forgotten that?

"They came in the night and burned down the village," Nelio said. "They killed many people. They also killed our dogs. They wanted me to kill my brother. That's when I ran."

Yabu Bata sighed in the dark.

"They kill so many," he said sadly. "In the end they will have killed everybody. The snakes will rule the earth. The spirits will search anxiously for all those who are dead and cannot be found."

"Have the bandits always existed? Who are their mothers?"

"We have to sleep now," Yabu Bata said crossly. "You should ask questions when the sun can laugh at all your stupidities. Tomorrow we'll no doubt have a long way to go. Who knows?"

They lay close together in the dark. Nelio could feel Yabu Bata's breath on the back of his neck. His steady breathing made the terror disappear, as if it too had retired for the night. Nelio's last thought before he fell asleep was whether Yabu Bata might be able to help him find a pair of pants.

Many days passed under the searing sun without Yabu Bata finding the path he had dreamed about. They often had very little to eat, and even though Yabu Bata had promised to get him a pair of pants, Nelio was still wearing the ragged *capulana* wrapped around his body. They put more and more distance between themselves and the high mountains, but that didn't mean they were getting farther from the bandits. They passed other villages that had been burned down, where solitary ghosts sat staring straight ahead. Several times Yabu Bata stopped when he saw people in the distance. If he had the slightest suspicion that they might be bandits, they would lie in the grass and stay there until they were alone again. Usually they walked in silence; Nelio realized that Yabu Bata was prepared to answer questions only rarely. Since he was afraid that Yabu Bata might suddenly tire of his company and chase him away, Nelio said nothing until he was absolutely sure that Yabu Bata had time for him. He learned that Yabu Bata's mood depended on whether or not they had food. One time, when they had corn and also several fish they had managed to catch in a river and they had eaten their fill, Yabu Bata began to sing in his shrill voice. He sang so loudly that Nelio was afraid the bandits a long way off would hear him and come up on them. But no bandits came. Later, after Yabu Bata had taken a nap in order to digest his food, snoring sonorously, he sat up without warning and looked at Nelio.

"I come from the Hunchback Mountains," he said. "If my father is still alive he certainly must have more animals than when I left. My mother wove mats, my uncle carved sculptures of black wood. I learned to be a blacksmith even though my arms are so short. If I hadn't had my dream, I'd still be a blacksmith. My wife may still be waiting for me, and my four children too; they're all tall and just as black as you are."

Nelio thought he must have been looking for his path for several months, maybe even since the rains had stopped. But when he asked, he received an answer he hadn't expected.

"You're still so young that you think a month is a long time," replied Yabu Bata. "I've been looking for my path for nineteen years, eight months and four days. With luck I'll find it before another nineteen years have passed. If I'm not lucky, or if my life is too short, I'll never find it. Then I'll have to continue my search for it when I begin my life with my ancestors."

Nelio sat in silence, pondering what Yabu Bata had said. He began to worry that Yabu Bata might be counting on him to go on carrying his suitcase until he found the path he had once dreamed about, maybe for another nineteen years. Nelio hesitated for a long time, wondering whether he should say what he was thinking, since Yabu Bata was so quick-tempered. But finally Nelio realized he had to tell him.

"I can't follow you for nineteen years," he said tentatively.

"I wasn't counting on that either," Yabu Bata said angrily. "I'm getting tired of seeing your face every day. When we reach the sea, we will go our separate ways. You'll have to manage on your own."

"The sea?" Nelio said. "What's that?"

His father may have told him a few times about a river that was so wide you couldn't see across to the other side. Nelio had vague memories of hearing about a gigantic body of water that could roar and heave itself up onto land, carrying off both people and animals. In those days he thought it was just one of the tales that his father liked to tell. Did the sea actually exist?

"I'd like to go with you to the sea," Nelio said.

"It won't be long before we get there," Yabu Bata said. "At least, it won't take nineteen years."

They reached the sea on an afternoon one week later. They had climbed up on to a ridge when Yabu Bata suddenly stopped and pointed. Nelio was following several paces behind him. He stopped short and didn't even have time to put down the suitcase before he caught sight of the blue water spread out before him. There and then, he had a strong feeling that he had arrived home.

So a person could feel at home in a place where he had never been before. Or is it imprinted on our consciousness, from the moment we're born, as a fundamental human trait, that we all must feel at home near the sea? Nelio stood next to Yabu Bata, gazing out over the water, which seemed to be growing bigger and bigger before his eyes, and thought about these things. They were thoughts that rose up of their own accord, effortlessly, thoughts that surprised him, since they were like nothing else he had ever thought in his life.

He didn't get far before Yabu Bata scattered his musings. "If you can't swim, the sea is dangerous," he said.

"Swim? What's that?"

Yabu Bata sighed. "I'm glad we're going to part soon," he said. "You know nothing. And you ask questions about everything. I'd grow old very fast if I had to answer all of your questions. Swimming means floating in water and at the same time moving forward."

Nelio, who had grown up near a river that was full of crocodiles, had never even imagined that a person could move around in the water. Water was for drinking, for washing, and for giving life to the corn and cassava. But to move around in it?

They walked down to the shore and to the sea, which was rolling back and forth.

"Don't put the suitcase down where it'll get wet," Yabu Bata said. "I don't want to be carrying a wet suitcase when I leave here." Then he walked out into the water, after rolling up his pants on his short, crooked legs. Nelio stayed behind with the suitcase so that he could move it quickly if the sea rolled farther in. The white sand was quite hot. Yabu Bata waded here and there, splashing water on his face. When he straightened up, he told Nelio to do the same.

"It's refreshing," he said. "Your heart slows down, your blood flows more quietly."

Nelio walked into the water. When he bent down to drink, it tasted bad. He spat as Yabu Bata laughed gleefully from where he was sitting on the sand.

"When God created the sea, He did it with great wisdom," shouted Yabu Bata. "Since He didn't want human beings to drink up all His blue water, He made it salty."

Nelio came back from the water's edge and sat down next to Yabu Bata on the sand. They sat there for hours without speaking and looked at the water, which was constantly changing, constantly moving. From several fishermen who passed by with nets and baskets over their shoulders Yabu Bata bought fish, which they cooked over a fire in the shelter of a sand dune. That night they stretched out on the sand and looked up at the stars. In the distance the water lapped the shore.

Yabu Bata suddenly broke the silence. "Tomorrow I'm going to leave you. I brought you to the sea, as I promised."

"You also promised me a pair of pants."

"You're an impudent young man," Yabu Bata said crossly. "People make lots of promises they'd like to keep. But it's not always possible to do everything you want to do. You want to live forever. But that's not possible. You want to see your enemies perish from their own misfortune. That's not possible either. You want a pair of pants. Sometimes that's possible. When you grow up, you'll understand."

"Understand what?" asked Nelio, unable to hide that he felt both displeased and disappointed.

"Understand that you have to learn to forget the promises that other people make."

"I don't believe that."

"You're not only inquisitive, you even object when older and wiser people tell you about life."

Again they lay silent. The stars were waiting.

"Tomorrow when I wake up," said Nelio, "will Yabu Bata be gone?"

"That depends, of course, on how early you wake up. But I hope to be on my way by the time you open your eyes. I don't like saying goodbye. Not even to an inquisitive child."

Nelio lay awake in the sand for a long time, long after Yabu Bata's breathing grew heavy, and even after he began to snore. Nelio seemed to realize for the first time that the next day he would be alone. He thought that this was the first thing he now had to learn, that he could no longer take for granted that he would always have someone else with him. Many times his father, Hermenegildo, had told him that the worst thing that could happen to anyone was to find himself alone. A person without a family was nothing. It was as if that person didn't exist. You could lose everything—your possessions, even your mind—if you drank too much *tontonto*. It was possible to survive all of that. But not being without other people, your family, all your mothers and sisters and brothers. Maybe that was the greatest injustice the bandits had done to him. They had robbed him of his family. Nelio felt very unhappy as he lay there in the cool sand with the snoring Yabu Bata at his side. Most of all he wanted to crawl over next to him, so close that he could hear his heartbeat. But he didn't dare. Yabu Bata would certainly wake up angry. Nelio stayed where he was and thought about everything that had happened ever since that night when the darkness had exploded in the white flash that came from the bandits' guns. He thought about his dead sister, about the man with the squinty eyes he had killed, and about his brother who was still alive.

Tomorrow he would be left alone, he didn't even own a pair of pants, and he didn't know where he should go. He thought that this would have to be the last question he asked Yabu Bata, the most important question he had ever asked in his life up until now.

Which way should he go? Where was his future? Was there any future at all? Had it vanished on that night when the bandits arrived and killed even their dogs? Or was it here, by the sea which he could not walk on, that his path would end? Was it here he would stay?

He fell asleep, dozing uneasily. All night long he dreamed that Yabu Bata had already got up and was preparing to leave. But when Nelio awoke in the early dawn, the suitcase was still at his side. Yabu Bata had taken off his sari and was standing naked in the water. His crooked body shone against the water as he washed. Nelio thought that someone standing naked in the sea was a very distinct individual. Against the water of the sea you could make out how a person truly looked.

Yabu Bata came back to the beach and did not seem glad to find Nelio awake. He pulled on his sari and shook the water out of his frizzy, pale yellow hair.

"I know that you think I ask too many questions," Nelio said. "That's why I'm only going to ask you one question before you leave."

At that moment Yabu Bata seemed sad that they were going to part. He sat down on the sand next to his suitcase and rested his head in his hands.

"Sometimes I wonder whether I'm ever going to find that path I dreamed about," he said. "Every night I dream that I'm back in my village near Hunchback Mountain, that I'm at my forge. But when I wake up, I'm always somewhere else. I often wonder why God gave people the power to dream. Why should you see a path in your dreams that you might never find? Why should you keep returning in your dreams to your forge, and then wake up lying on the sand near the sea?"

Yabu Bata sat there for a long time with his head in his hands, brooding over why people dream. Then he straightened up and looked at Nelio.

"What did you want to ask me?" he said.

"Which way should I go?"

Yabu Bata nodded thoughtfully. "That's the best question you've ever asked me," he said. "I wish I could answer it, but only you can say which direction you should take."

"I want to go somewhere I can find a pair of pants," said Nelio firmly.

"You can find pants anywhere," Yabu Bata said. "The best thing you can do is to follow the sea to the south. That's where there are people and towns. That's the way you should go."

"Is it far?"

"You said you only had one question," said Yabu Bata. "As soon as I answer it, you come up with another one. A road can be both long and short. It depends on where you're coming from and where you're going."

All of a sudden Yabu Bata started laughing. He grabbed a fistful of sand and tossed it over his head, as if he had suddenly lost his mind.

"I'll be damned if I'm not going to miss you!" he said after he calmed down.

He opened the lid of his suitcase and pulled out a little leather pouch. He took out several banknotes, which he gave to Nelio. "Use these to buy a pair of pants," he said. "Every time you take them off or put them on, you'll think about Yabu Bata."

"I have nothing to give to you," Nelio said.

"Give something to someone else when one day you have

something to give," Yabu Bata said, and he put the pouch back into his suitcase.

Then he stood and lifted the suitcase.

"There are only two roads in life. The road of foolishness, which leads a person straight to ruin. It's the road you take if you act against your own judgment. The other road is the one you must follow, the one that leads a person in the right direction."

Then he started walking along the beach. He did not turn around. Nelio followed him with his gaze until his eyes began to hurt from the harsh sunlight which was flashing against the white sand. The last thing he saw was a blurry dot, finally hovering like a wisp of smoke in the heat.

Nelio followed the sea toward the south. He tried not to think about the great loneliness surrounding him. He missed the suitcase he had carried for so long on his head as much as he missed Yabu Bata. But he knew that he would never see him again, and he would never know whether he found his path or not.

Two days later Nelio came to a little town, which consisted of low buildings along a single street. He stopped outside one of them where clothes were hanging on a rickety wooden rack. An Indian man who was so gaunt that he seemed emaciated, as if he had endured a long period of starvation, came out of the dark interior. Nelio bought from him a pair of pants made of dark red cotton. After he paid, he went behind the building, pulled off the tattered *capulana* and put on the pants. He wrapped the *capulana* artfully around his head as protection from the blazing sun. When he returned to the street, the Indian was standing outside his door, hanging a new pair of pants on the wooden rack.

"Where are you headed?" the Indian asked him.

"South," replied Nelio.

"Those pants will last for a long journey," said the Indian dreamily.

Nelio followed the line of the shore. Every night he slept behind a sand dune. At dawn he would take off his pants, wade into the water, and wash himself the way he had seen Yabu Bata do. When he was hungry he would stop and help the fishermen pull their boats on shore and clean their nets. They gave him food, and he would set off again after he had eaten his fill. The landscape changed, but the sea was always the same. In the distance he saw mountains and plains, forests with toppled grey trees, swamps and deserts. He walked without thinking about where he was headed. He was still moving away from something, and he was waiting for some sign that would tell him where he was going. At night he saw the moon wax from a slender crescent and become full, and then disappear. He thought about how he had already been walking for many days, and the sea seemed to him endless. Occasionally he met people and he would accompany them for a few days, but more often he walked alone. Everybody asked him where he was going. He told them about the bandits and about the burned village, but he always left out the fact that one day he had refused to shoot his brother and had instead killed a man with narrow, squinty eyes. When they repeated their question—where was he going?—he would say that he didn't know. During this time he learned that people always want to know where other people are going. That was the question that bound strangers and wayfarers together.

One day, early in the morning, he reached the mouth of a river. He saw a demolished bridge nearby and was thinking that he would have to find someone with a boat to take him across, when he caught sight of a person sitting on a stone by the water. When he got closer, he felt uneasy. Her skin was scaly and she looked more like an animal than an old woman. But she had heard him, and she turned her head and looked at him with piercing eyes. Then he understood that she was a *halakawuma* disguised as a human being, a woman. Or maybe the opposite was true—maybe she was an old woman disguised as the wise lizard. He approached, the whole time keeping a safe distance from her tongue. He knew that he was in luck. If you met a *halakawuma,* you could ask for advice. Even kings listened when the *halakawuma* whispered its advice about how a land ought to be ruled. Nelio had heard stories about how the first leader of the young revolutionaries had his whole garden full of lizards, which he regularly called upon for advice. Nelio sat down on the ground. The lizard followed his movements with her piercing eyes.

"I don't want to disturb you," he said, "but I need some advice. I've been walking for many days without knowing where I'm going. I've been waiting for some sign, but none has appeared."

"When one is as young as you are, there is only one road to take," replied the lizard in a voice that rang like bells. "Your road ought to lead you home."

Then Nelio briefly recounted what had happened. The whole time he was worried that the lizard would become impatient and, hissing, creep away into the tall grass that grew beside the mouth of the river.

When he fell silent the lizard pulled a bottle out of a bundle at her side and took several vigorous gulps. To his surprise, Nelio noticed the smell of palm wine. The lizard drank and then grimaced. Nelio thought that the world was full of unexpected events. Never had anyone told him that a *halakawuma* might also be fond of the liquors that people poured down their throats whenever they wanted to get drunk.

"I am old," the lizard said. "I don't know how good my advice is anymore. People have less and less respect for wisdom. Everyone seems to be taking the fools' roads, no matter what we say, those of us who still possess what is left of the old knowledge."

The lizard took another gulp and began rocking back and forth on the stone. Nelio was afraid that she would fall asleep before he got his answer.

"Cross the river," the lizard said at last, somewhat absent-mindedly, as if her brain were already full of other thoughts. "Cross the river and walk for a few more days. Then you will come to the big city where the houses clamber like monkeys along the steep cliffs facing the sea. So many people are already there that it won't matter if one more arrives. There you can vanish and reappear as the person you want to be."

Before Nelio had time to ask any more questions, the lizard crept away through the grass with a lumbering gait. He thought about what he had heard, and he decided that this was the sign he had been waiting for.

At the same moment he discovered that a man was just about to push a canoe into the river. Nelio jumped up and ran to the man, who already had a paddle in his hand.

An hour later, Nelio stepped ashore on the opposite bank of the river and continued his journey.

He came to the city late one afternoon. He had climbed a ridge, and he was very tired. How long he had been traveling, he could not say. But his feet were sore, and the pants he had bought were already ragged and quite dirty. Now he saw the silhouette of the city rising along the cliffs down toward the sea.

At last he had arrived.

Although he had never been there before, he was immediately

filled with the same feeling he had the first time he saw the sea with Yabu Bata. In the silhouette of the big city, the silhouette of something totally unfamiliar, something he could never have imagined, he felt himself at home. It was the second domain where he experienced an unexpected sense of belonging. This gave him with the idea that all people who are forced to flee from a war, a plague or a natural catastrophe, somewhere have another home waiting for them. It's only a matter of going on until you reach the point where all your strength has been emptied out. At that point, when exhaustion is transformed into an iron grip around the last remnants of your will, a home awaits you that you didn't know you had.

Nelio arrived in the city when the brief twilight was coloring the sky red. Some distance away he sat down on the soft sand and looked at the countless numbers of buildings, people, clattering cars and rusting buses.

Nowhere did he see any huts, nowhere in the city did he catch a glimpse of any villages.

He could also feel the fear inside him. Maybe the city belonged to the bandits. He didn't know. He still didn't dare go into the city. He would wait until the next morning. From a distance the city would be allowed to get used to his arrival. He knew that now his most important task was to stay alive. It's the most important task a person can have.

So Nelio found his home by the sea.

The following day he let himself be swallowed up by the people, the streets and the dilapidated buildings.

All of a sudden he was simply there.

Toward the end, at dawn, he was worn out. He had been speaking in such a low voice that I had to bend over his face to be able to hear what he said. Afterward, when he had stopped talking, he fell asleep almost at once.

I sat next to him for a long time, afraid that he would never wake again. And I thought that then I would never find out what happened on that night in the theater, the night that already seemed so long ago, the night when he was shot.

I put a wet towel on his hot forehead and went downstairs. From a distance I could hear Dona Esmeralda. Sometimes she came to the bakery early to check that everybody who was supposed to be there had arrived on time.

I stopped in the dark stairwell. Would she be able to tell from my face that Nelio was lying up there on her roof? Would she be able to tell that I had sat there all night long, listening to a story I never wanted to end?

I didn't know. So I continued down the stairs.

The Fourth Night

Dona Esmeralda didn't notice me as I came downstairs. A great commotion was raging that morning on the streets outside the bakery and theater. All the bakers, the dough mixers, the enticing girls who sold bread and the watchmen were standing around Dona Esmeralda in the doorway and looking out at the street. Since I am just as curious as everyone else, for a moment I forgot about Nelio who was lying up on the roof in his fever. Sometimes I think there is nothing that has as great a power over human beings as curiosity. So in a certain way I can forgive myself for not thinking about him for a little while. I asked the baker standing next to me—I think it was Alberto—what was going on. At the same moment I saw that huge groups of street kids were swarming restlessly back and forth along the street. They were blocking the traffic, throwing around garbage from the cans in front of the buildings, and yelling and screaming.

"Nelio has disappeared," Alberto said.

I felt something grip my heart. "Nelio," I said. "Nelio who?"

Dona Esmeralda, who has an exceptional ability to hear everything that is said in her vicinity, turned around and looked at me in surprise.

"Everybody knows who Nelio is," she said in a sharp voice. "The saintly Nelio whom no one has ever managed to beat up."

"Of course I know who Nelio is," I said apologetically. "So he's disappeared?" I turned back to Alberto since Dona Esmeralda had returned her gaze to the street.

"He's gone," replied Alberto. "The street kids suspect that he's been taken captive."

"Who could manage to capture him?"

"All the people who have never been able to give him a beating. The street kids think it's a conspiracy."

"That hardly sounds plausible," I said doubtfully. "Where would he be kept captive?"

"How would I know?" Alberto said.

The uproar continued all day long. The street kids, who seemed to number in the thousands, kept on causing a commotion. The police had been called out and kept a watchful eye on everything from the pavement. But their commanders, who were sweating under their heavy caps, wouldn't allow them to intervene. Someone also claimed to have seen the secretary of the interior, the feared mestizo Dimande, pass by in his armored car to survey the situation. Not until afternoon did the tumult of the street kids subside. They gathered in large bands and then broke up into small groups and vanished in all directions into the city. Although I was very tired, I had no peace to sleep during the day. My brother had also sent over one of his neighbors to find out if I had fallen ill since I had not been home for several days. I wrote a note on one of the brown bread bags, saying that at the moment I was working so much that I didn't have time to come home. But everything was fine, there was no reason to worry about me. I rinsed myself off behind the bakery, stripping off my clothes behind the rusty sheet metal from the roof that created a little partitioned space, and washing myself under the water pump. Then I went over to Senhora Muwulene's and bought new strips of cloth, which she dipped in her secret herb bath. I had the feeling she suspected it was Nelio who was in my care and that he had been injured in some way. As I stood in her dark garage reeking of ammonia and unknown spices, I seriously considered confiding in her about what had happened. Maybe I could ask her to come and take a look at Nelio as he lay on the roof. When I saw the thousands of swarming street kids, I realized what a responsibility I had assumed. What would happen if Nelio died and it was discovered that I had tried to nurse him on the rooftop, without getting him to a doctor? If Nelio could no longer speak, who would believe me when I said that it was his wish to be left alone on the roof? No one would believe me. Presumably I would be dragged out to the street, the police would look away, and I would be stoned, beaten to death, drenched in gasoline and set on fire.

So I said nothing to Senhora Muwulene. It seemed to be too late. I had taken responsibility for Nelio, and I would have to bear it alone until he asked me to move him from the roof. After my visit to Senhora Muwulene, I went to the big marketplace and shopped for food. I bought a prepared chicken and vegetables; I didn't have enough money for anything else. The marketplace was bustling. Even though no street kids were running around looking for Nelio, there were many hungry people begging, more than I had ever seen before. I knew that a steady stream of refugees had been coming to the city. The bandits were staging attacks all over the country, and there were rumors that the young revolutionary soldiers ran off whenever the bandits approached. More and more people were being forced to take to their heels, abandoning their homes. I thought about what Nelio had told me, and I understood something about the terrible fate that had befallen my country. The war that was raging was dividing families, brother against brother; and behind everything that was happening, from a great distance away in other countries, there were invisible hands pulling the strings of the bandits. It was the white people who had once been forced to leave the land and who now were seeking to return. In my mind I could picture how Dom Joaquim's statues would one day stand in the plazas again, and I felt a sudden rage at everything that had happened. The war had not only flung Nelio into a homeless vacuum, but it had sent people fleeing—innocent, simple people who wanted nothing but to try to live in peace with each other, people who never allowed a stranger to pass their homes hungry.

When I returned to the bakery from the marketplace, I seemed to see the city in a new way. It was the last rampart of defence against the bandits and the statues that threatened to destroy us.

I wondered how things would go. Without being able to explain it even to myself, it seemed to me important for everyone in the city that Nelio was up there on the bakery roof, and that he was still alive. The story he was telling me was a story that belonged to us all.

With the money I had left, I bought a shirt from a street kid. It was cheap and I could feel that it was of poor quality. But I didn't want Nelio to go on lying there wearing the same shirt. It was sweaty and dirty, and I needed time to wash it. When I got back to the bakery, I sneaked at once up to the roof to see if Nelio was still asleep. To my surprise I discovered that a gray cat had curled up at the foot of his mattress. At first I thought of chasing it away because it was probably flea-ridden. But I let it stay. Nelio was sleeping heavily and his forehead was not as hot as it had been at dawn. I sat down near the chimney and looked at him. I still could not decide whether he was a ten-year-old boy or a very old man lying there.

At dusk the cat abruptly got up from the mattress and

vanished over the ridge of the roof without a sound, slipping into the darkness. Nelio kept on sleeping. I ate half of the food I had bought at the marketplace and then went down to the bakery to start the night's work. As I supervised the dough mixer's work—he was new and still hadn't learned in what order to mix the flour, eggs, sugar, water and butter—I wondered if I should tell Nelio about what had happened during the day. I was not sure how he would react. Would he be pleased that he was missed? Or would it make him depressed? I also had to admit that above all else I was hoping it might make him tell me who had tried to kill him, and why.

I was convinced that it was not an accidental shooting. A servant of evil, unknown to me, had pointed the gun at Nelio. I thought it might have been the man with the hard, squinty eyes who had followed his tracks, which had led to the city, and who had now found Nelio. But I couldn't really believe it was him. And that wouldn't explain why it had happened on the spotlit stage, and in the middle of the night.

I argued with the dough mixer, who was lazy and uninterested in his work. I threatened to complain about him to Dona Esmeralda. But he only laughed at me and hummed his monotonous tunes, which he made up as he labored with the flour and water. Finally I was able to send him home; it was then almost midnight. I baked the first loaves and filled the baking pans. When they were in the oven, I hurried back to the roof. A mild breeze was blowing in from the sea. In the distance I could see lightning flashes from a thunderstorm that was moving past.

Nelio was awake. He smiled when he caught sight of me. I gave him the food I had bought and some water, which I mixed with Senhora Muwulene's herbs.

"I slept for a long time," he said. "And I've been dreaming. I've been retracing my steps. I dreamed that I saw Yabu Bata again."

"Did he find his path?" I asked cautiously.

Nelio looked at me in surprise. "Why would I ask him that? Yabu Bata was looking for his path in real life. So why would I ask him about it when I met him in a dream?"

Now, a year after the events on the rooftop, after those nights before Nelio died and I was given the strange explanation for everything that had happened, even now I still can't claim to understand Nelio's answer to my question about Yabu Bata's path. I have a feeling that he was trying to tell me something important. But my brain is still not ready to allow me to penetrate all his words. Sometimes I doubt that I will live long enough to experience that moment.

I changed the bandage. When I saw how the wound had grown even darker, I couldn't hide my horror. I thought that I could also sense the faint smell of death already present in the infected wounds.

"I have to take you to the hospital," I said.

"Not yet," replied Nelio. "I'll tell you when it's necessary."

His words were so resolute that I couldn't bring myself to object. The extraordinary aura of irrefutable naturalness that surrounded Nelio, ever since he crawled from the equestrian statue and showed himself to the world, had not deserted him even though he was now very sick.

On that night, the fourth night, he talked a great deal about the statue that had become his home in the city and the secret space where he could retreat with his thoughts.

Nelio went into the city at first light on the day after he arrived. He had spent the night on the beach under an overturned fishing boat. He followed the stream of people, overloaded trucks, rusty buses, handcarts and cars moving toward the city. He gawked at the tall buildings and was afraid that the people he glimpsed behind the broken window panes would tumble out and land on his head. He followed the hordes of people without becoming part of them; he drifted along, wondering where he was going. He remembered his first days in the city as a ceaseless wandering, day and night. At first it was confusing and frightening, then more and more pleasant, and finally with a feeling of having reached a focal point where everything converged—all events, all people were gathered at a single point. Then he got to know the city. He pulled mattresses out of garbage cans and learned to survive by copying the other children who lived on the streets as he did.

The next night he slept in the cemetery on the outskirts of the city. That was also where he thought he found a friend and then experienced a great betrayal. On the first day, which also was the longest day, his bare feet became covered with blisters since he wasn't used to walking on asphalt and rough cobblestones. He also stumbled many times and fell into the holes that peppered the streets and pavements. He learned that at any given moment he had to make a choice between looking at the wares on display in a shop window or continuing on. If he became absorbed in a fierce argument between a man and a woman, he couldn't keep moving at the same time.

When dusk began to fall, he found himself on the outskirts of the city. Behind a partially collapsed gate in a wall he saw several trees. He thought that he should climb up there, uncertain whether the city might have its own wild animals that hunted the homeless at night. But when he slipped in through the gate, he discovered he was in a cemetery. It didn't look like the place where they buried the dead in the burned village: simple mounds of earth, perhaps decorated with a few sticks tied in the shape of a cross. Here the graves had walls around them, with cracked, deteriorating photographs set in ceramic. Many of the graves were in shambles. He felt as if he were in a cemetery for dead grave monuments, not for people who had been reunited with their spirits. Some of the graves were so big that they resembled little houses, all of them adorned with white plaster crosses, and some of them had wrought-iron gratings in front of the openings. He was very tired. He saw other people curled up among the graves under blankets or pieces of cardboard. Outside some of the tombs, women were cooking food over fires while their families waited in the shadows. Nelio saw that the tree he had noticed from the street wasn't tall enough to climb. One of the tombs that was bordering on total collapse seemed deserted. That was where he crawled in and huddled in the dark. He fell asleep almost at once, secure in his conviction that he was surrounded by people and spirits who wished him no harm.

When he woke up at daybreak he discovered that he was not alone in the filthy tomb. A man was lying along the opposite wall. He had a mattress and a blanket, which he had pulled up to his chin. He had hung his clothes on a hanger: a suit, a white shirt and a necktie. A shaving mirror had also been set into the wall of the tomb where a piece of tile had fallen out. Nelio sat up cautiously and was preparing to sneak away when he noticed one of the man's feet sticking out from under the blanket. At first he thought the man was sleeping with his shoes on. But when he bent down and looked closer, he realized that they were not real shoes. The man had painted shoes on his feet, white shoes, with red edges and blue shoelaces. In amazement Nelio stared at the shoe-foot sticking out. At that instant the man woke with a start and sat up on the mattress. He was quite gaunt and had sharp, piercing eyes. Nelio had the feeling that he had yanked himself out of sleep the way a wrestler tears himself out of his opponent's grasp.

"Who are you?" the man asked. "You were sleeping here last night when I came home. I didn't want to wake you up, even though this is my house. I'm a kind man."

"I didn't know this was anybody's house," Nelio said.

"All of the houses in this city belong to somebody. There are so many people and so few houses."

"I'll go," Nelio said.

"Why are you sitting there staring at my shoes?"

"I thought they were feet," replied Nelio. "But now I see that I was mistaken."

"I always sleep in my shoes," the man said. "Otherwise there's a big risk that somebody might steal them. To steal my shoes, the thief would, unfortunately, have to cut off my feet. That would be a great calamity."

Then he showed Nelio how he had tied a string from his forefinger to the hanger where his suit hung. If anyone tried to steal his suit during the night, he would wake up.

"You can call me Senhor Castigo," said the man as he got up and began to dress. "Do you have a name? Do you know how to do anything? Or are you just as sluggish and ignorant as everybody else?"

"My name is Nelio."

Then he considered what he could actually do.

"I can carry suitcases on my head," he said.

Senhor Castigo gave him an amused look. "An excellent occupation," he said. "The world needs people who can balance suitcases on the wooden blocks they call their heads. Can you hold a mirror without dropping it?"

Nelio held the mirror while Senhor Castigo skilfully knotted his tie.

When he was satisfied he nodded with pleasure at the mirror, hung it back on the wall and folded his blanket. Then he motioned to Nelio to follow him. Before they passed through the gate, which was hanging crookedly from its hinges, the man with the painted shoes stopped and stared at Nelio.

"You're too clean," he said after a moment, and he bent down, picked up some dirt and rubbed it on Nelio's face. Nelio tried to resist, but Senhor Castigo hit him hard on the arm.

"Do you want to live? Do you want to survive? Or what?" he said. "I can tell that you've just arrived in the city. I'm giving you the opportunity to survive—so long as you do as I say. Do you understand?"

Nelio nodded.

"Walk a few paces behind me," continued Senhor Castigo. "We don't know each other. Stop when I stop, walk when I walk. Remember this for the time being. I'll teach you the rest later on."

They walked toward the town. At a street corner Senhor Castigo stopped and bought an onion. Nelio did as he had been instructed. He stopped a few paces away, and then continued to follow the man with the painted-on shoes. They walked along the base of the steep slopes until they reached one of the wide streets that Nelio recognized from the day before. They passed a café where many white people were sitting and drinking from glasses and cups. When they had left the café behind, Senhor Castigo drew Nelio into a dark stairwell that stank of urine.

"Carrying suitcases on your head is honest work, befitting a human being," he said with a smile. "But now you're going to learn the basis for all human labor, the most respectable profession that anyone can have."

"I'd like to learn that," said Nelio.

"Begging," said Senhor Castigo. "To arouse sympathy by means of your filth and your misery and your hunger. To help your fellow men express their generosity. Go out on to the street. When any white people come by, stick out your hand, start crying and ask them for money. For food, for your brothers and sisters for whom you have sole responsibility. Your father is dead, your mother is dead, you're all alone in the world. Do you understand?"

"My mother is alive," Nelio protested. "My father might be too."

Senhor Castigo flew into a rage. His eyes blazed. "Do you want to live? Do you want to survive? Or what?" he shouted as he shook Nelio; his hand on Nelio's arm was like a claw. "If I say they're dead, then they're dead. Right now, at this moment, while you're begging."

"I can't cry for no reason," said Nelio.

Senhor Castigo pulled the onion out of his pocket, bit it in half, and then grabbed Nelio hard by the neck. He rubbed the onion in Nelio's eyes until they stung and burned and his vision grew clouded with tears. Then he shoved Nelio out to the street. Nelio tried to do as he had been instructed. He stuck out his hand to the white people passing by. Mumbling, he tried to explain that he had not eaten for several days, for a week, for a month. A woman stopped. She was very fat and her skin was bright pink.

"Now you're lying," she said. "If you hadn't eaten for a month you would have been dead long ago."

She walked away without giving him a thing.

Senhor Castigo hid in the shadows. Every time anyone stopped and began searching in his pockets to give Nelio money, Senhor Castigo would walk past at exactly that moment, and then go back to the shadows from which he had come.

It wasn't until later that Nelio understood what was going on.

In the middle of the day, when the heat was overwhelming, and Nelio was wobbly with fatigue and lack of water, Senhor Castigo said that they should leave and take a rest. They walked down to the harbor area, which Nelio had seen from a distance the day before. In the wall of a building hung a curtain made of white plastic streamers, which Senhor Castigo swept aside. Inside, the room was dark. Nelio had trouble seeing since his eyes still smarted. A woman who was toothless and filthy and smelled of sour wine appeared with a bottle of beer and a plate of food for Senhor Castigo. He told her to bring Nelio a scrap of bread and some water. When he was ready to pay, he took a wallet out of his pocket and smiled.

"Do you remember the man with the blue hat who didn't want to give you anything?" he said.

Nelio nodded. When he saw the wallet he began to suspect something although he still didn't fully understand. Senhor Castigo drank so much with his meal that now he was drunk. Nelio felt a growing uneasiness about being in his company. Even if he didn't know what he was going to do, he knew he didn't want to beg. He couldn't understand how it could be the most respectable profession a person could have. Why had everybody in the burned village talked about beggars with either contempt or pity? It was often hard to distinguish the two feelings.

Senhor Castigo pulled another wallet out of his pocket, and then another, this time a red coin purse that belonged to a woman. Nelio realized, without comprehending how his fingers had done it, that the man with the painted shoes was a pickpocket. That was why he had approached the people who stopped to give Nelio money and then slunk away. Nelio decided at once to run away from Senhor Castigo. There must be some other way for him to survive in the city. But the man on the other side of the table seemed to read his mind. He leaned over the table, grabbed Nelio by the throat with one hand, and looked at him with glazed eyes.

"Don't even think about it," he said. "Don't even think of running away. No matter what you do, I'll find you. Every policeman in this city is a friend of mine. If I tell them to look for you, they'll do it."

He released his grip and then gave his full attention to drinking more beer and to emptying the contents of the wallets. The toothless woman appeared and stood at his side, watching. Now and then she would try to snatch a few of the bills, but Senhor Castigo was ever on the alert and slapped her hand. It was a brutal game they were playing. Nelio had slid his chair back, as far into the shadows as he could get. He could not understand how a thief could be such good friends with the police. He wondered if maybe that was the way things were in the city—the opposite of everywhere else. But even so, he was convinced that Senhor Castigo had said what he did only to frighten him. If Nelio didn't escape now, things were bound to get much worse. He would soon be blind from all the onion rubbed into his eyes.

His chance came when Senhor Castigo fell asleep on the other side of the table. His head fell back against the wall, and he started to snore with his mouth open. The toothless woman had disappeared into a back room. The smell of burning grease was coming from there. Nelio cautiously got up from his chair and retreated backward toward the door. Carefully he pushed aside the plastic curtain. A ray of sunlight swept quickly over Senhor Castigo's face without waking him. As soon as Nelio was out on the street, he started running. He expected at any moment to feel Senhor Castigo's hand striking the back of his neck. Or the man with the squinty eyes, who had returned from the world of the dead to take revenge. Or the man with no teeth. Not until he was far away, swallowed up by the mass of people who were swarming outside the big marketplace, did Nelio stop to catch his breath. He drank some water from one of the crumbling fountains, catching in his mouth the spray of water that shot out of the ornamental fish, and then he rinsed the sweat from his face. The whole time he tried to make himself invisible. He kept an eye on all directions, thinking that Senhor Castigo would surely come after him. There were also a lot of policemen outside the marketplace. Nelio noticed that they carried the same type of gun he had seen the bandits carry. The kind of gun he had held in his hands when he was supposed to shoot Tiko. How could it be that the police and the bandits had the same type of guns? Could it be true that the policemen were the pickpocket's friends? When the police came close to the fountain, Nelio ran off. In his pocket he had the money he had begged. When he counted it, he saw that he had a quarter of the amount that Yabu Bata had given him to buy a pair of pants. It was enough for food for two days if he ate as little as possible. For two days he would live like a beggar. Then he would have to decide what he was going to do to survive.

He walked down one of the long streets which followed the shoreline out of the city. It was lined with palm trees and decrepit benches. But there was a cool breeze from the sea and the palms provided shade. Nelio saw a stairway leading to the water. There he sat down and dipped his blistered feet in the sea. But he didn't dare stay for long. If Senhor Castigo found him, he would be lost. Then his only alternative would be to throw himself into the sea.

That night he slept in a broken-down car on a street on the outskirts of town. When he was sure that no one else was inside, he crawled into what was left of the backseat and tried to make it as comfortable as possible. Rats rustled around him. He slept fitfully; dreams groped over him like insolent fingers. He saw his father in his dreams, and the village when it was not burned down. His mother was also somewhere nearby, although he couldn't see her. It was one of those clear and cloudless days. But something was wrong; he felt a chill gust of wind in his dream. He didn't know at first what it was. Then he realized that the sun had disappeared. He looked up at the sky. The light was glaring, but it had no source. Someone had rubbed out the sun, removed it from the sky. But where was the light coming from? Then he realized that it was nighttime and the bandits had come; they were all around him, and he was trying to escape.

Nelio woke up because he had banged his knee. He saw a stray dog standing by the car, staring at him. In the distance he heard someone laughing and a radio blaring. It must be the middle of the night. His dream had made him sad. He thought that the hardest thing of all was loneliness. There had to be a way for him to find something to eat so that he could survive. But how would he cure his loneliness? He left the car at dawn without having found an answer.

That very day he discovered the statue that would be his home during the time he lived in the city. While he was wandering aimlessly, fleeing from the menacing shadow of Senhor Castigo and in search of a remedy for his loneliness, he came to a section in the center of the city that he hadn't yet seen. Squeezed in among the tall buildings he found a small open plaza, an almost circular marketplace. In the middle stood a tall equestrian statue. Nelio had never before seen a statue or a horse. At first he thought it was a donkey. But when he ventured to ask one of the old men sitting at the base of the statue, in the shadow of the mighty animal, whether such enormous donkeys really existed, all the men laughed at him.

"The biggest donkey is the one who asks such questions," they told him, chuckling with satisfaction at their own inventive wit. Nelio realized that he had asked a thoughtless question. He knew from experience that old men took great pleasure in accusing the young of stupidity. One of the old men, who had a cane and a hacking cough, nevertheless explained to him that it was a horse, an Arab *cavalo*, and that the man riding the horse was a famous conqueror who was one of the forefathers of the notorious Governor Dom Joaquim. Nelio also learned that a few oversights had occurred in the young revolutionaries' campaign to tear down and remove those statues, which they thought were an unpleasant reminder of the era that was now over.

"But you can't eradicate statues," said the old man pensively. "You can't eradicate a statue the way you stamp on an insect. You can cart them away, melt them down. But you can't eradicate them."

Nelio was told that the statue had been overlooked. A fierce debate had then broken out over who was to blame, and the debate was still raging. In the meantime, the statue had been allowed to stay. Nelio walked around it, again and again. The man sitting on the horse was wearing a helmet and holding a sword, which he pointed at the Indian shop selling cloth on the far side of the plaza. Nelio sat down at the base of the statue, at a suitable distance from the old men, and thought to himself that here, by this forgotten statue, was where he would stay. At this little marketplace, where people for a while stopped running and their pace was slow and dignified, where there were few cars and the sounds of the city were muffled by the tall buildings surrounding the plaza; this was where he would stay. It was like the calm space behind one of the sand dunes near the sea where he had slept during his long journey to the city. Or like a glade in one of the groves of black trees in the forest near his village.

All afternoon he sat at the base of the statue, moving along with the old men whenever the shadows shifted, and watched what was going on in the plaza. He saw the Indian shopkeepers and their women with veils draped over their heads and shoulders, standing motionless in the doorways to their dimly lit shops, waiting for customers. In the shade of the tall acacias, women sat on their reed mats. They had piled up little pyramids of fruit, vegetables and cassava roots, which they sold. Around them crawled their children. Whenever any of the women fell asleep in the heat, one of the other women would at once take on the supervision of her child. Usually they sat in silence, occasionally they would sing, now and then they would get into a violent argument, which ended as quickly as it had begun. Nelio couldn't make out everything they said; their language was not like his own. But from the contemptuous comments of the old men, Nelio understood that the women were true to their nature and were arguing about everything that was of little consequence. The old men then began arguing with each other over this, about what could be considered of value in life.

On the other side of the plaza there was a small church where a black-clad priest would from time to time peer out of the gate, as if he expected the church to receive an unannounced visit from restless souls in need of consolation. But no one came, and he would slam the gate shut, only to peer out again a little while later. The priest was a white man, bearded but with no hair at all on his head.

People lived in the other buildings surrounding the plaza, lots of people. Washed clothes hung everywhere; children screamed and played on the pavements. Whenever they got too loud, the old men would shake their fists at them, but the children hardly took any notice. Several times Nelio felt a burning desire to run over to them and take part in their games. But he knew that he could no longer do that. When he arrived in the city he left his childhood, his actual age, behind, like an invisible shell on the beach where he slept on the last night before he was swallowed up by the streets. The fact that he was sitting in the shadow of the equestrian statue alongside the old men was a sign of the great transformation that had occurred on the night the bandits burned his village down. Here in the open plaza Nelio felt for the first time that he could master the anxiety that filled him. It was as if he had found a village in the middle of the city.

That same evening he also found his home. One by one the old men had stood up and vanished into the darkness, heading toward the hovels where they spent their nights. The sun had set, the Indian shopkeepers had been reluctantly, almost remorsefully, forced to acknowledge that the last customers had gone, and they locked their doors, pulling the heavy wrought-iron gratings into place. In their stead appeared the black night watchmen, dressed in long ragged robes, who unpacked their blankets and greasy chicken legs. They lit their fires and began to make tea. Not until the Indian shopkeepers had left in their cars did they eat and then settle down to sleep. The children stopped playing, called inside by their mothers. The washing was taken down, and the smell of curry and *piri-piri* blended with the wind from the Indian Ocean. At last Nelio was all alone at the base of the statue. He had eaten a piece of chicken, which he bought from a man whose stove was an old, coal-fired oil drum. Nelio didn't want to leave the place he had found when he was fleeing from Senhor Castigo, and he thought about the fact that only in flight did you discover the world's secrets, which otherwise remained hidden.

In the twilight, he suddenly discovered a hatch under the belly of the horse next to the raised foreleg. When he pulled on the rusty handle, the hatch opened, and he saw that the horse had no entrails; there was only an empty space. He climbed up inside the horse. Faint rays of light, as if from the stars, shone in through the horse's nostrils and the eyeholes of the helmeted swordsman. Nelio knew that he had found a home. The statue was so big that he could stand up straight inside. He felt a great joy at discovering this home. Above his head there would always be a man with a drawn sword to keep watch over him. Inside the horse his dreams could safely roam. Here he could become a grown-up, find a wife and watch his children grow. He was filled with thoughts that night. His anxiety gradually receded. When at last he fell asleep, his head was resting on the left hind leg of the horse, and the bent knee formed a pillow for his head.

Nelio woke at dawn to the sound of a man laughing like a lunatic outside his statue. When he crept out of the hatch under the horse's belly, he saw that it was the black-clad priest, who was restlessly pacing back and forth near the gate outside the little church. He was flailing his arms and carrying on a mumbled conversation as if he were not alone but had an unseen companion at his side. He argued, threw his arms about in anger, and every so often he broke into maniacal laughter. Nelio thought he was arguing with evil spirits or lost souls that had assembled outside his church in the night. But later, when the old men had taken up their places again in the shade at the base of the statue, he learned that the old priest, whose name was Manuel Oliveira, had many years before lost his mind. When the young revolutionaries had seized power and marched into the city, the priest was struck by madness, whether from terror or from anger, no one could say for sure. He had preached such damning sermons against the young revolutionaries in his church that eventually none of his old parishioners dared to attend his masses, for fear that they would be seized by the security police, which the revolutionaries had immediately created and granted wide-ranging authority. The security police were supposed to watch for and arrest those who thought differently, particularly those who thought of the former colonial era as the good old days.

But Manuel Oliveira had continued to preach his sermons, although he was speaking to empty pews. Occasionally someone from the security police would attend one of his lengthy masses, whereupon Manuel, roused by having someone to preach to, would increase the intensity of his violent attacks. At first the authorities had shown tolerance toward the old priest, a victim of age and insanity. They had contented themselves with issuing a general prohibition against attending the church, and they allowed him to preach to an empty room. But when the priest began to preach outdoors, standing by the church gate on a wooden box, they had had enough. Manuel Oliveira was sent to a correction camp for those who thought differently in the remote northern provinces. The authorities also threatened to shoot him on the steps of his church if he didn't stop his wild ranting against the new regime. Nothing helped. At last he was allowed to return to his church. They thought that eventually he would grow tired, and he did. Now he spent his days in silence inside the church, waiting in vain for his God to explain to him why his church was empty and what had happened. Only in the early morning hours would vague remnants of his former insanity return. For the night watchmen, it was the daily signal for them to wake up in anticipation of the return of the Indian shopkeepers. They would confirm that everything was peaceful, and that they hadn't slept but had resolutely kept watch all night long. Later, at about the same time that Manuel Oliveira disappeared into the silence of his empty church, the night watchmen would pack up their blankets and hurry off to the jobs they had during the daytime. All of this the old men told to Nelio, and no one seemed to have any inkling that he had found a home inside the statue which protected them from the sun. Nelio saw that one of the women from a building next to the church placed a plate of food outside the church gate, and it occurred to him again that this place was like his home in the village which the bandits had burned.

In the days that followed, Nelio learned to survive in the city by keeping his eyes open. By chance he caught a glimpse of Senhor Castigo, very drunk, his suit stained and tattered. Nelio no longer feared him.

He spent much of his time watching the children his own age who lived on the streets. From a distance he observed their labors: washing cars, begging, selling and stealing whatever they could find. He saw how the older boys ruled the younger ones, and he thought that it was among them that he belonged. During his wanderings through the city he also came upon a neighborhood that was especially quiet, where the streets were not full of garbage or potholes. Big white houses without cracks were nestled in wide expanses of garden, hidden behind tall wrought-iron fences. There were children there too, the same age as he was. But he quickly discovered that they didn't see him; their eyes looked right through him. It was among the other children that he belonged—among those who, like himself, were living in order to survive.

He also realized that it was very difficult for kids who suddenly found themselves on the streets to force their way in and become accepted by those who were already living there and keeping watch over their territory. Many were turned away and beaten; they retreated, but then came back because they had nowhere else to flee. In the end, many of them disappeared, and no one ever asked about them. Nelio sometimes lay awake in the horse's belly with his head resting against the left hind leg, wondering whether there was a separate heaven for the street kids who vanished without a trace. A world solely for street kids, where they could continue their stubborn life of dancing and starving and laughing.

Nelio fell silent, practically in the middle of a sentence. It was almost dawn; the sky in the east had already begun to shimmer with the faint reddish-yellow light which heralded the sun. I could tell from his face how tired he was. I thought he had dropped off to sleep but then he began to speak again.

"The chance came unexpectedly. One day I had the chance to join a group of street kids—the ones you know, the ones who live right outside on this street. One day something happened that changed everything. It was pure chance that I was there. But isn't life made up of a long chain of chance moments?"

I waited for more, but it never came. Nelio had closed his eyes. Soon he was asleep. His breathing came in gasps. I was already dreading what I would see when I changed his bandage. And yet I knew that life was still holding on to him. He would never leave me ignorant of what had happened when he became one of the group of street kids that lived and plied their trades on the street outside the theater and bakery.

I knew that there would be more.

I got up, went to the edge of the roof and looked out across the city. I was very tired.

Later that day, after I had paid another visit to Senhora

Muwulene, I went to the plaza where the equestrian statue stood. The old men were sitting there in the shade, exactly the way Nelio had described them. I sat down next to the horse's leg and saw the hatch which led to Nelio's secret room. For a second I was tempted to open it and crawl inside. But I didn't do it. That would have been an affront to him. I left quickly. From one of the enticing girls I borrowed money to buy some food. There were still ten days left before Dona Esmeralda might pay me my small wages, if she happened to have any cash, and that was not always the case.

The day was exceedingly hot. A thunderstorm was brewing on the horizon. I hurried back to the rooftop where Nelio lay, fast asleep, and rigged up the rain canopy I had earlier put together from old flour sacks.

I had just finished when the rain came.

Nelio noticed nothing. He slept.

The Fifth Night

The rain had moved off and the night, which was fresh and clear, had settled in over the city. I had slept for several hours next to the chimney on a pile of old newspapers since the roof was still damp from the heavy downpour. It was almost midnight, and I was about to go down the winding stairs to the heat of the bakery to check on the slovenly baker's work when Nelio broke the silence and said that he needed to use the toilet. Since he had eaten so little during the days and nights he had lain on the mattress, I had forgotten to make any arrangements. I went downstairs and out to the backyard where one of the enticing girls from the bread counter had retired with one of the bakers from the day shift. I caught them in a situation that was not at all easy to ignore, and I could feel myself blushing, but I hastily grabbed one of the buckets that was used for emptying the garbage and went back to the roof. Behind me I heard the baker's fury at being disturbed and the girl's embarrassed giggles. I tore pieces of newspaper and put them next to the bucket. Then I helped Nelio up and left him in peace. When I returned, he was lying on the mattress again. I saw that he was sweating from the effort, and I blamed myself for not making better arrangements for him.

"Your work is waiting for you," he said.

"I'll be back soon," I told him. "The dough mixer doesn't know how much flour or how little salt to mix for the bread to meet Dona Esmeralda's standards."

With the bucket in hand, I left. It took me two hours to get the night's work in order. The dough mixer's eyes were glazed. When I realized that he had been smoking *soruma* and was off in a land far away, I could no longer control myself, and I punched him right in the face. I yelled at him that I had had enough and that Dona Esmeralda would fire him the moment I told her how unreliable he was. After that, everything took even longer. The dough mixer could scarcely stay on his feet, and I had to haul up the heavy flour sacks myself, since I didn't dare to let him go to the storeroom alone. On top of that, the wood in the ovens was bad that night. It took a long time before I got them hot enough so I could shove in the first baking pans. I rolled out the dough and baked the bread as fast as I could. But it was the small hours of the morning before I could kick the dough mixer out and go back to the roof. Nelio was awake when I got there. To my joy, he had eaten the fruit and the slice of bread with the thick layer of butter, which I had left for him next to his mattress. He had also put on the shirt I had washed for him earlier in the day. I thought that a miracle might be in the making. The fact that he had needed to use the toilet was a sign that his stomach was not seriously damaged. The fact that he was eating meant that life was trying to return inside him. Maybe Senhora Muwulene's herbs were healing his wounds.

But when I changed his bandage, I felt disheartened again. The wounds had grown darker; they were festering and smelled very bad. I knew I had to tell him how things stood—that he would die if he wasn't taken to a hospital where doctors could cut out the bullets that were poisoning his body. But he only smiled and shook his head.

"I'll tell you when it's time," he said.

I cleaned the wounds as thoroughly as I could, without causing him too much pain. I could see that he made the utmost effort not to show me how much it hurt. Afterward I put on the clean strips of cloth and gave him some water to drink. He sank back on to the mattress. In the glow of the kerosene lamp I could see how haggard his face had become during the four days I had spent with him. His black skin was stretched taut over his cheekbones, his eyes seemed to have sunk into their sockets, his lips were cracked, and his curly hair had begun to fall out. I thought that he should rest instead of devoting his nights to telling his story. I couldn't deny my curiosity—I wanted to hear his words, every one of them, since I sensed that his story was in some way also about me. I realized that I had to be patient. In the silences, when he allowed the story to rest, he would have a greater chance of regaining his strength.

But when he asked me to sit down on his mattress and then continued his story, I was never able to tell him to stop, to think about himself and how important it was not to exert himself. As he had on the previous nights, he continued his wandering through the city and through his life. A little before dawn a few scattered raindrops fell. But that was all. Otherwise we were surrounded by silence, now and then broken by dogs growling and barking at each other somewhere in the dark.

Nelio had often pondered the power that chance has over human beings. Those little words "if" and "if not" were more important than all other words. No one could ignore them, no one could deny that they were always close at hand, like symbols of the unpredictability that shapes our lives.

One morning he had been out on one of his aimless meanderings through the city—which often brought him the most significant experiences—when quite close to the theater and bakery he caught sight of several policemen who had grabbed a street boy and were furiously beating him with their black batons. Nelio had noticed the boy before; he was the leader of a band of street kids, and his name was Cosmos. Like most of the others who led bands of children and guarded their territories, Cosmos was somewhat older than the others, maybe thirteen or fourteen. Nelio had noticed him because he seldom hit the smaller boys, rarely even yelled at them or ordered them to run errands for him unnecessarily.

When Nelio saw Cosmos being beaten by the police, he knew that he had to help, even though he didn't know what had happened. Quickly he tried to work out what he could do. Once again chance came to his aid. He was standing on a street corner where there were traffic lights and an extremely busy intersection. One day a few weeks before, he had watched the light being repaired. Two men in overalls had opened a rusty iron box that stood next to the traffic light, and they controlled the light by flipping several circuit breakers off and on. Ever since, the lock had been broken, but no one would suspect this unless they knew about it. Nelio didn't stop to think any further. He knelt down next to the metal box as if, like any other street kid, he was just sitting down or stretching out right there on the pavement to sleep because he felt tired. He prised open the metal door, stuck his skinny arm inside, found the circuit breakers and began wiggling them as he pretended to sleep. The traffic instantly erupted into chaos. The red and green lights seemed to be engaged in some sort of contest, and cars came to a halt in a complicated tangle in the middle of the wide intersection. Everyone was honking; the cars backed up farther and farther. The people who were sitting in the cars and couldn't see what was going on, got out and started yelling at bystanders. The police noticed that something was happening; they saw the violent turmoil that had developed at the intersection, released Cosmos, and plunged into the fray. By then Nelio had slipped away from the metal box, the lights were functioning as they should, and no one could later explain what had happened. Cosmos, who was swollen-faced and red-eyed and furious, was sitting on the curb when Nelio went over and sat down beside him. He told him what he had done. Nelio did not doubt that he would be believed and he was not disappointed. Cosmos began to laugh, and when the other boys in the ragged group had gathered around, he told them what had happened.

"Who do you belong to?" he asked Nelio.

"I don't belong to anyone."

"Now you belong to us."

From that moment, Nelio left his great loneliness behind. He began a life with Cosmos, Tristeza, Mandioca, Pecado, Nascimento and Alfredo Bomba. With them he shared almost everything. The only thing he kept for himself was his statue. At first Cosmos wondered why Nelio didn't sleep with the others on the cardboard boxes in the stairwell of the Ministry of Justice. Nelio told him that he had a sickness that required him to sleep in a different place every night. He said it so convincingly that Cosmos believed him. He even suggested that they should try to collect enough money to visit a *curandeiro* who might be able to cure this strange illness. Without hesitation, since he knew that they would never manage to find the money, Nelio replied that he had no greater wish.

Nelio took his place in the group without encroaching on anyone else. Everyone had his position to guard, and it could be weakened or elevated, although it was always Cosmos who decided, sometimes on a whim, sometimes wisely and with good judgment. But from the very beginning Nelio went his own way. First Cosmos, then the others—even, at last, Tristeza, who was slow-witted—understood that Nelio was not like anyone else. As a person, he was his own breed. He acted like the others, learning their language and their customs quickly, but he was still an outsider, though in such a manner that no one even thought to ask him why this was so.

One night Cosmos had a dream which he told to Nelio much later on, but never to the others. He dreamed that Nelio was a sun-dried person, like a fruit or a fish, that tasted better than anything else and that lasted for as long as anyone was hungry. Cosmos asked Nelio whether he could explain this dream. He asked him about it when they happened to be alone, since it wouldn't look good for him, as the leader of the group, to be asking questions. He was supposed to have all the answers. Nelio said the dream was surely a divine revelation that only Cosmos could interpret. Nelio himself did not have the power to do so; he came from the remote regions where people very seldom received divine revelations in their dreams. Cosmos was so moved by Nelio's answer that on the following Sunday he ordered the whole group to get cleaned up and accompany him to the big cathedral to attend evening prayers. But when Tristeza could no longer hold back his laughter and when Alfredo Bomba fell asleep on the stone floor of the church, they were all thrown out, and they never went back.

"God exists even in the garbage cans," Cosmos had shouted derisively at the church officials who had angrily expelled them. They ran as fast as they could, scattering in all directions to avoid arrest, and later they regrouped outside the theater. Cosmos was so mad that he even forgot to give Mandioca a thrashing. And he forgave him for losing during their hasty retreat the liturgical book which Cosmos had swiped from the wide pocket of one of the dark-clad padres and then passed swiftly over to Mandioca, who had the biggest trouser pockets. For a long time afterward

Cosmos mulled over the idea of starting his own religious movement, which would be devoted exclusively to the street children. Through him the ragged bands' god, who must exist somewhere, would be reborn. But since they were heading into the hottest time of the year, he decided that the whole thing was far too strenuous, and he let the matter drop.

Cosmos recognized early on that Nelio had not come to the group in order to challenge his leadership or to seize power at some advantageous moment. At first it made him uneasy, since he had never experienced this before or even heard of such a thing. In the beginning he suspected that Nelio was deceiving him, and in secret he told Pecado and Mandioca to ask sly questions and to try to work out whether Nelio was other than the modest and reserved person he appeared to be. But at last Cosmos was convinced that Nelio was exactly the strange person he seemed to be. Nelio was nothing other than what he was. Cosmos had never met such a person before. How could someone be exactly what he was? Apart from his peculiar sickness, Nelio did not seem to have any unexpected secrets. Cosmos told Nelio about all these thoughts much later on, when he was planning, in great secrecy, to leave the group and start off on his long journey to another world. Nelio was surprised by what he heard. He had never imagined that his presence in the group could have aroused so many emotions in Cosmos. On the other hand, he had felt for a long time that the others in the group, especially Nascimento and Pecado—and later Deolinda, after she had forced her way in among them—had great difficulty accepting his presence. That was when the rumor was born that he had an unmatched ability to avoid being beaten.

Nascimento was the one who challenged him most, the aggressive Nascimento who could barely speak, who instead used his clenched fists and leaps and kicks as the language with which he described and commented upon the world he was forced to live in. He bore the name of his own origins. Everyone in the group had his own story; everyone, in spite of his youth, was a full-grown personality. And they were regarded as the most filthy but also the most respected group of street kids in the whole city. Much later Nelio came to understand that it was this respect, clothed in filthy and threadbare rags, which had so provoked the police that they decided to pound some fear into Cosmos, a fear that he would then spread to the others of the group. But the police had never succeeded, and Nelio felt as if he were living inside a roaming, jumping, dancing, laughing fortress under whose protection he and the others were invulnerable. Gradually he came to know them all, one by one, and he discovered that they were grown up even though they were kids, that they were old men even though they had scarcely reached puberty. Their stories stretched over infinite spaces of experiences, and each was a hero, a scoundrel and a victim in his own drama. Their names and their black bodies were as if celebrated in song.

Mandioca, the tall boy with the big feet and the crooked little finger on his left hand, had the biggest trouser pockets, and he had onions and tomatoes growing in them. The earth which he poured into his pockets and watered each morning was constantly dribbling out around him. And it was his vow, his yearning, to return some day to the village he could not remember, but which existed in the depths of his consciousness—the village his family had fled from when the warning came that the bandits were on their way. They had traveled by bus, they were many in number, but when they thought they had reached safety, the attack had come suddenly. The bus was set on fire, and Mandioca was flung into a thicket where later, half dead and dehydrated, he was found by several foreign nuns who rattled off a litany of prayers and then took him along to an orphanage in the city. When he had learned to walk—and it was his opinion that the only reason he wanted to walk properly was to be able to run away—he set off for his home in the countryside. But he never got farther than to the center of the city, and he had been living on the streets since he was four. Different charitable organizations based in all parts of the world and people of goodwill would often take him to orphanages, but he always ran away, back to the streets, since he knew that it was from there that he would one day start his journey home. He did not want to bathe or sleep in a bed or wear clean clothes. He wanted big trouser pockets to hold the earth that was just as important to him as his own blood. In every person he met on the streets he looked for some reminder of his father or mother, without remembering what they actually looked like. He searched for his siblings, his brothers and sisters, his uncles and aunts, his cousins and his neighbors, and for those he had never seen and didn't even know whether they existed at all. Often he would sink into a furious grief. But just as often he would balance on the stone walls adorned with lions outside the Ministry of Justice and dance to the music that only he could hear.

If Mandioca was tall and carried earth around in his pockets, then Nascimento was his complete opposite: short and stocky, with stones and sharp iron-points stuck in his hair and in the frayed edges of his tattered clothing. Nascimento woke up screaming every night; he saw contorted monsters coming toward him out of the dark. The others who slept around him on the cardboard boxes under ragged blankets had grown used to being woken up each night. They took turns telling Nascimento that there were no monsters, there were no bandits, there was only the deserted city and the cardboard boxes and the ragged blankets. In the daytime, when it was light, Nascimento continued to chase his monsters. Then they became his fear of the night that would inevitably come, the endless series of nights and monsters that he would continue to battle as long as he lived.

He never uttered an unnecessary word. He wore a pink swimming cap pulled all the way down to his eyes, and he always expected that whoever he met meant him harm. That's why he defended himself by going on the offensive. He fought with everyone and everything: with the rusting and broken-down cars, with the garbage cans, with rats and dogs and cats, and with the others in the group. Sometimes he would even lose control and go after Cosmos, who of course was much stronger and who would be forced to dip Nascimento's head into the broken sewer pipe behind the garage where the thieves from the suburbs ordered the new license plates they needed for the cars they stole during the night.

Nascimento had a secret that no one knew anything about; he was hardly aware of it himself. One time when he found a half-full bottle of wine and drank it down in one gulp, he was overcome by an intoxication that seemed to make him reveal at least part of the truth. And Nelio, who was the one he confided in, gradually understood from his stuttered, incoherent and poorly formulated sentences that Nascimento had once been forced to do what Nelio had managed to escape: he had killed someone in order to save his own life. Nelio understood that Nascimento had been forced to kill his own father with a cudgel or an axe, and that he had then become one of the feared child-soldiers that the bandits always sent in advance whenever they were going to attack a village or a bus or people working in their fields. How he had ended up in the city, nobody knew. But he had not arrived alone; from the very beginning he had brought along his swimming cap and his invisible companions, the monsters who never ceased to torment him.

Pecado did not have imaginary monsters; he had real-life

monsters, out in one of the suburbs. His father had disappeared without a trace. Pecado seemed only able to remember that his father had laughed when he left the hovel where they lived, never to return. His father was a faceless laughter. There were seven children. His mother sold vegetables at the marketplace. She would get up at four in the morning and walk over to the decrepit old bullring where she could buy produce cheaply. Then she would carry her baskets to the marketplace, and she wouldn't come back home until it was dark. Pecado never saw her laugh. But he didn't remember her being sad either, only worn out, exhausted and dejected. If his father was a faceless laughter, his mother was a face in which all contours had been worn away; her nose had crumbled, along with her eyes, her teeth and the smile which once must have existed.

One day a new man entered their house. Everything was supposed to be fine: a new husband, a father who would sit in the shade and shout for food. Pecado began hating the man the minute he saw him step across the threshold; he didn't want any *padrasto*. And the man seemed to have read his thoughts, because he announced his presence by knocking Pecado to the ground and twisting one of his shoulders out of its socket. Then he hit each of Pecado's siblings in turn. He devoted his days to beating them while their mother was out on her endless wanderings with the baskets of vegetables, which kept them alive. Finally Pecado had had enough. He decided to live up to his name, and he heaved a roof tile at the head of the man who had moved into his mother's bed. He threw it with all the strength of his siblings gathered in his fists; he was six years old at the time. Then he fled to the streets, because nothing could be worse than being at home. During those first years he hoped that his mother would try to find him. But she never came. He saw her only from a distance, when she stood at her stall selling *alface* and sometimes tomatoes. Pecado never went back home, and in the end his mother had become as vague and remote a memory as his father with the faceless laughter.

Then there was Alfredo Bomba, the youngest, who had only one arm. He had been born a pariah with a stunted shoulder in another town, and he came with an older brother to the big city to seek, if not happiness, then at least less misery. He was the one who constantly hid behind an unwavering good humor except when he begged—then he would cry, and he knew all the tricks. He was missing an arm, but he could make those who saw him believe that he was missing everything. They saw only his hand stretched out, and they gave him money for their own salvation. He was the one who each day could give Cosmos the greatest amount of money; it was his mission in life. He bore with joy and pride the fact that he was always the one who could contribute the most.

At his side almost always was Tristeza, the slow-witted boy. He was the hopeless stepchild of poverty; his brain had never been given the nutrition it needed as much as it needed oxygen. He had never learned to think except very slowly. For his mother, he was the twelfth painful reminder that she was still alive, and after naming the eleventh child Miseria, she had had only one name left: Tristeza. And she died the same day that he was born after having whispered to an exhausted and starving nurse that she wanted his name to be Tristeza, the only thing that she had left.

Nelio listened in amazement to their stories, and he realized that he was one of them; they had the same origins and the same experiences. In their stories he recognized himself, in the way that they all carried the burned village inside them. Often, as he lay in the horse's belly waiting for sleep, he would think that they all seemed to have been born of the same mother. A woman who was young and full of energy, but who had been broken by bandits, by monsters and by poverty to become a toothless, shrunken shadow. He knew that this was what they actually had in common: possessing nothing, having been born into a world against their will, and having been flung out into a misery created by bandits and monsters.

They had only one mission in life: to survive.

In the daytime he would see the rich climbing in and out of their shiny cars on the wide avenues in the center of the city: white men, black men, Indians. From Cosmos he had learned what one of those cars cost. It was such a dizzying sum that it was as if Cosmos were talking about the distance to a star rather than the price of a car. By looking at the rich, Nelio also discovered his own poverty. Between the rich, who always seemed to be setting off to conduct some urgent business, and the group of street kids there was a chasm which Nelio saw widening every day. The kids would cross it whenever they popped up and offered to watch over a car or to wash it while the black or white or Indian man who stepped out with his briefcase was conducting his important business.

Nelio once asked Cosmos who these men were, what they had in their briefcases, and why they were always in such a hurry. Cosmos didn't have any answers, but admitted that it might be worthwhile to find out. At an advantageous moment a short time later, he instructed Mandioca and Tristeza to break into a car and steal the briefcase that was inside. Afterward they took cover behind the gas station and opened the bag. Mandioca had imagined it full of money. But when he opened the lock and lifted the flap he found only the shrivelled remains of a lizard. That was a magic moment, since they would never have imagined that a dead lizard could be the secret of great riches.

"They carry around boxes with dead animals," Cosmos mused. "Maybe there are special lizards that ward off evil spirits."

"It's an ordinary lizard," said Mandioca after he pulled it out, studied it carefully and then sniffed it.

"But it must mean something," Cosmos said.

"Anyway, let's make it perfectly clear that we know what's in their bags," said Nelio.

Where he got the idea from, he didn't know, no more than he could explain so many other things he brooded about. He imagined that he had a secret space in his head where the unexpected thoughts waited for the proper moment to slip free.

"How can we do that without getting caught?"Cosmos said.

Nelio thought about it, and suddenly he knew.

"We catch a live lizard and put it in the bag," said Nelio. "Mandioca and Tristeza open the car door without being seen. Then we put the briefcase back in the car. The man will have something to wonder about for as long as he lives. We've seized power over him. We know how it was done. But he doesn't."

Cosmos nodded. Then he called to Alfredo Bomba and told him to catch one of the lizards that were skittering up and down the tree trunks or hiding in the cracks of the buildings. Alfredo Bomba stood motionless next to a tree, put his hand on the trunk and waited for a lizard to come near. Then he flicked his wrist and the lizard was caught between his thumb and forefinger.

Nelio wondered where he had learned this skill. Alfredo Bomba was surprised by the question.

"I learned it by watching the way lizards catch insects," he said.

Since Tristeza was the one watching over the car, he and Mandioca had no trouble opening the door again and putting the briefcase back inside. When the man who owned the car returned, he gave Tristeza a bill for all of 5,000 because he had looked after the car so well.

From then on, Cosmos and Nelio were obsessed by the discovery they had made. They could control the world by invisibly slipping inside wherever they wanted and leaving their mysterious signs, which would seem inexplicable and sometimes even frightening to those who found them. They looked around the city. The lizard in the briefcase had given them the upper hand, and they decided to challenge their poverty. Cosmos made all the decisions, but it was Nelio who whispered in his ear. Then they parceled out tasks to the others, and afterward they would all admire the trophies.

One night they made their way through winding sewer pipes, beneath the feet of armed guards, into the city's largest department store. Cosmos had to give both Nascimento and Alfredo a thrashing to stop them from filling their pockets with valuables from the store. They weren't there to steal but to leave their sign and take back a trophy. Taking instructions from Cosmos and Nelio, they moved everything in the store around; they put radios inside the big freezers, filled the empty bread baskets with shoes, and hooked frozen chickens onto hangers in the women's clothing department. The last thing they did was to unscrew the brass plaque hanging near the main entrance commemorating the occasion when the president dedicated the big department store. Then Pecado pinned up a dead lizard he had from Alfredo Bomba, and they left the nighttime store as soundlessly as they had come. The next day Cosmos and Nelio stood outside the entrance when the store opened. They saw the disbelief in the guards' eyes, then the astonishment of the bosses who came hurrying up when they realized that nothing apart from the brass plaque had been stolen. When the police eventually arrived, Alfredo's dead lizard was lying on a silver tray, and no one dared to touch it.

On another night they visited the big white hotel which stood on a cliff above the sea. They sneaked in through a ventilation shaft which had its intake in the slope facing the sea. By climbing like monkeys onto each other's shoulders they were able to reach it, and at last they found themselves inside the vast halls with marble floors and meter-high urns for flowers. They moved with great caution because the clerks at the front desk, the guards and sleepless guests were keeping vigil in the dimly lit halls. In the café with the soft easy chairs they gobbled up the pastries that were still in the gold-framed cooler counter. Here too they stole a shiny plaque posted between two columns in the great lobby to commemorate the day many years before when Dom Joaquim had dedicated the newly built hotel. Alfredo Bomba stuffed his dead lizard into the hollow where the plaque had been. Nelio carefully placed a pastry next to the lizard's mouth before they slipped back through the ventilation shaft.

What happened the next day they never found out because they wouldn't have made it past the guards stationed at the hotel's swinging doors. But they thought they could imagine what had gone on.

Nelio and Cosmos grew bolder. They slipped inside the parliament building, unscrewed the handle of the speaker's gavel and poked a dead lizard inside in its place. They challenged each other by starting to show their superiority to others. They challenged the overblown self-righteousness of the wealthy by toppling two escort motorcycle cops outside the theater when a minister's cortège passed by. Nelio and Cosmos had noticed that the lead motorcycles in every cortège always took a short cut across the wide avenue's center lane just before the big intersection. When the wail of the sirens was heard in the distance and all the drivers had pulled over, Tristeza and Nascimento poured splinters of black-colored glass over the center lane and then hid behind a parked car. Afterward, when the motorcycles had fallen and the cortège was forced to stop, a dead lizard was found among the shards of glass.

Cosmos and Nelio discussed at length what would be their greatest challenge. They weighed the possibility of releasing all the prisoners in the municipal jail, each with a dead lizard in his hand. For a long time they considered disrupting the transmissions of the city's radio station one night. But what they finally agreed on was that they would sneak inside the president's palace, into the very room where he slept, and put a lizard on his bedside table. That would be their last challenge. After that, the lizards would stop appearing. But no one could ever be sure that they wouldn't turn up again.

It took them a year to prepare for their visit to the president's bedroom. During that time they continued their restless, uneasy life on the streets. They fought with the other groups over territory; they waged a constant battle with the Indian shopkeepers, with the police, and with themselves. They washed and guarded cars, scavenged for food in the garbage cans, and refined Alfredo Bomba's begging techniques. Once in a while they would be accosted by the outside world, most often in the shape of white people who spoke their language very badly. Apparently they wanted to take the group of kids with them to some place they described as a big house where there was food and bathtubs and a god. Cosmos used to assign Mandioca to go along and investigate what it was all about. But Mandioca would usually be back the next day, saying that it was just another institution where they wanted to change the kids and rob them of their right to live on the streets.

Sometimes people would arrive wearing visored caps, carrying big cameras and wanting them to pose. Cosmos would immediately demand payment, whereupon the men with the cameras and the skinny women with pens in their hands would usually leave with disgruntled looks. If the men with the cameras were prepared to pay, the kids would gladly pose. They would show off with expressions of hunger, pain, yearning, filth, vulgarity, larceny and innocent joy. Cosmos gave the instructions, and each of them had his assignment. They used the money to buy food, usually chicken, which they would grill down by the decaying wharf. The days with the cameramen and the skinny, pen-wielding women were sated days. Afterward they would lie in the shade of the palm trees and talk. Cosmos let Nelio lie next to him while the others kept a respectful distance. Cosmos would look out over the ocean, gnawing on the last chicken leg, and talk about everything except himself. Cosmos's origins were something that Nelio often pondered. But he knew that Cosmos would never answer if he asked him any questions. Nelio sometimes thought that Cosmos had always been a ready-made person. He was born the way he was and he would never change. That could also be the reason why he never spoke of his past. He didn't talk about it because it didn't exist.

The sated days sometimes led Cosmos into a philosophical and dreamy reverie.

"If you ask Tristeza or Alfredo or any of the others what they want most in life, what do you think they will say?"

Nelio thought for a moment. "Various things," he said.

"I'm not so sure about that," said Cosmos. "Isn't there something that is greater than everything else? Greater than mothers and full stomachs and distant villages and clothes and cars and money?"

They lay there in silence while Nelio considered. "An ID card," he said at last. "A document with a photo that says that you are who you are and nobody else."

"I knew you would think of it," said Cosmos. "That's what we dream about. ID cards. But not so that we'll know who we are. We already know that. But so that we'll have a document proving that we have the right to be who we are."

"I've never had an ID card," Nelio said pensively.

"We should get ourselves some," said Cosmos. "After we've visited the president's bedroom we'll get some ID cards."

"What happens if they catch us?" asked Nelio. "What happens if the president wakes up?"

"He'll probably yell for help," replied Cosmos. "He'll be like Nascimento. He'll think he's dreaming about monsters."

"If I was our president," Nelio said, "what would I do?"

"Eat your fill every day."

"Eat my fill every day. And then what?"

"Rebuild the village that the bandits burned down. Go in search of your mother and father and your sisters and brothers. Try to find Yabu Bata. Throw the man with no teeth into jail. You'd have a lot to do."

Cosmos yawned. "If I was our president, I would resign," he said, turning on to his side to go to sleep. "How would the leader of a band of street kids have time to be president?"

Usually they finished off the sated days by paying a visit to the fairgrounds, which were in a fenced-off area between the harbor and the crowded alleys where the bars did not close until the sun came up. Even if the kids had had money, it was a repugnant thought to pay an entrance fee. They had their own entryway behind one of the smoky restaurant kitchens where the grease burned on stovetops that were never cleaned. They would crawl through a hole in the wall which they had made themselves and then covered up with clumps of earth. They knew the enormous Adelaida who stood there holding her spatula while the sweat ran down her face. She was a mulatto and weighed close to 330 pounds. When she started as cook in the restaurant ten years earlier, the owner had been forced to enlarge the kitchen to make enough room for her. She danced and sang while she cooked. The food she made was nothing extraordinary, but a rumor had spread that what she served had a magic effect on the desires and prowess of both men and women. This meant the restaurant was always full. Adelaida was paid a high salary, since she was aware of her value, and she was happy to keep watch on the secret entrance that the street kids used.

The fairgrounds were a labyrinth of restaurants and bars, cramped stalls where you could have your fortune told or get a tattoo from small, dark and mysterious men from the remote islands of the Indian Ocean. In the middle of an open plaza there was a Ferris wheel which no one had dared to ride for the past twenty years because the chains of the caged seats had rusted through. The owner, Senhor Rodrigues, who had imported the huge wheel more than sixty years before during the time of Dom Joaquim, was still to be found at his position each evening. As if it were a wishing well, people would buy tickets from him without taking a ride, and then wish for a long life. Senhor Rodrigues, who had a fierce smoker's cough and lived on raisins, sat in his little ticket booth and played chess with himself. During all the years he had spent at the fairgrounds, he had developed a great proficiency at losing to himself. He knew that he was a bad chess player, but inside him there was a secret genius who was an unbeatable master.

Next to the Ferris wheel were several lottery stands and a track for small electric race cars. The big carousel, whose motor had stopped functioning several years before the young revolutionaries seized power, was now driven by hand. The owners had fled in terror, thinking that all whites would be decapitated by the new rulers. They had drained off all the motor oil and let the carousel break down. They did it one night when they were alone at the fairgrounds; they drank great quantities of wine and rode on their carousel until the motor ground to a halt. The next day they were gone. They had chopped the heads off the wooden horses, as vengeance against the new era which would not allow them to continue to lead their comfortable colonial lives. No one ever found the chopped-off heads, and no one ever replaced them with new ones either. That's why the carousel horses were still missing their heads. Cosmos ordered everyone except Alfredo to push. Alone in his kingdom of headless horses, Alfredo sat on the lead horse and rode around and around the world. For that moment of happiness he was prepared to beg on the others' behalf for as long as he lived. They roamed the fairgrounds and looked at everything that was going on. They were keen observers of the fights that erupted and just as quickly died out; they studied with interest the half-naked women looking for customers, and they discussed the women's physical attributes so loudly that they were usually chased off. The sated days were days when time stood still, when life was something more than mere survival.

At the beginning of the second year in which Nelio lived with the group led by Cosmos, they made their nighttime visit to the president. They slipped into the walled and heavily guarded palace by crawling into the big laundry baskets, which once a month were delivered to the palace from the government laundry. They waited in one of the cellar rooms until it was night, and then they made their furtive way through the silent building. Over a long period prior to that night, they had asked innocent questions of various people who worked in the presidential palace and found out how the building looked and where the stairs and the guards were located; they also knew in which room the president slept. Sometimes he visited his wife, who had her own bedroom, but he always returned to his own bed. As they were on their way up to the upper floor of the palace, they heard a door open and close somewhere overhead. They crouched in the darkness of the stairs. Then they saw the president approaching in the moonlight, and he was naked. Soundlessly he passed above them on his way back to his own bedroom. That was a moment none of them would forget. Cosmos threatened to give them a beating every day for three months if they ever revealed what they had seen. No one needed to know that their president had shown himself naked before some of his subjects.

They waited on the stairs until Cosmos thought the president must be asleep. Cautiously they approached and opened his door. In the light from the window they saw the shadow of the black man in his bed, and they heard his calm breathing. They stood around him, holding their breath. Then Alfredo Bomba placed the dead lizard on the bedside table, and they left the room.

What they never found out was that a moment later the president had woken up. He was dreaming that something smelled bad—it was the foul smell of poverty. When he opened his eyes in the dark, the smell was in the room, as if it had followed him out of his sleep. He lay there for a long time, wondering what the dream was trying to tell him. That he did too little to alleviate the poverty that seemed to be spreading like an epidemic through the country? Anxiously he looked for an answer without finding one until he fell into an uneasy slumber shortly before dawn.

But he did not see the lizard on his bedside table. In the morning, when the president had bathed and then dressed with bleary eyes, he still hadn't noticed it.

A horrified servant called for the man in charge of the president's security department, who in turn, and under the greatest secrecy, summoned the head of the security police. After a number of highly confidential meetings, it was decided not to inform the president. But they did, again in secrecy, increase threefold the guard on the president's palace.

A short time after this, his final triumph, Cosmos was struck by a melancholy that came as a great surprise to everyone, even to himself. One evening when Nelio was about to leave for his statue, Cosmos pulled him aside and told him that as of the next day Nelio would be in charge of the group. Cosmos would be gone by then, and he was making Nelio responsible until he came back. There was a freighter in the harbor that would set sail for the East at sunrise. Cosmos was going to sneak on board and set off on a journey which he saw as the only way to regain his good spirits.

"They'll never accept me as their leader," said Nelio. "They'll say that I killed you."

"They'll miss me, said Cosmos. "That's why you are the only possible leader, since you're the one who is closest to me."

Nelio tried to object.

"Say no more," replied Cosmos. "I think it's important for people to go away once in a while. I'll be fine."

Then he pulled a dead lizard from his pocket and smiled.

The next day he was gone. No one ever heard from him again. He had vanished with the ship that had sailed into the sunrise.

At the very moment that Nelio was telling me about the disappearance of Cosmos, the sun rose over the horizon. The African sun, red like silk, spread its rays across the city, which was starting to awaken. I could see from Nelio's face that he was tired. As I was about to leave him, he began to cough. When I turned, I saw blood running from his mouth. It occurred to me that it was over now. Nelio was going to die. Then he raised his hand and gave a dismissive wave.

"It looks worse than it is," he said wearily. "I'm not going to die without you knowing it."

A moment later the bleeding stopped. I asked him whether he wanted anything.

"Just water," he said. "Then I will sleep."

I stayed on the roof until he fell asleep. Then I went down to the bakery. Dona Esmeralda had already arrived, and I told her about the useless dough mixer I worked with during the night.

I listened to my own voice, to the words I uttered. They sounded alien and unreal, as if I were about to be devoured by the dying Nelio and his story, but Dona Esmeralda didn't seem to notice. She got up from her stool, tied the hat ribbons under her chin, and said that she would immediately replace the incompetent dough mixer with a better person.

Then I went into the city. Some distance away I turned and looked up at the roof of the theater.

The evening and the night were still far off.

The Sixth Night

That day a cold wind suddenly swept in over the city. During the hottest time of the year this was not uncommon, but even though people knew this, it always took everyone by surprise. One time, long ago, when the city consisted of nothing more than several low buildings along the unspoiled estuary, rumor had it that icebergs could be seen at just about that spot where sharks now prowl with their fins barely visible above the surface. For several days the estuary froze solid, and people were able to cross the mouth of the river by walking on water. Even if this tale is in all likelihood a fiction, today whenever the cold winds sweep across the land from the sea, you still see people—especially old people—standing by the city docks, scanning the horizon to see whether the icebergs are about to return after all these years. Then the truth would be revealed: what had happened in the past was not just a fable.

I fell asleep in the shade of a tree down at the wharf where the rusty ferry that shuttles back and forth across the river puts in. I woke up suddenly because I was cold. It was already late in the afternoon, and I hurried back to the bakery. I was just on my way up to the roof to see whether Nelio was still asleep when I heard someone calling me. It was one of the girls from the bread counter, who said that Dona Esmeralda had been asking for me. I was supposed to go and speak to her at once, even though she was now over in the theater rehearsing a new play with the actors.

I was instantly nervous. It was extremely rare for Dona Esmeralda to want to be disturbed when she was in the theater. I asked the woman—I now remember that it was Rosa, who was big and fat and who passionately loved a tailor who had left her more than fifteen years before—what it was that Dona Esmeralda wanted.

"Who knows what she wants?" Rosa said. "But I think you'd better hurry. She's been waiting a long time."

I thought Dona Esmeralda must have discovered that Nelio was on the roof. She would know that I was the one who had taken him there. Now she was going to fire me because I had been hiding something from her.

I stepped cautiously inside the dim theater, full of evil forebodings. Onstage, in the same spotlight where I had found Nelio lying in his blood, I saw the actors performing. They were stuffed into strange gray suits that seemed to be pumped full of air. From their faces hung long pipe-like objects that looked like lengths of rough rope, making it hard for them to move. I stopped inside the doorway, entranced by the balloon-shaped creatures onstage who were tripping over their long noses.

It took a while before I realized that they were supposed to be elephants. I could see Dona Esmeralda's back. She always sat in the same place, in about the middle of the house, when she was directing rehearsals. Since the rehearsal was under way, I waited to approach to her. I had a hard time working out what the play was about since the actors' words were impossible to hear from behind the long trunks hanging in front of their faces. But it seemed to me that they sounded annoyed. They kicked irritably at their trunks, moving awkwardly and ponderously in the balloon-like suits, which must have been quite hot.

As the rehearsal continued without interruption, I thought that I shouldn't wait any longer, so I walked tentatively down the middle aisle toward where Dona Esmeralda was sitting. She had taken off her hat and laid it on the floor near her chair. She was totally still. When I got close, I saw that she had fallen asleep. But she was sitting erect; her chin had not sunk toward her chest. The actors onstage shouldn't notice that she was asleep. I was about to retreat when she woke with a start and looked at me. She gestured with one hand that I was to sit down beside her. Carefully I moved the bottle of cognac from next to her chair and sat down. All the while the elephants were bellowing incomprehensibly at each other on the stage. Then Dona Esmeralda leaned toward me and whispered in my ear.

"What do you think of our new play?"

"It looks good," I whispered back.

"It's about a herd of elephants that is afflicted by religious problems," she said. "It's a reminder of those evil days when my father still ruled this country. Toward the end of the play he appears onstage himself, with a drawn sword. If I can find anyone to play him, that is. The elephants are actually revolutionary soldiers."

I have to admit that I had no idea what she was talking about. Since the actors up onstage seemed annoyed, I assumed that they didn't understand what the play was about either. But I didn't dare to venture any remark except to repeat what I had already said, that it looked good. Dona Esmeralda nodded contentedly and then seemed to forget I was there. She was following the rehearsal with a rapt expression of childish delight. I watched her surreptitiously, thinking that it was exactly this child's sense of joy that was keeping her alive, despite the fact that she was at least ninety or maybe even a hundred years old.

I thought she had forgotten that I was sitting there at her side when she suddenly looked at me again.

"I fired the dough mixer," she said. "What was his name?"

"Julio."

"I told him to get himself an instrument and try to be a musician. I think he'd be good at it."

Even though Dona Esmeralda always went to great lengths to avoid firing the people she employed, it could not be totally avoided. And she never let anyone go without recommending what type of work they ought to take up in the future. I knew that she was nearly always right. I tried to imagine what instrument would suit Julio, but I couldn't come up with anything.

Dona Esmeralda interrupted my thoughts. "A new dough mixer is coming tonight. That's why I wanted to see you. I've hired a woman."

"A woman? But the flour sacks are heavy!"

"Maria is very strong. She's as strong as she is beautiful."

The conversation was over. Dona Esmeralda signaled to me that I could go. I left the dark theater, thankful that she had not sent for me to talk about Nelio.

She had said that Maria was as strong as she was beautiful. And God knows, she was right! When I went into the bakery late that night to start my work, there stood the most beautiful woman I had ever seen. I fell instantly in love with her. At that moment no one else existed but her. We shook hands.

"My name is Maria," she said.

"I love you," I thought of saying. But of course I didn't. I simply told her my name.

"My name is also Maria," I said. "José Antonio Maria. The flour sacks are very heavy."

I placed a sack—a white one with blue-and-red stripes—right next to her feet. She leaned forward, bent her knees and lifted it high over her head.

How could a woman be so strong? How could a woman be so strong and yet so beautiful?

"Have you worked in a bakery before?" I asked.

"Yes," she said. "I know how to mix dough."

And she did. I just had to tell her how many portions of dough we needed to make each night and what Dona Esmeralda's special wishes were. Maria nodded, and I never had to remind her again.

She was so beautiful that several times I forgot all about Nelio. It wasn't until I let her go home around midnight that he once again entered my consciousness, although not until I had gone out into the street to see whether some man was waiting for Maria. But she went off alone into the night. At that moment I married her in my mind.

It was not until I was on my way up the winding stairs to the roof that I remembered where I was going and why. I immediately felt guilty. A human being was dying on the roof, and I had only my new dough mixer Maria on my mind. I forced myself to feel ashamed, though it was difficult, and then I rushed up to the roof.

Nelio was awake when I got there. Earlier in the evening, before Maria arrived, I had borrowed an old tattered blanket from the night watchman outside the Indian photographer's shop. I gave him a loaf of bread and a matchbox filled with tea leaves in return for the loan of the blanket. I had spread it over Nelio to protect him from the cool winds blowing over the city. I had given him some of Senhora Muwulene's herbs and sat beside him while he had one of his attacks of fever. The cool air seemed to have done him good. He smiled now when he caught sight of me.

At that moment he was a ten-year-old boy. The next moment he could once again be a very old man. He switched back and forth all the time. I never knew which one I would find before me. The only thing that was certain was that he had been lying on the roof for five days and five nights; it was now the sixth night, and the wounds in his chest were getting darker and darker.

Maybe it was meeting Maria that had influenced me—I don't know. But when I changed the bandage and saw that Nelio now showed the unmistakable signs of blood poisoning, I could no longer refrain from speaking my mind.

"You're going to die if you stay here on the roof."

"I'm not afraid to die," he said.

"You don't have to die. Not if you let me take you away from here. To a hospital. The bullets in your body have to come out."

"I'll tell you when," he said, as he had so many times before.

"Now it's my turn to say when," I replied. "I have to move you now. Otherwise you will die."

"No," he said. "I'm not going to die."

What was it that made me believe him? How could I allow myself to go along with something that I knew wasn't right?

The answer is that I don't know. But Nelio's power was so great that I yielded to him.

That night he told me about the time after Cosmos crept on board a ship and disappeared into the dawn. Toward daybreak, when Nelio began to grow tired, I could feel that the cool air had once again vanished. When I stood up to leave him and looked at the ocean, I could not see any icebergs.

On the morning when Cosmos left, when Nelio told the others that from now on he would be the leader of the group, everything had proceeded quite calmly. A transfer of leadership might be accompanied by unrest and murky feelings of resistance seeping to the surface. But Nelio told them the truth—that some day Cosmos would come back and then everything would revert to the way it was. He had no intention of changing anything—what he knew about being a leader he had learned from Cosmos.

But this was not entirely true. During the night, when he lay in the horse's belly and sleeplessly waited for dawn and the ranting morning prayers of the maniacally laughing priest, Nelio thought that he would be exactly like Cosmos, but even more so. He would be a little more patient with Tristeza; he would laugh a little more at the endless stories that Alfredo Bomba told. In this way Nelio hoped to be able to exercise the authority that Cosmos had established in the group.

The only one to challenge him during those first days was Nascimento.

"You know where Cosmos is," he might suddenly say in the evening as Nelio was dividing up the money they had earned during the day by watching over and washing cars.

Tension would instantly spring up among the others. Nelio knew that he had to accept the challenge and once and for all make clear to Nascimento why Cosmos had chosen him as his successor.

"He appointed me as leader because he knew that I was the only one who wouldn't tell where he was going," Nelio said. And then he continued, unperturbed, to divide up the money.

Nascimento pondered what this answer actually meant. That night he said nothing more.

"We can't have a leader who doesn't sleep with the rest of us," he said on another evening.

Nelio was prepared for this. He had suspected that Nascimento would make use of the differences between him and Cosmos. And he had come to the conclusion that there were two significant differences between them. One, that Nelio lived separately, and two, that he was not several years older than the others.

"Everything will be the same as it was under Cosmos," Nelio said. "That's why I will continue to sleep wherever I like."

"A leader should be older," said Nascimento.

"That's something you will have to discuss with Cosmos," replied Nelio. "I'm sure he'll be able to give you an answer that will satisfy you."

Nascimento soon stopped challenging Nelio. He realized that it was getting him nowhere. The group was content with the fact that a change had occurred without anything threatening to split them up. Before long the other street kids in the city knew that Nelio, despite his young age, had taken over leadership from Cosmos, who had set off on a mysterious journey.

It was also during this period that Nelio began to speculate more and more about why the world looked the way it did. Before him he saw life teeming in the streets of the city. One day, when he was an old man and about to eat his last meal, would he have to dig that too out of the garbage cans the way he did now? Was life really nothing more? Was that all? He remembered the words that the white dwarf, Yabu Bata, had spoken before they parted. "There are two roads. One will lead you in the right direction, the other is the path of foolishness and will lead a person straight to ruin." Which road had he chosen when he entered the city on that morning? Should he have continued to follow the endless shoreline instead? Nelio had only one mission in life: to survive. When he understood this, he grew uneasy. I have to do more than that, he thought. I have to do more than simply survive.

During that period he also acquired some habits which contributed to creating the image of him as a remarkable person. But he was never aware of the rumors circulating about him.

Every morning when he woke up he would ask himself whether he wanted to spend another day under the name Nelio. On those days when his name felt like a burden, he would choose another. He used to ask one of the boys playing by the equestrian statue what his name was and then take that name for the day. So far no one had discovered that he had turned the statue into his home. He always opened the hatch with caution when Manuel Oliveira began laughing outside his empty church, and he would slip out as quickly as possible. Then he would hurry through the city to the stairwell at the Ministry of Justice, where the others had begun to wake up at about the same time. They didn't want to be caught sleeping there when the guards arrived to open the doors or they would be brutally driven off and their cardboard boxes might be kicked to shreds.

The days of the street kids were always much the same without ever repeating themselves. Something would always happen that no one could have foreseen. But Nelio kept more and more to himself, and he would grow annoyed if the others didn't leave him in peace. His thoughts were often interrupted by Nascimento starting a fight with Pecado or someone in another band of street kids. Then Nelio would be forced to intervene to restore order and stop the strife from spreading.

When he stepped between the two combatants, silence would fall at once. No one had ever lifted a hand against Nelio, not even Nascimento. And no one could understand why he always managed to avoid being drawn into a fight. The rumor began to circulate that his father was some unknown *feticheiro* with exceptional powers which he had passed on to his son. Where the rumor stemmed from, where it had started, no one could say. But suddenly one day, a shadow fell across Nelio as he sat leaning against a tree right next to Dona Esmeralda's bakery, studying the torn and stained atlas of Africa that Alfredo Bomba had found in a garbage can the day before. When Nelio glanced up, a young woman holding a child was standing before him.

"My daughter is ill," said the woman plaintively.

"Then she ought to be given medicine," replied Nelio. "But I have no medicine to give you."

Nelio sank back into his thoughts. The woman did not move. Time passed. After more than an hour Nelio looked up at her again.

"I have no medicine," he repeated. "If your child was sick an hour ago, she must be even worse now."

The woman had the child bound to her breast. Now she undid the wrappings, knelt down and held out the child toward Nelio. Many people had gathered around. Nelio felt ill at ease. He had great respect for the *feticheiros* and *curandeiros* who possessed the secret powers, who could talk to the restlessly hovering spirits, who could drive out the evil and liberate the good that every person has inside him. Nelio realized now that the woman who was holding out her child thought that he was a *feticheiro*. That scared him. Dead *feticheiros* would punish him severely if he pretended to be one of them.

"You're making a mistake," he told the woman. "Go to a *curandeiro*. I'll give you money, if you'll just go away."

The woman didn't move. Nelio saw that Nascimento and the others were watching what was going on with interest. He had started to sweat.

"Go away," he repeated. "I can't help you. I'm only a boy."

Suddenly the woman began to appeal to the circle of bystanders, which was getting bigger all the time.

"My child is sick," she lamented. "He refuses to help her."

A murmur of displeasure erupted among those who stood there watching, and they immediately sided with the woman. Nelio saw that the only thing he could do was to take the child and hold her in his arms. He noticed that her lips were cracked and parched.

"Give the child boiled water with salt," he told the woman, remembering what his mother had given him.

The woman took her child, smiled and placed a few crumpled bills at Nelio's feet. The crowd began to disperse.

"Not even Cosmos was a *curandeiro*," said Pecado in amazement. "Can you make the fleas stop sucking my blood?"

Several days later the woman with the sick child came back. Her daughter was now well. Nelio assumed it was the boiled water and salt that had had an effect. But from that moment on, the story spread that Nelio possessed the sacred, healing powers. Not wanting to be caught as a *curandeiro* who was not genuine, Nelio understood that all he could do was to spread another rumor. He gathered the group around him.

"If too many people start coming to ask me to make them well, then it will be impossible for me to continue to be your leader. That's why we're going to spread the news that I will only receive sick people when I'm sitting at the exact same spot where the woman found me. Only there. Nowhere else."

From that day on, Nelio avoided sitting in the shade of that tree where he used to withdraw to ponder his many unanswered questions. Even though he never again held a sick child in his arms, he had acquired an invisible cloak over his shoulders, from which no one could free him. Nelio—he who was so young and yet had taken over as leader after Cosmos—was now a man with supernatural and magic powers. Nelio became a well-known figure in the city. Many started coming to him to ask advice. Nelio never tried to give a clever answer. He simply said what he thought. If he didn't understand a question, he would say so. If he had nothing to say, he would keep quiet. Rumors began to circulate that one day Nelio would perform a great miracle. Nobody knew what the miracle would be, but everyone expected it to be something magnificent, which would make their city famous around the world.

But Nelio had no intention of performing any magical or miraculous acts. He was striving only to do something that would make his life mean more than mere survival. At the same time, he took seriously his responsibilities as the successor of Cosmos. He was constantly trying to make sure that the kids in the group washed and didn't get sick. Several times he smashed half-empty wine bottles that Nascimento had found, determined to get drunk. During those brief times when they were not preoccupied with surviving, and they lounged on the pavement in a spot where they could find some shade, Nelio would listen to their dreams. He had discovered that the others' dreams were just as powerful as his own. He believed their dreams would always endure, no matter how hard their lives might be. Each and every one of them possessed a core that was as resilient and precious as a diamond. It was the dream of another day, a reunion, a bed to sleep in, a roof over their heads, an ID card.

Nelio decided that knowledge meant being able to see relationships between things. If anyone had asked him what was the fundamental need of every human being, he would have known the right answer at once: a roof and an ID card. That was what a person needed, in addition to food, water, a pair of pants and a blanket. It was by having a roof over their heads and ID cards in their pockets that human beings differed from the animals. These were the first steps toward a decent life, an escape from poverty—building yourself a roof and obtaining an ID card. When the time was ripe, Nelio would see to it that the kids Cosmos had entrusted to his care would set off on that long journey away from the streets.

Nelio listened to their dreams, and he was often annoyed when they were both absurd and unrealistic. Even though he always tried to hide his irritation, there were times when he couldn't help putting his foot down. When Tristeza had disturbed their afternoon siesta over a long period of time with his endless pronouncements about how he would one day open his own bank, Nelio put his foot down. He woke up those who had managed to fall asleep and gave a lecture.

"Everybody is entitled to talk about their dreams. You dream when you're dreaming, and you keep on dreaming when you talk about what you have dreamed. That's fine. But what Tristeza is doing is not fine. It's not a good dream to believe that one day you will open a bank. Especially if you can't even count. It's idiotic. So from now on Tristeza will not talk about his bank. Especially when the rest of us want to nap."

After that it was quiet. Everyone was happy to be allowed to sleep in peace. But Tristeza, who had a hard time understanding things and whose mind was sluggish, asked Nelio to repeat what he had said, and this time to say everything move slowly. Nelio was overcome with remorse when he saw how sad Tristeza felt when his dream was forbidden. He saw that he had to give him another dream at once so that he wouldn't lose his spirit.

"You must practise thinking faster," Nelio said. "That's what you should dream about. That one day you'll be able to think as fast as the rest of us. When you've learned to do that, we'll collect enough money for you to buy a pair of sneakers."

Tristeza gave him a look of disbelief.

"I mean it," Nelio said. "Do I usually make promises that I don't keep?"

Tristeza shook his head.

"You can go to the shop yourself and pick out whatever shoes you want," Nelio said. "Then you can take the money out of your pocket and pay for them yourself."

"I'll never learn to think that fast," Tristeza said.

"You'll get your shoes when you've learned to think just a little bit faster than now."

"I don't know how to do that."

"You think about too many things at once. That's why your head is always in such a muddle. Learn to think about only one thing and nothing else."

"What should I think about?"

"Think about how hot it is," Nelio said. "Think about how soundly we're going to sleep and how seldom we'll be annoyed with you if you're not always talking about your bank. Think about that until you fall asleep. Later I'll give you something else to think about."

"Sneakers," Tristeza said.

"Yes," Nelio said. "Sneakers. Quiet now! Think. And sleep."

Afterward, when Tristeza too had fallen asleep, Nelio lay awake in the shade of his tree. He tried to imagine Tristeza in ten years, in twenty, as a grown man. He grew sad at the thought that Tristeza probably wouldn't live that long. The world wasn't made for slow-witted street kids.

*

One morning Alfredo Bomba came over to Nelio, who was absentmindedly scraping dirt off his feet with a dull, broken knife blade. He told Nelio that during the night he had dreamed that the next day was his birthday.

"But you don't know what day you were born," said Nelio.

"I dreamed that I knew," replied Alfredo Bomba. "Why would I dream something that wasn't true?"

Nelio looked at him thoughtfully. Then he clapped his hands and stood up.

"You're right," he said. "Of course it's your birthday tomorrow, and we're going to celebrate it. Leave me alone now so I can think about your birthday in peace."

Whenever Nelio had to solve a problem or think something through until there was nothing more to think about it, he always wanted to be left alone. He couldn't think when the others were jabbering all around him. He would sit in the scorched-brown grass behind the gas station where his only companions were a few scrawny goats. That was where he went now to think about Alfredo Bomba's birthday. After an hour he knew what they would do. He called the group together for a conference. Nascimento arrived carrying a box of half-rotten tomatoes that had fallen off the roof of an overloaded bus. With quick and practised hands they tore off the parts of the tomatoes that were rotten and gobbled down the rest. Nelio waited until the box was all but empty before he began to speak.

"Tomorrow is a great day. It's Alfredo Bomba's birthday. That's what he dreamed, and so it has to be true. I assume he's going to be nine or ten or maybe eleven. But that's not important. Nothing is preventing Alfredo Bomba from being as old as he wants to be. And tomorrow we're going to celebrate Alfredo Bomba's birthday."

Nelio pointed to a house a short distance from the gas station.

In Dom Joaquim's day it had belonged to a wealthy plantation owner who had vast fields of tea in the remote western provinces. After the arrival of the young revolutionaries, the house stood empty for a long time and fell into disrepair. But during recent years various whites had lived there who had come to this country to offer assistance—people who were called *cooperantes*. Right now a man was living there who had bright yellow hair and who came from a country that no one had heard of. Nelio had once overheard that the man was a *marques*, without understanding what that meant.

Nelio had often wondered about these *cooperantes*. They wore shorts and sandals and carried small pouches of money in belts around their waists. Nelio thought this might be their uniform. They had big cars, and they were almost always friendly to the street kids and gave them too much money for guarding their cars. They liked getting red in the face from the sun and always tried to show that they weren't afraid of all the blacks who always wanted money from them—although Nelio had, of course, perceived that they were actually terrified.

Nelio pointed at the house.

"Tomorrow is Saturday. That means the *marques* will pack up his car with mattresses and chairs and food boxes. He won't be back until the following day, on Sunday. His *empregada* has the day off, and the night watchman always sleeps soundly. Nascimento can also try to get hold of a bottle of wine to give him. Then he'll sleep even more soundly. Since the man who lives there is a *marques* and *cooperante*, he's here to help the poor people of our country. We are poor. And he can help us by celebrating Alfredo Bomba's birthday. We'll hold the celebration in his house."

He encountered a storm of protest. Nelio knew that everyone thought his idea was excellent, and they were trying to help by pointing out anything that might be a problem.

"We can't break into the house," said Mandioca. "The police will come. We'll have to have the birthday party in jail. They'll beat us badly. Especially Alfredo Bomba, since his birthday is to blame for it all."

"We're not going to break in," Nelio said. "I'll explain later."

"Since it's not our house, we'll have to be quiet," said Nascimento. "But we can't be quiet. We've never been able to do that. How can we celebrate a birthday without making a racket?"

"We won't open the windows," Nelio said. "And we won't break anything."

"We can't turn on the lights," said Pecado. "Are we going to walk around in the dark in a strange house? A lot of things will get broken, whether we like it or not."

"The *marques* always leaves the lights on when he's away," said Nelio, "so that no robbers will break in."

He countered all their objections and then explained how they would get inside the house.

"Mandioca is the one who can do two things better than anyone else. First, he can look more pitiful and starving than the rest of us. Second, he can keep quiet and sit still for a long time. That's why, Mandioca, you will go up to the house and ring the bell. The *cooperante* will open the door. Then you will faint and collapse just inside the threshold. The *cooperante* will get worried; he'll bring you water to drink. After a while you'll start feeling better. You ask to use the toilet. When you're alone in there, you unlatch the window. Do it so no one will notice. Then you thank the *cooperante* for everything he has done for you. He'll probably give you some money, since you're so hungry. And then you come back here to us."

"If I'm supposed to look hungry, I'll have to be full," said Mandioca. "If I'm really hungry when I'm supposed to look hungry, I'll just look crazy."

Nelio pointed to the box of tomatoes.

"The rest of the tomatoes are Mandioca's," he said. "There's just one thing you should remember when you're inside the house. If you have to pee when you're in the bathroom, pee into the chair with the lid. Don't pee in the bowl with the faucets. Do you understand?"

"I won't pee," Mandioca said. "What kind of bowl?"

"You'll see when you get there," said Nelio. "Now we'll wait here until the *cooperante* comes home."

"What happens if he doesn't leave tomorrow?" asked Nascimento.

"All the *cooperantes* lie on the beach and turn red on Saturday and Sunday," said Mandioca. "Nelio's right."

"I've never had a birthday party," said Alfredo Bomba. "What do you do?"

"You eat and dance and sing," said Nelio. "And that's exactly what we're going to do. And we'll get cleaned up and sleep in beds and have a roof over our heads. We can look at the pictures on his TV."

"Maybe he doesn't have a TV," Nascimento said.

"All *cooperantes* have a TV," said Nelio. "They have yellow hair and they have TVs. You have to learn that once and for all."

Mandioca fainted on the threshold of the *marques*'s house, unlatched the window in the bathroom, and was given 20,000 when he had revived and was able to leave the house. The next day they stood in the street and waved to the yellow-haired man as he left in his car. Late in the afternoon Nascimento managed to get hold of a wine bottle that was half full. By eight in the evening the night watchman was asleep, and they crept into the garden at the back of the house. By climbing up on Mandioca's shoulders, Tristeza reached the window and slithered inside. A few minutes later he opened the outer door as Nelio had instructed. They hid in the shadows and waited for a couple of policemen to pass by on the street. Then they slipped swiftly out of the shadows and disappeared through the door. Nelio told them sternly to stand still and not touch anything until he checked to see that all the curtains were drawn. Then he gathered them around him in the hall.

"Now everybody will go and get cleaned up. It's especially important that you all have clean feet."

Since he mistrusted their desire to wash properly, he locked them in the bathroom and said that he would let them out, one by one, after he had personally checked to see that they were clean enough. Then he walked through the house, opened the two refrigerators, decided where they would sleep, turned on the TV, and finally put away two porcelain vases that might easily fall to the floor and break.

Nascimento had to wash his feet three times before Nelio was satisfied. Then he gathered everyone in the kitchen.

"*Cooperantes* always have a lot of food in the refrigerator," he said. "I'm convinced that the man who lives here will be pleased that we're celebrating Alfredo Bomba's birthday with a proper meal. So let's cook."

Nelio went into action as if he were organizing an invasion. He put Mandioca in charge of the vegetables, while he told Pecado and Nascimento to cook the rice. Alfredo Bomba and Tristeza helped the others while Nelio cut up a big piece of meat into small pieces and started to fry them. When the food was ready, they sat down at the big table. They had found some juice in the pantry, and they looked at Nelio and waited for his permission to begin.

"Today might well be Alfredo Bomba's birthday," he said. "At least he dreamed that it was. So let's eat."

Several times during the meal Nelio had to intervene when fights threatened to break out over the meat. When Nascimento started getting loud without being aware of it, Nelio sniffed at his glass and realized that Nascimento had mixed his juice with alcohol. Without his noticing, Nelio exchanged Nascimento's glass with his own, and later poured it into the sink. Afterward, when they had also found two big cartons of ice cream in the huge freezer, they started dancing to a radio that Nelio brought in from the enormous living room. He thought it best if they stayed in the kitchen, where there were no carpets to get dirty; the floor was tiled and easy to wash. At first Nelio sat off to one side and watched the dance. Deep inside his head he seemed to hear the sounds of a *timbila* and the drums in the village that the bandits had burned. Suddenly they were all around him in the *marques*'s kitchen: the spirits that were looking for him, all of the dead and all of those who might be dead or might still be living. He could feel that he was about to become so sad that he might disrupt Alfredo Bomba's party with his mournful face. He got up from his chair, and joined the dance. He danced as if in a trance until the sweat ran down his forehead. They kept on dancing late into the night; they danced until they didn't have a single dance step left in their legs or hips.

By then Alfredo Bomba had already fallen asleep under the big table. Nelio showed them where they should sleep—some in the *marques*'s bed, others on the sofas. When it was quiet in the house, Nelio went back to the kitchen and cleaned up. By daybreak, no one could have said that anyone had been there as long as they didn't look into the refrigerators or the freezer. Nelio walked through the silent rooms and looked at the group of kids as they slept.

He had the feeling that he was wandering through many different times and worlds all at once. It was as if he could remember the little forest grove outside the village where he grew up, the village the bandits had come to burn.

They never burned the trees, he thought. The forest has been growing for hundreds of years. Each time a child is born, a tree is planted. You could see from his tree how old a person was. The tall and thick tree trunks, which gave the most shade, belonged to people who had already returned to the spirit world. But the trees of the living and the dead stood in the same grove, sought their nourishment from the same soil and the same rain. They stood there waiting for the children that were not yet born, the trees that had not yet been planted. In that way the forest would grow, and the age of the village would be visible for all time. No one could tell from a tree whether someone was dead, only that he had been born.

Nelio looked at the sleeping children and thought that he was wandering through a world that might not yet exist. In some future they would sleep in beds and on sofas, and they would dream the dreams that only people with full bellies can dream. Maybe the future would look like the *marques*'s house.

He thought he could see something that the elders had talked about, as the greatest miracle that a person might be privileged to experience. To see what has been and what would come, all in the same moment.

He would never forget the night they spent in the *marques*'s house. Alfredo Bomba would remember his birthday; Nelio would remember the feeling of floating freely through time. It's possible to fly without visible wings, he thought. The wings are inside us, if we're privileged to see them.

The first to wake was Tristeza. "What should I think about today?" he asked.

"Think about how it feels to have clean feet," Nelio said.

The others woke up and rubbed the sleep out of their eyes.

First they looked around in amazement; then they remembered. It was still early dawn. By peeking through a curtain Nelio could see that the night watchman was still asleep.

"It's time to go," he said. "The same way we came."

"How did you know there would be so much food in the cupboards that are cold?" Nascimento asked him.

"A man who comes home every day with big baskets of food can't be eating everything himself," Nelio said. "You've seen it for yourself. You could have answered that question without my help."

They left the *marques*'s house as stealthily as they had come.

"What will he say," Alfredo Bomba said, worried, "when he discovers all the food is gone?"

"I don't know," Nelio said. "Maybe like other whites who live in our world, he'll say that Africa and the blacks are inscrutable."

"Are we?" asked Alfredo Bomba. "Are we inscrutable?"

"No, we're not," Nelio said. "But the world we live in can sometimes be hard to understand."

They went out on to the street, knowing that they shared a great secret. Nelio could see that they started rummaging through the garbage cans and begging to guard cars with greater energy than usual so early in the morning.

He thought that what they had done was a good thing. That's why they would never do it again.

That morning Nelio was very tired. He said that he was going to sit in the shade of his tree and that he didn't want to be disturbed. They should also do their best not to fight or make a lot of noise around him.

But when he reached his tree he gave a start and stopped. Someone was sitting there. Someone he had never seen before. He was annoyed that his place beside the tree had not been respected. No one else was allowed to sit there.

He went over to the tree. It was a girl sitting there. And she was just as white, just as much an albino, as Yabu Bata.

I waited for more, but it never came. Nelio had cut short his story and slipped into his own thoughts. Then he looked up at me.

"I remember that I thought it had to mean something important," he said. His voice was quite faint now, and I thought about the wounds that smelled bad and were growing darker under the bandage.

"First Yabu Bata showed me the way to the city," he went on. "And now a girl in ragged clothing was sitting in the shade under my tree. I thought it had to mean something. And it did."

I thought about my own woman. The new dough mixer whom no one had escorted home in the night. I felt already a tense anticipation about seeing her again that evening.

"I see that you're thinking about something that makes you happy," Nelio said. "If I wasn't so tired, I would like to hear you talk about it."

"You must rest," I said. "Then I will take you to the hospital."

Nelio did not reply. He had already closed his eyes.

I stood up and left the roof.

The sixth night was over.

The Seventh Night

Can you hear from a man's footsteps that he's in love? If that's true, and I think it is, then Maria must have known that my heart was already burning for her when I entered the bakery on the second night that we were going to bake Dona Esmeralda's bread together. It was very hot, and she was wearing a thin dress through which the contours of her body were quite evident. She had started work by the time I came down from the roof, and she smiled when she caught sight of me.

Now, more than a year later, I can imagine that if everything had been different—if Nelio hadn't died and I hadn't left my job at Dona Esmeralda's and later reappeared as the Chronicler of the Winds—then maybe Maria and I would have become a couple. But we never did, and today it's no longer possible since she is bound to another man. I have seen her in the city, and she had a man quite close by her side. I think he was selling birds at one of the city's marketplaces, and her stomach was enormous. Even though our time together was so brief and even though I never found out whether my feelings for Maria were reciprocated, I hold on to my memory of her as the greatest joy of my life. A joy which also contained within it the seed of the greatest sorrow.

Something in my life seemed to come to an end during those days when Nelio lay on the roof of the theater, slowly languishing from the black wounds that poisoned him and finally took the life from him. I think that's the way it has to be expressed: that his life was taken from him. Death always comes uninvited; it disrupts and causes disorder. But in Nelio's case, death arrived with a crowbar and broke its way into his body and stole his spirit.

Afterward, when I had taken off my white cap, hung up my apron and left Dona Esmeralda's bakery behind, it was a different life that I began. I could not have taken Maria into that life, even if I had wanted to. How could I have asked her to follow me out into the world as the wife of a man who had chosen to be a beggar? How could I have made her understand that, for me, this was a necessity?

But I did see her in the streets of the city. And she was still extremely beautiful. I will never forget her. One day when I know that my time has come, when the spirits are calling me too, I will close my eyes and in my soul I will see her again, and with the image of her I will leave this world. It will make death easier for me. At least I hope so. Because as an ordinary, simple man, I feel the same fear of the unknown that everyone feels. I don't think my fear comes from the fact that life is short. The trembling and darkness that seize hold of me tell me that I will be dead for such an extremely long time.

I hope my spirit will have wings. I can't sit motionless in the shade of a tree during all the time I will have to spend in the unknown landscape of eternity.

I think you can hear from a man's footsteps that he's in love. His feet barely touch the ground, all fear is conquered, and time is dissolved like the fog in the first light of dawn.

Maria was the best dough mixer I ever had. I asked her where she had worked before and how Dona Esmeralda had found her. But she merely laughed at me, and never did give me an answer.

To watch her work was like listening to someone sing.

When you see someone working the way she did, you start to sing yourself.

I baked the best bread of my life during those nights when Maria mixed the dough and I followed her out to the street after midnight to watch her disappear into the dark. I was already longing for the next night when she would come back. In a childish and perhaps naive way I would worry that she had vanished into the darkness, never to return. But she did come back, her dresses were always thin, and she would smile her beautiful smile when I came down from the roof.

I wish that I could have told her about Nelio. She would have changed his bandage better than I did, and maybe she also would have persuaded him that the time was right to be carried down from the roof and taken to the hospital if he wanted to live.

But I never told her anything. And I never mentioned her name to Nelio either.

Up there, beneath the stars, only he and I existed.

When I went up to him on the roof after shoving the first baking pans into the hot oven, I felt that he was lying there waiting for me. Was it still true that he was trying to get better? His wounds had darkened more, and I held my breath as I unwrapped the bandage because the stench was so awful. But could a healing process be under way that was not apparent to me? I felt his forehead. It was hot again. I diluted some of Senhora Muwulene's herbs with water, and he drank the solution but with greater effort. It occurred to me that he had never asked me what kind of herbs I was giving him. From the moment I carried him up to the roof, he never once questioned my ability to take care of him.

Or was it because he already knew, from the moment the shots were fired, that there was no saving him?

I might have wished that I had not been alone with the responsibility. It was too great for me to bear alone, and yet I had no one to share it with. It was quite simply too late.

I helped him put on a clean shirt after I had changed his bandage. Since it was so warm, I took away the blanket and folded it beneath his head as an extra pillow. He was very tired, but his eyes were strangely clear. Again I had the feeling that he could see right through me.

At those moments when he looked at me, he was a ten-year-old boy lying there, with two bullets in his body. But when the fever returned, he was transformed once more into a very old man. I thought that it was not only his consciousness that seemed able to switch unhindered between what had been and what was to come, between the spirit world and the world that we lived in together. His body could also switch between ages, between the child that he was and the old man he would never be.

"Do the spirits of our ancestors have faces?" I asked him. Where that question came from, I didn't know. It was as if I didn't know what I was saying until after I had said it.

"People have faces," replied Nelio. "Spirits don't have faces. And yet we recognize them. We know who is who. Spirits don't have eyes or mouths or ears either. And yet they can see and speak and hear."

"How do you know that?"

"The spirits are all around us," he said. "They're right here, but we can't see them. What's important is that we know they can see us."

I didn't ask any more questions. I wasn't sure whether I had understood what he meant. But I didn't want to tire him unnecessarily.

That night he told me about the arrival of the *xidjana*.

She was the one who turned up on that morning after they celebrated Alfredo Bomba's birthday in the *marques*'s house. She was wearing a ragged dress, her face was covered with burns from the scorching sun, and she truly was an albino. She heard Nelio approach and quickly turned.

"What are you doing sitting in my place under the tree?" asked Nelio.

"A shadow is not a house that can be owned," the *xidjana* said. "I'm thinking of staying here."

During all his days on the streets, Nelio had never been as challenged as he was by the *xidjana*. Yet he sensed that she was uncertain and maybe even weak. He squatted down a short distance away.

"What's your name?"

"Deolinda."

"Where are you from?"

"The same place as you. Nowhere."

"What are you doing here?"

"I want to stay here."

They were interrupted by Nascimento who had caught sight of the girl under the tree from his place on the bed of the rusty truck which he happened to be guarding. With a howl he came running over.

"What's this *xidjana* doing here? Don't you know that a *xidjana* means bad luck?"

"I'm not bad luck," said the girl, standing up.

"Get away from here," screamed Nascimento, rushing at her with clenched fists. Nelio didn't have time to intervene. But it wasn't necessary anyway. Reacting swiftly, the *xidjana* knocked Nascimento to the ground. He lay there, staring in amazement up at Deolinda who stood leaning over him.

"I'm not bad luck," the girl said. "I can beat anyone and I want to stay here."

"We can't have a *xidjana* around," Nascimento said, getting to his feet.

"Her name is Deolinda," Nelio said. "Go back to the truck. She's stronger than you are."

Nascimento left. Nelio watched him summoning the others to the bed of the truck. None of them would want an albino in the group. He too thought it best if she disappeared. The band of kids should never be allowed to get too big: he would lose control, and the group, in turn, would lose control of itself.

"You're sitting in my place," Nelio said. "That's forbidden. Get out of here! We don't want a girl in our group. You can't do anything we can't do."

"I can read," Deolinda said. "I can do lots of things."

Nelio was sure that she was lying. He pointed at a word that someone had scratched on the side of the building.

"What does this say?"

Deolinda squinted as if the harsh sunlight was hurting her eyes.

"*Terrorista.*"

Nelio, who couldn't read, realized that he wouldn't be able to tell whether she was right.

"It's just because the letters are so big that you can read them," he said evasively.

He picked up a piece of newspaper from the street.

"Read this," he said, handing the paper to Deolinda.

She held it up close to her eyes and started to read.

"'A number of children will be given the chance to live in a big house. Nobody's children will become Everybody's children.'"

"What does that mean? 'Nobody's children?' What's that?"

She frowned and thought for a moment. Then her face brightened.

"Maybe that's us."

She continued to spell her way through the words. "'A European organization will give money to the project . . .'"

"'The project'?"

"We're going to be projected. I've been projected once. They gave me clothes and I was supposed to live in a house with lots of other kids. I was supposed to stop living on the street. But I projected myself out as fast as I could."

Nelio begrudgingly acknowledged that Deolinda actually did know how to read. He realized that she had a good head, even though it was white and covered with permanent burns. And yet he still was not sure whether she should be allowed to stay with the group. Maybe it was true that an albino brought misfortune. But he also reminded himself that he had heard the opposite from his father. A *xidjana* could never die; a *xidjana* possessed many extraordinary powers.

But the big problem was something else entirely. She was a girl. Not many girls lived on the streets. Things were often much worse for them than for the boys.

Nelio needed to be alone to think.

"Go away," he said. "Get two grilled chickens. Show us what you can do. Then I will decide."

Deolinda left. Slung over one shoulder she had a little bag made from woven strips of raffia. Her dress was hanging in tatters, but she carried herself as if at any moment she might start dancing. Nelio sat down in his spot in the shade under the tree. What would Cosmos have done? he wondered. He tried to picture Cosmos on board a ship, far away, quite close to the sun. He tried to hear his voice.

"You're crazy if you let her into the group," he seemed to hear Cosmos saying.

"But she can read," Nelio protested. "I've never heard of a street kid who could read. Least of all a girl."

"Did you see her eyes?" Cosmos said, and Nelio thought his voice sounded annoyed. "Did you see that they're red and inflamed? That's the kind of eyes you get from reading. And then you go blind."

"All *xidjanas* have red eyes," Nelio said. "Even the ones who can't read."

He heard Cosmos sigh. "Let her stay then. But chase her away as soon as there's a problem."

Nelio nodded. He would let her stay. But only if she came back with the grilled chickens.

By evening she still hadn't returned. Nelio thought that she must have realized that she wouldn't be allowed to stay, and so she wasn't going to bother to get the chickens or come back. Nascimento was pleased and said that he would kill her if she ever appeared on their street again. When Mandioca pointed out that Nascimento had been knocked down by a *xidjana,* a violent fight broke out, and Nelio had great difficulty stopping it. It began with Nascimento throwing himself at Mandioca. But when Alfredo Bomba got mixed up in it, their anger turned on him. Nelio had learned that fights among street kids followed their own rules and could develop in the most unexpected directions.

"She's gone," he said when the fight was over. "Maybe she'll come back, maybe she won't. For now we can forget that she was ever here."

They started getting ready for the night.

"What should I think about now?" asked Tristeza.

"Think about the night at the *marques*'s house," Nelio said.

"I've stopped thinking about my bank," Tristeza said proudly.

"You can think about it once a week," said Nelio. "But never in the afternoon when we're having our siesta."

In the morning of the following day Deolinda came back. Nelio found her once again sitting under his tree. When he went over to her, she pulled two chickens out of her bag.

"Where did you get them?"

"An ambassador was having a big dinner in his garden. I climbed over two fences and went into the kitchen when no one was looking."

Nelio didn't know what an ambassador was. He hesitated for a moment, wondering whether he should tell Deolinda that he didn't know. Then his curiosity got the better of him.

"An ambassador?" he said.

"An ambassador for a country far away."

"What country?"

"Europe."

Nelio had heard people talk about Europe. That's where the *marqueses* came from, and all the others who were *cooperantes* and had small pouches with money on their bellies.

He tasted one of the chickens.

"Not enough *piri-piri*," he said.

Deolinda opened her bag and took out a little glass jar.

"*Piri-piri*," she said.

The group had cautiously approached. Nelio divided the two chickens among them. At first Nascimento refused to take his share, but finally he snatched a piece and sat down a short distance away. From that moment on, Deolinda was one of them. Nelio remembered Cosmos asking him who he belonged to, and then from that moment on he was one of them. Now they had taken in Deolinda, and Nelio knew that the group was complete. No other new members would join unless one of them disappeared.

When the chickens had been eaten, Nelio told Nascimento to come closer.

"From now on Deolinda will be one of us. This means that no one can hit her without first asking my permission. Since she's new, she'll get only a half-share of our money. When we think that she deserves it, she'll get the same as everybody else. And no one calls her a *xidjana* unless she agrees to it. At the same time, Deolinda can't take advantage of the fact that she's a girl. She has to act exactly like the rest of us."

Nelio thought about whether he had forgotten anything. After a moment's hesitation he added one thing.

"If Deolinda wants to be alone when she pees, she can. And she can also have a blanket if it's cold at night. But she has to get the blanket herself."

Nelio looked around to see if anyone wanted to say anything.

"What do we need her for?" Nascimento said. "She's neither black nor white, and she'll bring bad luck."

To everyone's surprise, it was Tristeza who spoke up. "Maybe that's a good thing. When she's with us, she's a *xidjana*. When she's with the whites, she's white. She can be both them and us."

"A good answer," Nelio said. "Soon you will earn your sneakers."

It didn't take long before Nelio saw that he had been right about taking Deolinda into the group. She was clever at begging, and she was quick to see possibilities in various situations that cropped up on the street. And besides, she could fight and defend herself. Soon nobody dared to accost her without risking that she would demonstrate her superior strength. Only Nascimento openly continued to show his dissatisfaction. Nelio began to suspect that one day Nascimento might leave them to join another band of street kids. He took Nascimento behind the gas station and asked him straight out if he was thinking of leaving.

"No," Nascimento said.

Nelio could hear that he was lying. But there was nothing he could do if Nascimento decided to leave.

It took a long time before Nelio began to understand what had driven Deolinda to the streets. Whenever he asked her about it, she would only snarl that it was nobody's business. It wasn't until Nelio opened her raffia bag while she was asleep and found inside a photograph of a man and a woman that he began to have some inkling of what some of the reasons might be. The man's face had been obliterated. The facial features had been scraped away with a nail or a stone. Nelio put the photograph back, ashamed that he had looked in her bag. No one should ever be forced to reveal a secret; and no one had the right to obtain information by stealth to satisfy his curiosity.

Nelio recalled something his mother had once said: No one is allowed to break his way into another's person's heart like a thief in the night.

Nelio soon noticed that Deolinda and Mandioca had become friends. They often squatted on the street, whispering to each other until they burst into laughter. If Nascimento was nearby he would angrily prowl around them without daring to interrupt their camaraderie. But they didn't seem to pay any attention to him.

One evening when Nelio was on his way home to his statue, he noticed that Deolinda was following him. His first thought was to stop and tell her to go back to the others. Then he realized that he might have a chance to find out what had driven her onto the streets. When he reached the small plaza, which was now deserted except for the sleeping night watchmen and the man who sold chicken thighs from his coal-fired drum, Nelio sat down at the foot of the statue. Deolinda had stopped at the street corner and was trying to hide in the shadows. But he called out that he had seen her. He thought she might be embarrassed at being caught.

"Who gave you permission to follow me?"

"I wanted to see where you live," she replied, looking him straight in the eye.

"You can follow me for the rest of your life, but you'll never find out where I live."

"Why not?"

"Because I just disappear."

"I'd like to see that."

Nelio nodded. "If I manage to disappear without you noticing, what will you give me in return?"

She took a step back. "I won't do *xogo-xogo*."

Nelio was embarrassed. He knew what *xogo-xogo* was, but he had never done it. He knew that he wasn't old enough yet even to want to do it. "I just want to know where you're from. Nothing else."

"Why do you want to know that?"

"You can't go on being part of the group if I don't know where you're from. What did you do on the day before you sat down in my place in the shade of the tree? Why did you sit there? I have lots of questions."

She was thinking about this. Then she nodded. "You won't be able to disappear without me noticing. So I agree to answer your questions."

"Turn around and close your eyes. Cover your ears. Count to ten. Can you count?"

"I can do everything. I can count and read and write."

"Where did you learn all that?"

She didn't answer.

"Turn around," he repeated. "Close your eyes and count out loud to ten. And cover your ears too. If you cheat, you'll be struck blind."

Nelio saw that she shuddered. She had heard about his supernatural powers.

She turned, shut her eyes and started counting. Nelio opened the hatch and quickly crawled inside the horse. He could see her through a hole next to the horse's mane. She finished counting and turned around. The plaza was deserted, there was no place he could have hidden, and he wouldn't have had time to run to the corner and disappear.

Nelio tried to decipher Deolinda's thoughts from her expression. She was confronted with something she hadn't expected.

Then she walked away. Nelio waited until he was sure that she had left the plaza. Then he crept out of the hatch and dashed through the night-empty streets, taking the shortest route he knew, until he was back at the Ministry of Justice building where the rest of the group was already asleep. He sat near his tree and waited. When he saw Deolinda coming, Nelio stood up and walked toward her. She gave a start when she caught sight of him.

"I disappeared and I came back," he said. Then he stretched out his hand to her. "Touch my hand. It's warm. I'm not a shadow or a phantom standing here."

She touched his hand with her fingertips.

"People sleep too much," Nelio said. "Let's use the night to talk."

He took her to the botanical gardens, up on the hill near the hospital. The gates were locked with heavy chains and padlocks, but Nelio knew of a hole in the fence. That's where they crawled through, and he led Deolinda over to a bench that was still sturdy enough to sit on. Next to the botanical gardens was a hotel, and its sign lit up the area around the bench.

Deolinda's face was stark white.

Nelio looked at her ragged dress and thought that soon they would have to get some money together so that she could buy a new one.

He didn't have to ask a single question. She started talking about her life of her own accord. He sensed that it was a relief for her, and he listened attentively.

She was born in one of the poorest suburbs of the city, a collection of shacks and hovels surrounding the city's swamplike dump. She was born and she was albino. Her father refused to look at her. He accused her mother of conceiving the child with a dead man that she had secretly met in a cemetery at night. Then he had chased her out of his house. Deolinda later learned that this was the time of her mother's greatest despair. But she would never have killed her daughter, she would never have strangled her and buried her in the garbage so that she could return to her husband. She took her daughter to a town that was many days' walk from the city. There she had a sister, and there they would be able to live. Her three other children remained with their father, and she grieved for them so fiercely that for long periods of time she was close to death. One day, many months later, a message arrived from her husband, telling her that she didn't need to come back; he had found a new woman who would never give birth to an albino. The children would stay with him, and he cursed the dishonor she had brought upon him by being unfaithful to him with a ghost in a cemetery.

"I was born with a ghost for a father," Deolinda said, and it sounded as if she were spitting out the words. "Today, now that I'm grown up and smart, I realize that it's true. My father is a ghost, even if he's alive."

"How old are you?"

She shrugged. "Eleven. Or fifteen. Or ninety."

"I think you're twelve," Nelio said.

"If I'm twelve, then I'll stay twelve for the rest of my life," she said. "Why do we always have to exchange one age for another?"

"I've had the same thought," Nelio said. "I think I'll go on being ten until I get tired of it. Then I'll be ninety-three."

Frogs were croaking in the pond of the botanical gardens. Deolinda had several half-rotten bananas in her woven bag which they shared.

After she learned to walk and already had four rainy seasons behind her, Deolinda became aware that she was different. Then, at the very time when she must have needed her more than ever, Deolinda's mother was struck by madness, which not even the renowned *curandeiro,* sent for from another village, was able to cure. She stopped eating altogether, she refused to braid her hair, and she started wandering around the village with no clothes on. Finally her sister locked her up in a hut and nailed the door shut. They gave her water through the slits in the wall. That was also where she died one night, after having poked out her eyes with a splinter from one of the bamboo poles supporting the roof. The last memory Deolinda had of her mother was of her hands sticking out of the slits in the wall of the hut. As if that was all that was left of her—two empty hands, ceaselessly wringing.

After Deolinda's mother died, her aunt changed. She blamed

Deolinda for her sister's death, she frequently beat her, and sometimes she even refused to give her food. Deolinda tried to find out why she had changed, but no one could give her an answer. And so she started to believe that she actually deserved all the blame people placed on her. In her the ancestors had gathered all their misdeeds; they had chosen her to bear them. Deolinda realized that she couldn't stay in the village, and the only person she could think of who might help her was her father. She left the village one night when everyone was asleep, and she never went back. When she arrived in the city and found her father's house near the stinking dump, he chased her off with a stick and warned her never to come back. After that, the streets of the city were all that remained for her. Many times the nuns took her to an orphanage. But she never stayed more than a few days. On the city streets there were others who were as white as she was. Some of them even had cars. They had jobs, and they lived in proper houses. She had discovered, above all, that they also had black children. On the streets of the city she was not alone in being different.

"I'm going to stay alive so that I can have children," she said. "I'm going to have thousands of children, and they're all going to be black. Then, when I can't have any more children, I'm going to kill my father."

"That's probably not a good idea," Nelio said. "If you absolutely have to have him dead, it would be wiser if you asked someone else to do it. I don't think it's good to sit in jail."

"I want you to teach me how to disappear," Deolinda said.

"I can't do that," he said. "I don't know how I do it myself. Tell me instead why you want to stay with us."

For a long time she sat in silence. Nelio closed his eyes and dozed on the bench while he waited.

He woke up with a start when Deolinda touched his shoulder.

"You're asleep," she said.

"I don't like waiting for anything," Nelio said. "Instead of waiting, I do something else. Just now I was sleeping."

"Cosmos is my brother."

He was astounded. He thought about what she had told him for a while. Could it really be true?

"He saw the way my father chased me off with a stick. He was still living at home then. Our father started beating him too. He came to the city. He became the leader of the kids sleeping over there on the steps. We would sometimes meet in secret. He said that I could come here after he had set off on his journey. He was the one who taught me to read and write and count."

"But how could he know that I would take you in?"

"He thought that you would."

Nelio kept thinking about this strange piece of news.

"Was that why Cosmos set off on his journey?" he asked. "So that you could come to us?"

"Maybe."

"Cosmos ought to be hung on the wall of a church," Nelio said. "Not Cosmos himself, but his picture. His face carved out of wood, like a saint."

They left the botanical gardens and crept out through the same hole they had used to get in.

"When I grow up, I'm going to sing for the whole world," Deolinda said as they made their way through the empty streets.

"Can you sing?"

"Yes," said Deolinda, "I can sing. And my voice is very black."

"Everybody's tongue is red," Nelio said. "Just like everybody's blood. There's so much to think about. So much that is strange."

Deolinda wrapped herself in her blanket next to Mandioca. Tristeza and Mandioca lay on either side of Nascimento, who had crawled into his cardboard box and pulled down the lid. They lay there like two guards, ready if Nascimento should be attacked by the monsters that were always lurking in his dreams. Nelio stared thoughtfully at the ragged band. Then he went to his statue, thinking about what Deolinda had told him. On the way he passed a big hotel where festively dressed people were getting into their cars. He stopped for a moment and stared at all that wealth. Then he continued on his way.

But when he had crawled into the statue and rested his head on the left hind leg of the horse, he couldn't sleep, even though it was late. He started thinking back on the life he had lived in the past, before the bandits had come creeping out of the night and burned his village. He felt as if he were being drawn back in time by an invisible wind. Suddenly the horse's belly was filled with spirits scattering memories over him. He was overwhelmed by a great sorrow—so great that it was almost too heavy for his thin body to bear.

It's dawn. The dry earth is whirling outside the hut. His mother is pounding corn. And she is singing. He wakes up on the reed mat in the darkness of the hut. The smell of burning wood blows in through the opening of the hut. The smell of burning wood, which every morning reminds him that he will live another day. When he goes out into the strong sunlight, he can see that it's all true. His mother, who is pounding the heavy stick against the corn, his newborn sister, who is hanging on her back . . .

Inside the horse Nelio stood up straight, with his head inside the rider's ribcage. The horse seemed to be alive. He thought that soon he would have to return home. He had to find out what had happened, who was still alive, and who was dead.

The spirits hovering around him had no faces. The whole time he was afraid that he would suddenly recognize the presence of his father or his mother or his sisters and brothers. They would be dead, and it would be even harder for him to go on living life as he did now, which was only surviving.

Nelio would remember the days that followed as the time when he never danced and never smiled. He couldn't hide his gloomy mood, and he saw no reason to try. He was often annoyed at being disturbed all the time—by Nascimento who was always on his way from one fight to the next, and by Tristeza who came each day and asked what he should think about and when he was going to be allowed to buy his sneakers. Nelio would lose his temper, and afterward he would feel even gloomier at the thought that he had done something that was foreign to Cosmos. Deolinda, noticing that Nelio wanted to be left alone, tried to protect him. She chased off the others when she could, and she always saw to it that Nelio had something to eat without having to climb around on the garbage heaps himself to search for scraps.

Nelio often thought about Cosmos as he sat in the shade of his tree. He wondered whether he was still alive, whether he had drowned at sea, or whether he had come so close to the sun that he caught fire and burned up. He wondered whether Yabu Bata had found the path he had spent more than nineteen years searching for.

When his thoughts grew too burdensome, he would leave the street and set off on long, solitary wanderings. The others would send someone to follow him, to see that he didn't walk straight into the sea and disappear. Of course, Nelio noticed that someone was following him at a distance. Ordinarily he would have turned around and said that he wanted to be left alone. But he didn't have the energy to do that. He walked and walked, sometimes so far that he reached the place where he had spent the night on the eve of his first entrance into the city. Often he would come back after it was already dark.

It was Mandioca who suggested that they should try to cheer him up by giving him a dog. They often sat and talked anxiously about Nelio's remoteness and melancholy.

"He thinks too much," Nascimento said. "Cosmos never had so many thoughts. He's sick in the head. His brain has swollen up from all the walking and brooding that he's doing."

"What he needs is a dog," Mandioca said. "If you have a dog, you don't have time to think."

"What do you know about dogs?" Deolinda said.

"I had a dog once," said Mandioca sadly.

"What happened to him?" asked Deolinda.

"He ran away," replied Mandioca. "I look for him every day. Maybe he's looking for me."

"He died a long time ago," Nascimento said angrily. "Dogs die faster than people."

It looked as though a fight would break out between Mandioca and Nascimento. But Pecado stepped between them and said that they should be worrying about Nelio instead of fighting.

After discussing the pros and cons of getting a dog for Nelio, they decided it was worth trying. The next day they captured a brown dog by the harbor. The dog bit Nascimento on the hand, but they succeeded in tying a leash around his neck and dragged him back in triumph. Nelio was sitting in the shade of his tree when they appeared with the dog.

"We want to give you a dog so you'll be in a better mood," Pecado said. "He doesn't have a name, and I'm afraid he'll have to be tamed. He bit Nascimento on the hand. But I'm sure he'll be good company."

Nelio stared at the dog, which was alternately barking and

whining. He thought about the dogs that the bandits had killed when they burned the village.

He took the leash that Alfredo Bomba was holding.

"I thank you for catching a dog for me. I accept, and I will call him Rico. A stray dog is even poorer than we are, but I can still give him a good name. I will keep him until tomorrow. Then I'll let him go. But he will still be my dog. Tomorrow I will also be in a better mood. Now go away and leave me in peace."

That night the dog stood tied up outside the equestrian statue, barking. In the early dawn Nelio let him loose. He ran off at once, and Nelio never saw Rico again. That night, as he lay awake because of the dog's barking, he realized that he would have to do something about his bad mood. He couldn't continue to be the leader of the group if he was always impatient and angry. And yet he couldn't leave them because he had made a promise to Cosmos. And none of the others could take over the leadership.

The only one he could imagine doing it was Deolinda, but that would never work. An albino who was also a girl could never be the leader of a group of wild street kids.

The next day he called them together behind the gas station.

"I've had a lot to think about lately. And it was hard because you are always making such a commotion, but from now on everything will be different. I won't sit alone in the shade of my tree so often."

His words had the effect he had hoped for. He could see that they were relieved. To further emphasise that he was back to normal, he told them that they should all work extra hard and not take any unnecessary siestas. Tristeza would be allowed to use the money they earned to go to the shoe shop and choose a pair of sneakers. And from now on Deolinda would get the same share as everybody else. And they would also buy her a new dress.

"That we go around in rags is one thing," Nelio said. "But Deolinda is a girl. She should be properly dressed. But you have to wash well before you put on the new dress. And keep the old one. That's what you can wear when you climb around the garbage heaps looking for food."

A few days later Tristeza, his head held high, went into a shoe store, and when he came out he was wearing a pair of white sneakers. The same afternoon they bought Deolinda a new dress that was red with white trim around the sleeves.

"I thought all gloomy thoughts could be chased away," Nelio said at last, as dawn drew near on the morning of the eighth day. "But I was wrong. Because several days later something happened that made Deolinda disappear and never come back. And Alfredo Bomba started acting strangely."

Nelio fell silent, as if he had said too much.

"Alfredo Bomba," I said, trying to coax him to continue.

Nelio looked at me for a long time before he spoke again. With the red glow of the morning on his forehead, I could see that he was sweating. He was slipping once more into a fever.

And then, just as I was starting to fear that he was asleep, he began speaking again.

"Alfredo Bomba started acting strangely. And then everything else happened, ending with you finding me and carrying me up here to the roof."

Then I knew that we had come to the end of the story. Now I was going to find out what had happened on that night down in the empty theater. Maybe I would only have to wait one more night before I had the answers to the questions I had been pondering.

Nelio lay there with his eyes shut. I had put a cup of water next to the mattress. I got up carefully to go down to the yard and wash. I also had to wash my clothes, which were starting to smell bad.

Then Nelio began to speak again, without opening his eyes.

"It's not easy to die," he said. "It's the only thing that no one can teach us."

He said nothing more. As I went down the winding stairs, I felt frightened. I could no longer push the thought aside; I could no longer fool myself with false hopes.

Nelio was going to die on the roof. He had known it all along.

I sat down in the dark of the stairs and wept. I don't cry very often. I couldn't even remember the last time it had happened. I am a man who laughs. But on that morning I sat in the dark stairway and cried, and I thought that it was all too late, and that a ten-year-old boy who is an old man is still only a child.

A child should live, not die.

I borrowed money from one of the girls at the bakery counter and then went over to one of the city's *barraccas* and drank *tontonto*. It didn't take long before I was quite drunk, and I fell asleep on the ground.

When I woke up many hours later someone had stolen my shoes, and I had to walk barefoot back to the bakery.

I remember that the day was very hot. The sea was dead calm.

I stood at the pump in the backyard for a long time, washing myself.

When Maria came walking toward the bakery I was out on the street waiting for her. I couldn't get enough of her smile. But all my thoughts were with Nelio, who was lying up there on the roof. No one had taught him how to act when he was about to die.

Is there any greater loneliness? When a person realizes that he has to die and there's no one to teach him how to do it?

I thought about that great loneliness, and the feelings I had then have never since left me in peace.

At midnight I followed Maria out to the street again. When she had taken a few steps, she turned and waved.

Then I went back up to the roof.

It was the eighth night.

The Eighth Night

When I went up to the roof and looked at Nelio, he was already dead.

I stood there motionless, and something hard clamped around my heart.

What I thought at that moment, I no longer remember. But I think it's true that when another person dies, the life you have inside you defends itself by mobilizing all its forces to keep mortality at bay.

In the presence of death, life always becomes very clear.

But what I was thinking I can no longer recall.

Then I saw that I was mistaken. He wasn't dead; he was still alive. Or if he had died for a brief moment, then he returned to life because I had called him. I had whispered his name: Nelio. And suddenly he moved, quite feebly, but there was a definite movement on the mattress. I knelt down beside him and put my face close to his mouth; I could feel that he was still breathing.

But was he still there or was he about to leave? I must have been seized by panic because I started tugging and shaking him and calling out his name. If sleep and unconsciousness are the only experiences we have that teach us something about what death is, then he had already sunk very deep. I was shaking a body that felt already far away. Since he weighed so little, it was like shaking a bunch of feathers or an empty shell from which the spirit had departed.

At last he came back to life, though reluctantly, and opened his eyes. He was very tired and also seemed lost and confused. I wasn't sure that he recognized me, and it was a long time before he seemed to be calm again. I gave him some water with Senhora Muwulene's herbs to drink.

"I dreamed that I was dead," Nelio said. "When I tried to make my way back up to the surface, something was holding on to my legs. Then I managed to kick myself free. But I only did it because I wasn't finished with my story."

I changed his bandage. His whole chest was now inflamed. The dark edges of the infection had spread far down toward his groin and up to his shoulders. The stench was almost unbearable. I thought my efforts were pointless—the bullets were spreading their poison through his body more and more rapidly, and his resistance had finally succumbed.

"I have to take you to the hospital," I said.

"I'm not finished with my story yet," he replied.

I said nothing more. I knew that he would never let me take him to the hospital. He would stay on the roof until he died.

Nobody had any money to lend me. That month, like so many others, Dona Esmeralda was late in paying us our wages. To give Nelio something to eat I had boiled some eggs from the bakery and mashed them up in a cup. I had to feed it to him, and he ate very slowly. Afterward I rearranged the blanket under his head. The night was muggy, without a breath of wind. Nelio looked up and gazed at the clear night sky with the glittering stars.

Suddenly he said, "*Opixa murima orèra. Mweri wahòkhwa ori mutokwène, etheneri ehala yàraka.*"

I was surprised by his words. I remembered that I had once heard an old woman in my village say the same thing: "*The moon disappears after growing big, the stars continue to shine even though they are small.*"

I looked up at the sky. "The moon will come back," I said.

"The stars have no memory," Nelio said. "For them, the moon is every night a stranger coming to visit and then leaving again. Among the stars, the moon is an eternal stranger."

The dogs were barking restlessly on that sultry night. Drums could be heard in the distance from the other side of the estuary. Fires blazed, and I thought I could see small, dwarf-like shadows moving to the rhythmic pounding of the drums.

Nelio thought that Deolinda had come to stay, but he was mistaken. Since he slept in his statue at night, he wasn't at first aware of what was going on. It wasn't until Mandioca came and sat down next to him in the shade of his tree one day that he realized that everything was not as it should be. Mandioca was hesitant and embarrassed. He sat there twisting an onion between his fingers. It was unusual for Mandioca to seek out his company alone, so Nelio understood that Mandioca must have something important weighing on his mind.

"What is it you want?" Nelio asked after waiting a suitable amount of time in silence.

"Nothing," replied Mandioca.

More time would have to pass before Mandioca felt ready to start talking.

"The shadow is still long," Nelio said. "I'll stay here until it's gone. Before then you must tell me what you want."

Mandioca dug into his pockets where his plants grew. He folded back his pockets so the sun could shine on the leaves. Earlier, to his astonishment, Nelio had seen that plants really could grow in Mandioca's pockets. It was as if Mandioca himself were a plant, a sapling whose arms were like spindly branches without leaves.

"Something isn't right," Mandioca said at last, when the shadow had already begun to narrow.

"What you said just now doesn't mean anything," Nelio said. "Speak clearly if you want to talk to me. Stop mumbling."

"It's Nascimento," said Mandioca.

Nelio thought that Mandioca seemed to be in a wrestling match with his words.

"What about Nascimento?"

Silence again. Nelio sighed and continued to watch the shadow as it narrowed. A lizard darted between his feet and disappeared into a crevice between the cobblestones.

"What about Nascimento?" he repeated.

After the long, drawn-out preliminaries to the conversation, Mandioca's reply came surprisingly fast.

"Nascimento wants to do *xogo-xogo* with the *xidjana*," he said. "But I don't think the *xidjana* wants to."

Nelio considered what he had heard for a moment before he asked his next question.

"Did he say that?"

"He already tried it."

"What happened?"

"The *xidjana* didn't want to."

"Don't call her *xidjana*. We said we would use her real name."

"Deolinda didn't want to."

"When was this?"

"Last night."

"What happened?"

"Nascimento thought everybody was asleep. But I was awake. Nascimento pulled off the *xidjana*'s blanket."

"Her name is Deolinda."

"Nascimento pulled off Deolinda's blanket."

"Then what happened?"

"He pulled up her dress to see what she looked like underneath."

"Did he see anything? Doesn't Deolinda wear anything underneath?"

"I don't know. She woke up."

"Then what happened?"

"Nascimento wanted her to pull up her dress and show him what she looked like."

"Did she do it?"

"She got mad and lay down to sleep again."

"What did Nascimento say?"

"He said that the next night they would do *xogo-xogo*, whether she wanted to or not. Otherwise Nascimento would beat her."

"And the next night is the night that's now on its way?"

Mandioca nodded. The long conversation had taxed his strength. Nelio moved further into the shadow, which was now quite narrow, and thought about what he had heard.

"If Deolinda doesn't want to do *xogo-xogo* with Nascimento, she'll know how to stop it from happening. She threw him to the ground once before."

Nelio considered the conversation to be over. But Mandioca didn't move.

"Is there something else?"

"Nascimento might not know that it's dangerous to do *xogo-xogo* with an albino."

"Why should it be dangerous?"

"Everyone knows that you get stuck."

"Stuck?"

"Nascimento is going to get stuck. He'll never be able to get out again. It's going to look very strange."

"That's just a story. It's not really true."

"Deolinda might not know that."

Nelio realized that Mandioca's real worry was whether Nascimento would get stuck or not.

"Nothing's going to happen," Nelio said. "Now the shadow is gone. We don't need to talk about this any more."

But that night as Nelio lay sleeping in the horse's belly, he was jolted awake from disturbing dreams. He had seen Deolinda's face before him—it was contorted with terror or rage, and she had talked to him, but he couldn't understand what she said. Filled with foreboding, he pulled on his pants and crept out through the hatch. Then he ran as fast as he could through the city. But when he reached the stairs where the group lay tangled up among cardboard boxes and blankets, Deolinda was gone.

Mandioca was awake.

"Where's Deolinda?" Nelio asked in a low voice so as not to wake up the others.

"She's gone."

"I dreamed about her. What happened?"

"Nascimento did *xogo-xogo* with her. Even though she didn't want to. But he didn't get stuck."

Nelio felt his fury rise. "Where's Nascimento?"

"He's sleeping in his box."

Nelio kicked at the cardboard box where Nascimento spent his nights in a ceaseless battle with his monsters. He lifted the lid and told Nascimento to come out. Gradually the others began to wake up too. As Nascimento clambered out of his box, Nelio saw that his face was scratched. This made him so angry that he was about to lose control. The marks on Nascimento's face were Deolinda's attempt to defend herself. Nelio yanked at Nascimento's shirt and pulled him clear of the box. The others sat around nervously. They had never seen Nelio so angry before.

"Where's Deolinda?" Nelio said with a quavering voice.

"I don't know," replied Nascimento. "I was asleep."

"But not before you did *xogo-xogo* with her!" Nelio screamed. "And she didn't want to. I wasn't here. But she came to me in my dreams and told me what happened."

"She wanted to do it," Nascimento said.

"Then why did she scratch up your face? You're lying, Nascimento."

Nelio let him go and began tearing the blankets off the others, who cowered before his fury.

"Nobody is going to sleep any more tonight!" he shrieked. "Go out and look for her. Don't come back until you've found her. She's one of us. Nascimento has done something very bad to her. Did anybody see which way she went?"

Picado pointed toward the harbor.

"Get going!" Nelio shouted. "Go and find her. But not you, Nascimento. You stay here and guard the others' blankets. Get back in your box, and don't come out unless I say so. The rest of you get moving! Don't come back without her!"

They searched all night for Deolinda. They kept on looking for her the next day, but she was gone. They asked other boys who lived on the streets whether they had seen her, but she had vanished without trace.

After four days Nelio realized that it wasn't worth it any longer. There was great unrest in the group, and he decided to call off the search. During all this time Nascimento was confined to his box behind the gas station as if it were a jail. Nelio had worried about how to punish Nascimento for his attack. But it had been in vain. He couldn't decide what to do. Finally he gave up. He gathered them together and said that they would no longer search for Deolinda.

"She's run off, and she probably won't come back. We don't know where she is. When you don't know where to search any more, you have to give up. She left because Nascimento did something to her that he shouldn't have done. What we should really do is beat him every day for weeks on end and keep him locked up in his box for a whole year. But I don't think it was Nascimento who did the thing that made Deolinda leave. I think it was the monsters inside Nascimento's head that did it. That's why we're not going to beat him. And he doesn't have to stay in his box either. But what happened wasn't right."

Nelio looked around. He wondered whether they understood what he was trying to say. The only one who seemed pleased was Nascimento. Nelio thought that the next time anyone attacked Nascimento, he wouldn't intervene. Nascimento did have monsters inside his head, but not everything could be blamed on them.

Secretly Nelio continued to search for Deolinda. He missed her, and he worried about what she might have done to herself. Sometimes he thought that she was right next to him, walking at his side with her woven bag slung over her shoulder. Nelio knew that an albino could be alive and dead at the same time. Maybe she had chosen to leave this world and move on to the next world where no one could see her, but where she could see everything she wanted to see.

One day Nascimento stumbled and fell to the ground, opening a big gash in his forehead. Afterward Nelio went over and examined the spot where he fell. There was nothing there that could have made Nascimento stumble. The explanation had to be that Deolinda had stuck out her invisible leg.

She was somewhere close by. But she would not be coming back.

During that time Nelio spent long hours in the shade of his tree, studying the tattered atlas of the world that Tristeza had found in a garbage can and given to him as a present. The Indian photographer Abu Cassamo, whose dimly lit shop was next door to the theater and the bakery, had told him the names of the various oceans and countries. He told Nelio what the big mountain ranges looked like, where the deserts were, and where the kilometer-high ice sheets reigned. Abu Cassamo, in whose shop there were hardly ever any customers, had a melancholy face, and he never spoke to anyone unless spoken to first. He was exceedingly polite and bowed even to Nelio when he came to the shop and stepped inside the murky room where the photograph lamps were turned off, the cameras were covered with black cloths, and the smell of curry was overwhelming. Through Abu Cassamo, who talked in a low and lilting voice, the world was explained to Nelio.

Nelio leafed through the stained pages of the atlas, thinking that he was living in an evil world. Where were people supposed to get enough strength and joy to endure? He was living in a world where bandits burned villages, where people were constantly fleeing, where the roads were lined with all the dead and all the bombed and burned wrecks of cars and buses and carts. He was living in a world where the dead were not allowed to be dead. They were chased out of their graves or out of their trees; they were in flight just like those who were still alive. And the living—they were so poor that they were forced to send their children to live on the streets like rats. But even the rats were better off, because at least they had their fur coats when the nights were cold.

Occasionally Nelio would glance up from his maps and look

at the people who rushed past without seeing him. Were they alive or were they already dead? Sometimes he would go down to the wharf at the harbor and look for the sharks that could sometimes be seen beyond the mouth of the river. Were the breakers rolling toward the beach dead too? Where was there life in these evil times? Where could they get the strength and the joy that they needed to endure?

He pored over his maps. At night he lay sleepless in the horse's belly, and in the afternoon he stood looking out across the sea, immersed in thought. He had the feeling that no matter where he stood, he was in the center of the world and its evil. That had to be true because he thought the same thing no matter where he was. If Deolinda had still been there, he might have talked to her about everything he was brooding about. The others wouldn't understand. They would just get worried and then run off and find him another dog.

But Deolinda reappeared in his dreams, and sometimes she had Cosmos with her. Nelio asked her where she had gone on that night when she was attacked by Nascimento's monsters. But her answer was unclear, and he understood that she didn't want anyone to look for her.

"I don't need any house, she told him in one of his dreams. "I've built myself a hiding place. There I have all the freedom I need."

That's the way the world is, Nelio thought as Manuel Oliveira greeted the morning, waking him with his demented laughter outside the horse. *People no longer build houses, they build hiding places.*

Deolinda was gone. Violent storms swept in over the city. It rained steadily for eleven days and nights, and the poorly erected shacks perched along the slopes above the estuary were washed away, and the sharks tugged and tore at the dead bodies all the way to the beach. No one had ever seen anything like it, not even people who were so old it was questionable whether they were alive at all. It was a time of omens. The bandits had now come so close to the city that they sometimes broke into houses and burned and killed in the nearest suburbs. Nelio sometimes thought that if he died inside the horse's belly, his life would have been incomprehensible. How could he explain to his ancestors, when he met them, that he who had been born of good people in a village that was not a hiding place but a home where people lived, had in the end stopped breathing inside the belly of an equestrian statue hidden away in a forgotten plaza in the big city? They would think he was lying, that he was trying to deceive them, and they would chase him away; they would chase him back to life again, and there would be the bandits, waiting for him with their knives and their rifles and their unquenchable lust for killing anything alive and laying waste to the earth.

Often he looked at his hands, or looked at his reflection in the piece of a mirror that Pecado used to start fires. He searched for signs that he had already started to age. It was plain to him that a ten-year-old who had so many thoughts would grow old very quickly. He searched for wrinkles in his face, the first gray hairs, a sudden weakness or trembling in his legs. He was often struck by great fear that one morning he would wake up as a dazed old man with no teeth, who couldn't remember his own name, no matter how hard he tried. His thoughts were like a terrible illness he carried within him, which might break out when he was least expecting it.

All this time it was the group that kept him alive. In their daily struggle to survive, he could find moments when his thoughts stopped pursuing him.

But the whole time he had a premonition that something was about to come to an end. Each morning he woke up with a feeling that something was going to happen and he should already be afraid of it.

The storms passed. The rain stopped, and the muddy streets began to dry out. The weather turned hot again. Each day they would seek out the shady plazas to take a siesta.

That was when Nelio discovered that something was wrong with Alfredo Bomba. When the siesta was over he always wanted to keep on sleeping. Nelio asked him if he was feeling all right. He complained that he was always tired, as if sleep were draining him of all his strength.

"Are you in pain?"

"A little," replied Alfredo Bomba.

"Where?"

Alfredo pointed to one side of his belly.

"Stomachache," Nelio reassured him. "It'll pass."

Alfredo Bomba nodded. "It only hurts a little."

After a few days Nelio knew that Alfredo Bomba did not have a stomachache. He was running a fever, he didn't want to eat and he was very pale.

"We have to get a pushcart or a wheelbarrow," Nelio told the others. "Alfredo Bomba is sick. We have to take him to the hospital."

"We can borrow a *xuva shita duma* outside the marketplace," said Pecado. "But they'll want to be paid."

"They'll get their money," Nelio said. "Give me whatever you have."

A heap of crumpled thousand-escudo bills accumulated at his feet.

"That should be enough," Nelio decided. "Mandioca and Pecado will go and get the cart. But don't stand around talking to everybody you know."

They took Alfredo Bomba to the hospital in a ragged procession. Many who saw them thought the pale boy in the cart was already dead. They would kneel down, make the sign of the cross, or turn away. When the boys reached the hospital, they carried Alfredo to the emergency room, which was full of sick and injured people.

"You'd better wait outside and watch the cart," Nelio told Nascimento. "Otherwise somebody might steal it."

"It smells bad in here," Nascimento said.

"Sick people never smell good. Now go! And don't fall asleep!"

Pale and in pain, Alfredo Bomba sat in a corner. An irritable nurse came over and asked him what was wrong.

"He's sick," Nelio said. "You're the ones who have to tell us what's wrong with him."

Several hours passed before anyone else took an interest in Alfredo Bomba. Nelio had kept Pecado with him to help and then sent the others off in search of food.

It was evening when two nurses wheeled in a stretcher and lifted Alfredo Bomba on to it.

"Does he have any family?" one of the nurses asked.

"He has me," Nelio said. "He doesn't need anyone else."

"Are you his brother?"

"I'm his brother and his father and his uncle and his cousin."

"What's his name?"

"Alfredo Bomba."

"Bomba isn't a real name, is it?"

"Then he has a name that isn't real. But he has pain in his stomach. And the pain is real."

They wheeled the stretcher into an examining room that was

full to overflowing with people whimpering and moaning. The smell of sweat and filth was overpowering. Nelio swatted away a cockroach that was groping its feelers over Alfredo Bomba's sweaty face.

A doctor who was tall and fat came into the room. He stopped at the stretcher and looked down at Alfredo."You're having stomach pains?" he asked brusquely.

"He's very sick," Nelio said.

The doctor muttered something inaudible and then pulled up Alfredo Bomba's filthy shirt and began pressing on his stomach. Another doctor passing by stopped at the stretcher. They talked to each other, but Nelio didn't understand what they said. The other doctor began pressing on Alfredo Bomba's stomach too.

"Why are they pressing so hard?" groaned Alfredo Bomba.

"Doctors press hard so that their fingers can speak to the sickness inside."

"We should have gone to a *curandeiro*," Alfredo Bomba said. "It hurts so much."

The two doctors stopped pressing.

"He'll have to stay here," said the fat doctor. His voice was now much less brusque.

"What's wrong with him?" asked Nelio.

"That's what we have to find out," replied the doctor.

"Maybe he has worms," suggested Nelio.

"I'm sure he does," the doctor said. "But this is something else."

That night Alfredo Bomba slept in a hospital bed that he shared with another patient. Nelio sent the others off with the cart and then lay down under Alfredo's bed. The next day they took blood samples from Alfredo Bomba. His arms were so thin that the person drawing the blood could hardly find a vein. The following day they took more blood.

Then nothing happened. After three days had passed Nelio

started to think that the doctors had forgotten about Alfredo Bomba, but the next morning a nurse came to get Nelio. He followed her through the corridors, which were so crowded with sick people lying on the floor everywhere that they could hardly make their way through. She showed Nelio to a room where a piece of cardboard was tacked up over a broken window. Behind a desk sat the fat doctor who was the first to press on Alfredo Bomba's stomach.

"Doesn't this boy have any parents?" he asked, and Nelio noticed that he sounded terribly tired.

"He only has me. He lives on the street."

The doctor nodded slowly. "Then you're the one I have to talk to," he said. He stretched out his hand and said that his name was Anselmo.

"Alfredo Bomba is very sick," Anselmo said. "He's going to die soon."

"I don't want that to happen," Nelio said. "I can get money for all the medicine he needs."

"It's not a matter of money or medicine. Alfredo Bomba has an incurable disease. He has a tumor in his liver. Since neither you nor he knows what a liver is, I won't try to explain. The tumor has already spread through his body. There's nothing we can do to save his life. We can ease his pain, but that's all."

Nelio sat in silence.

He felt as if the doctor's words had transferred some of Alfredo Bomba's pain to his own stomach. He refused to think that Alfredo Bomba was going to die. And yet he knew that it was true.

"He really doesn't have any parents?" Anselmo asked again. "Doesn't he have any *tia*, any *avô*?"

"He has me and the others," Nelio said. "How long does he have to stay in the hospital?"

"He can stay here until he dies. Or he can leave with you now. With the medicine, his pain will almost disappear."

Nelio stood up. He realized that the man on the other side of the desk thought he was talking to a ten-year-old. But Nelio himself felt as if he were a hundred.

"He'll come with us," Nelio said. "His last days will be the best ones he's ever had."

They left the hospital. Nelio had been given a paper cone with pills that he was supposed to give to Alfredo Bomba when he was in pain. Nelio asked him whether he wanted to ride in the cart back to their street, but Alfredo Bomba said no. They walked along the shady side of the street, down the steep slopes.

"I know I'm going to die," said Alfredo Bomba.

"You're not going to die," Nelio said. "I have medicine in my pocket."

"Even so, I know that I'm going to die," Alfredo Bomba said after a while.

"Didn't you hear what I said?" said Nelio angrily.

They walked in silence.

Later that day, when Alfredo Bomba was asleep, Nelio told the others what the doctor had said.

"He can make a wish for whatever he wants," Nelio said. "And whatever it is, we'll give it to him."

"He can have my sneakers right now," Tristeza said.

"Alfredo Bomba has never liked wearing shoes," Nelio said. "And besides, his feet are smaller than yours. He's the only one who can tell us what he wants."

That night Nelio didn't go to his statue to sleep in the horse's belly. They made a fire behind the gas station. They had all done their utmost during the day to earn enough money so they could cook a feast over the open fire. Alfredo Bomba sat closest to the fire, wrapped in a blanket because he was cold. Nelio had given him a pill. The pain was gone, but Alfredo could do little more than taste the food they had made for him.

"I'm sure you'll be well soon," Nelio said. "But until then, I want you to make a wish for whatever it is you want most."

Alfredo Bomba didn't seem to understand what Nelio was saying. "Whatever I want?" he said slowly.

"Whatever you want."

"I've never heard of anybody wishing for what he wanted most and then actually getting it."

"Then you'll be the first," Nelio said.

Alfredo Bomba sat for a long time, pondering what Nelio had said. Nascimento and Mandioca disappeared every once in a while to look for more wood to keep the fire going. The city grew more and more quiet; silence descended over the group sitting around the fire.

Then Alfredo Bomba began to speak. "I remember that my mama once told me about something amazing when I was little. She said it was true, but I've always thought it was a fairy tale, the kind that you tell to children. But I've never forgotten what she said. Maybe now I should try to find out if it was true or not."

"A mother doesn't lie to her children," Mandioca said.

"Quiet," Nelio said. "Don't interrupt. Let him talk in peace."

"There's supposed to be a place where the living and the dead meet," Alfredo Bomba said. "It's supposed to be a huge garden, with a river running through it. In the middle of the river there's an island that's nothing but sand. If you ever visit that island, afterward you'll never be afraid of anything for the rest of your life. If it's true that I can wish for whatever I want most, then I wish that I could go there."

"Yes," Nelio said when Alfredo Bomba had stopped. "I've heard of that river and an oval-shaped island made of sand. I've also heard there's a kind of lizard there that sings. But maybe I'm mistaken. I think you're right—you should visit that place."

"I don't know where it is," Alfredo Bomba said. "How can you go someplace without knowing where it is?"

"We'll deal with that," Nelio said. "I have an atlas of the world. The one that Tristeza found in the garbage can. I'll talk to Abu Cassamo, the photographer, tomorrow morning. He might know."

"Do you really think it's possible?" asked Alfredo Bomba.

"Yes," Nelio said. "I think it's possible."

Alfredo huddled under his blanket next to the fire and fell asleep.

"So we're going on a journey," Nelio said a little later. "We'll need a lot of money, and we have to find out where that place is. And we don't have much time, either, before Alfredo Bomba gets too sick to make the journey."

"There's no river and there's no island," Nascimento said. "I won't be part of this deception. It's better that we let him go to the movies every night. I don't think Alfredo Bomba has ever been to the movies."

"They'll never let him in," Mandioca said. "He doesn't have any shoes. You have to have shoes and a ticket to go to the movies. If you only have a ticket, you can't get in."

"Sometimes all of you talk too much," Nelio said, not hiding his annoyance. "We're going to find that place, and we're going to get enough money together so that we can go there. Now we'd better get some sleep. We have a lot to do tomorrow. And to show you that I'm serious, I'm going to sleep here tonight."

"It's no good if you get sick too," Tristeza said, worried.

"Alfredo Bomba is sicker than me. That's the only thing that matters."

They settled down for the night. Nascimento crawled inside his cardboard box and pulled the lid shut. Nelio curled up next to Alfredo Bomba. He lay there thinking that he had taken on a great responsibility. Alfredo was counting on getting what he had wished for. No one had the right to disappoint someone who was dying.

That night Nelio slept badly, tormented by disturbing dreams. The dreams that plagued him all had faces and reminded him of the young bandits who had clung to their bloody weapons. They had taken away his trousers and his ability to think and feel. He found himself near a river and caught sight of his face in the water. He was looking at a ghost, an old man with sunken eyes and a grimy stubble on his face. From the other side of the river Yabu Bata shouted something to him, but he couldn't understand what he said. Nelio woke up before it was light. Alfredo Bomba was sleeping next to him, on his back with his mouth open, like a little child. Nelio thought it would be wise for him to start this important day by trying to understand the dreams he had had during the night. From his father he had learned that dreams often contain omens. They might be puzzling, but it was a person's task to interpret the omens and to act accordingly.

"People sleep in order to dream," his father had told him. "The reason we wake up afterward is so that we have the chance to interpret our dreams."

Nelio thought that it would have been easier if he were lying inside the horse's belly. There he was used to studying his dreams. He needed to be alone if he was going to listen to the voices of the night that spoke to him. Here, surrounded by the sleeping band, he had no peace.

With the first glow of morning light in the sky, Nelio got up, carefully so as not to wake the others, and walked across the deserted street to Abu Cassamo's shop. He listened at the door and could hear the sound of shuffling footsteps inside. He knocked gently and waited. Abu Cassamo peeked from the doorway after undoing all the locks and the safety chain, which were his security against the world he mistrusted. His eyes that were always melancholy regarded Nelio standing outside.

"I've brought my maps again," Nelio said. "And I also have a question to ask you."

Abu Cassamo let him into the dim studio. Then he squatted down next to the spirit stove where he was making coffee according to a complicated ritual. Nelio sat on a stool and waited. On the walls hung torn tourist posters in gaudy, implausible colors, and Nelio assumed that they were scenes from the Indian subcontinent, which Abu Cassamo would never see.

When Abu Cassamo had emptied his little coffee cup, he wiped his mouth and sat down on a stool facing Nelio, who was already holding the tattered atlas in his hands. He explained to Abu Cassamo why he had come. But he spoke of Alfredo Bomba's wish as if it were his own.

"I once made a promise to my father to visit this island," Nelio said. "Last night I dreamed it was time for me to make the journey. My father will be very annoyed if I don't do as we decided."

"I assume that your father is dead," mused Abu Cassamo.

"He'd be angry even if he was alive," replied Nelio. "I don't think it's got any better since he drowned in a ditch full of water when he was groggy with malaria."

Abu Cassamo took the book of maps and turned on the last of the glaring photographic lamps that still worked. Nelio waited, aware that he was slowly being pulled back in time, to a point long before the bandits came and burned his village. Not until many hours later, as Abu Cassamo turned the final page of the maps, did he come back to real life again.

"I can't help you," Abu Cassamo said. "The island where your father is waiting for you isn't shown. This is a very poor atlas."

"I found it in a garbage can," Nelio said. "Now I understand why someone threw it away."

"The world can only be shown on poor maps," Abu Cassamo said. "How could anyone make a complete map of something that is so badly tended as our world?"

They were quiet for a moment.

"How do you find an island that isn't shown on any map?" asked Nelio at last.

"You can't find it," Abu Cassamo said. "The best thing you can do is to drink *uputso* and dance and talk to your father. Sometimes the dead can show us ways that we didn't realize we knew."

Nelio couldn't help noticing the faint undertone of scorn in Abu Cassamo's voice. He knew that Indians were like whites in the sense that they had never understood why black people often danced and talked to their ancestors. Just like the whites, Indians were afraid; they hid their fear by showing their contempt, although with much greater discretion than the whites, because they were businessmen and they didn't want to make enemies with anyone who might some day unexpectedly become a customer.

"I'm going to take your advice," Nelio said. "But I have another question. Who might give me all the money I need to make the long journey and also buy a new suit for my father?"

"I didn't know that the spirits wore suits."

"My father claims they do. When I dream about him, he's always wearing the same suit, which is now much too shabby and worn."

"I only know one person who might be able to give you the money," Abu Cassamo said. "His name is Suleiman, and he's just as rich as the great Khan, but everybody pretends he's not because he doesn't give any money to build new mosques."

"Why would he give me the money?"

"He's Indian, like me," Abu Cassamo said. "But his soul has

gone astray by living so many years among blacks, like you. He's so afraid of evil spirits and omens now that he doesn't even dare to conduct business any more. He has shut himself up in his house and never goes out. If you give him my greetings, he might let you in."

"How do you happen to know him?"

"He was my last customer," Abu Cassamo said sadly. "In the last photograph I took, you can see the fear shining in his eyes."

"Maybe he ought to go with me to the island," Nelio said. "Where does this man named Suleiman live?"

"There's a house next to the old prison that looks as if it's had its top chopped off. Suleiman tore down the upper floor with his bare hands after he was swindled in some big deal. He was punishing himself for being so gullible. That happened many years ago, before he believed that the evil spirits and omens could harm him."

Nelio got up to go. It was already late afternoon. He was very hungry.

"Don't you ever eat?" he asked.

"Only when I'm hungry," Abu Cassamo said. "But today is not one of those days."

"I'll let you take my picture," Nelio said, "when I come back from my journey. And you'll take pictures of the others that I live with here on the street. You'll develop the pictures, we'll pick the best ones, and then we'll frame them. And we'll pay you for your work."

"Which wall should we hang the photos on?" asked Abu Cassamo after he had shown Nelio out.

"At the back of the gas station," Nelio said. "There's a beautiful wall there. When it rains, of course, we'll have to cover them with sacks."

*

The next day Nelio walked through the city to Suleiman's chopped-off house. He opened the gate and walked into a yard that looked like an overgrown cemetery. In the dry grass lay rusty dog chains, a reminder of furious barking. Nelio knocked on the door. A tiny slot opened just above the doorstep. A fat brown finger stuck out and indicated that Nelio should lie down so that his face was level with the slot. The finger disappeared, Nelio lay flat and stared straight into an eye.

"I've come to talk to Suleiman about an island where fear is erased," he said. "Abu Cassamo sent me here."

The eye vanished and the door opened a crack. It occurred to Nelio that all Indians open their doors only halfway, maybe out of fear, but also out of thrift. Nelio went into the chopped-off house where all the curtains were drawn. There was an unfamiliar smell, and it was very dark. When his eyes had grown accustomed to the darkness, he saw that the house had no furniture at all. The only thing inside the house was money. There were bundles and stacks of bills everywhere, all tied up with string. It was the money that was making the smell that Nelio hadn't recognized. In the midst of all the money, as if surrounded by protective walls of cash, stood Suleiman. He was short and very fat. His hair had fallen out, his beard was skimpy, and the frames of his glasses were held together with dirty tape. Nelio explained to Suleiman the purpose of his visit. He listened with his eyes closed. When Nelio stopped talking, Suleiman threw out his arms in a gesture of weary resignation.

"I don't have any money to spare," he said. "The little I have left, which you see here, is already spoken for. And I can't go with you on your journey either. Beyond these doors all those who wish me ill are waiting. At night I hear them scratching and scraping on the walls of the house. They've lured my watchdogs away with poisoned pieces of meat."

"We could leave after dark," Nelio suggested.

"Even worse," Suleiman said. "It might have been possible in the daytime, in bright sunlight, but I don't dare. And besides, I'm too fat and my eyes are too feeble. I have to stay here and guard the money that's left. Once I was a wealthy man, as rich as Khan. Now my wealth has made me poor by dwindling away in some manner that I don't fully comprehend. Everything is already spoken for."

"I believe one of the small bundles would be enough," Nelio said cautiously, lowering his voice so that his request would seem smaller because it was presented so quietly.

"I have no money to give away," Suleiman said, and Nelio could tell that he was beginning to get annoyed. "Everybody wants money. I can't leave the house without being surrounded by all the beggars. It's easier to count the ones who don't want anything. The beggars even beg from each other. The dead in the ground shout for money. I've given away everything I once owned. What's left here is for paying my debts after I'm dead. The money in the corner by the window will pay for my funeral, the money beyond the door there will pay for my cousins' weddings and for my faithless sons' illegitimate children, whom no one will acknowledge except me. I have the alms ready, the fines and the bribes, and everything is spoken for. There's no money for a suit for your father or for a journey to the island that you're talking about. Even if it doesn't exist, even if you're actually a con artist and I choose to let you deceive me, I have no money to give you."

"A little boy is going to die soon," Nelio said. "His soul could protect you."

"My house is full of all the dead souls that people who have asked me for money have given to me as guarantees which I can redeem when they die. But what good have they done me?"

Nelio left Suleiman's house. He realized that the paths he had taken during the past few days had not led him any closer to his goal.

That evening Nelio gathered the group. He waited until Alfredo Bomba was asleep before he began to speak.

"Abu Cassamo couldn't find the place that Alfredo Bomba's mother talked about. Since Abu Cassamo never has customers who want to be photographed, he has been able to devote all his time to studying the maps. So it won't do any good to ask anyone else. And we don't have time to go searching for Alfredo Bomba's mother; no one even knows if she's still alive. We haven't managed to get hold of any money, either."

He looked around. They all avoided meeting his gaze since they had nothing to say.

It was Tristeza who broke the silence. "Maybe it would be better if we gave him my sneakers after all. Now that he's so sick, maybe his feet have grown bigger."

"Why would that happen?" asked Nelio.

"Sick people swell up," muttered Tristeza. "The blood hides from death in their feet."

Nelio pondered Tristeza's strange remark for a while. He had learned that Tristeza, even though he thought slowly, sometimes could say things that were worth considering.

"Alfredo Bomba doesn't want sneakers," he said. "He wants to visit the island where people lose their fear. Our first problem is to find out where it is. Our second problem is that even if we find it, we have no money to pay for the journey."

"There's no such island," Nascimento said.

"Maybe not," said Nelio thoughtfully. "But that's a only minor problem."

They were looking at him with surprise. What did he mean? Nelio raised his hand dismissively. Right now he didn't want to hear any more questions. Somewhere inside his head a plan was being hatched. He had discovered an unknown path in his mind which he was now following, and it would give him the answer to how they were going to grant Alfredo Bomba's wish. Nelio stood up and walked past the gas station out to the street, and crossed to the other side where Abu Cassamo's photo shop stood, next to the bakery and the theater. One of Dona Esmeralda's performances had just finished. The audience was pouring out and heading off in the dark in various directions. The watchmen were starting to lock the doors, and the lights outside the entrance were extinguished, one by one. Nelio stood and watched all this at the same time as he followed a winding path between dense brambles in his head. He was seeing with his gaze turned inward, and he now knew how they would make the journey to the island in an unknown part of the world, or maybe in a world that didn't actually exist.

He went back to the waiting boys. Alfredo Bomba was asleep.

"I've found the island," he said. "It's not on the maps that Abu Cassamo tried in vain to read. And it's so close that we don't need any money to make the journey."

"Where?" asked Nascimento.

"Right across the street," Nelio said. "It's right where Dona Esmeralda has her theater. At night the theater is empty. The stage is deserted, because the actors are asleep. What doesn't exist you have to create yourself. Even an island that no one can find can be created. Even a dream can be plucked out of your head and shaped for a purpose. Tonight when the watchmen outside the theater are asleep, we'll climb in through one of the broken windows in the back, where Dona Esmeralda has her wardrobe room. Then we'll turn on the lights on the stage and start rehearsing a play about Alfredo Bomba's visit to the island that his mother told him about."

"None of us knows how to do that," Mandioca said.

"Then we'll have to learn," Nelio told him.

"Some of the watchmen outside the theater have guns," said Nascimento.

"We'll be quiet," Nelio said.

That same night, just after midnight, when the watchmen had fallen asleep outside the theater's entrance, they sneaked around to the back and climbed in through the broken window of the wardrobe room. They had assigned Tristeza to stay with Alfredo Bomba, since he would never be able to learn to say lines or to move in a disciplined way onstage. They found their way by striking matches, and then turned on the glaring spotlights that hung above the stage.

The stage was deserted.

They stood below in the house. At that moment Nelio thought that the stage looked like a mouth, an open mouth waiting for the food they would give it.

Then they began creating the island.

Nelio smiled his weary smile in the dawn light. In the distance, on the other side of the river, a thunderstorm was brewing. I realized that we were now approaching the end, both of his story and of his life.

I said nothing. I just looked at him and smiled. What was there to say, after all?

Then I got up and went down the stairs to the bakery.

The Last Night

On the last day of Nelio's life the sun was quite close to my spirit. When I emptied my lungs the air would flare up and fall like black-singed ashes to the cobblestones in the street. I have never—either before or afterward—experienced heat as I did on that day. There was no relief anywhere; even the wind which crept in over the city from the sea seemed to be panting with exhaustion. I wandered restlessly through the streets, squeezed into the parched shadows where people were vainly seeking respite, and fought off a growing dizziness that was constantly threatening to topple me to the ground. I felt as if I no longer knew who I was, as if everything that had happened to me was a mistake that no one was responsible for or even cared about. For the first time I saw the world as it was, the world that Nelio could see through even before he was grown up.

What was it I thought I saw? The rusted engine in a burned-out tractor spoke to me like a scornful poem about a world that was on the verge of collapsing before my eyes. I saw a boy, a street kid, who was furiously lashing at the sand as if punishing the earth for his own misery. A solitary vulture sailed soundlessly overhead. It floated on the whirling updrafts, oblivious to the rays of the sun that were boring into its plumage. The bird's shadow passed over my head like an iron weight that was pressing me down to the ground. I saw an old black man standing naked at a water pump, washing himself. In spite of the heat he was rubbing his body vigorously, as if he were tearing off an old, worn-out skin. On that day, beneath the unrelenting sun, I discovered the true face of the city. I saw how the poor were forced to eat their lives raw. There was never any time for them to prepare their days—not those who were constantly forced to fight on the outermost bastions of survival. I looked at this temple of the absurd, which was the city and maybe also the world, and it resembled what I saw all around me. I was standing in the center of the dark cathedral of powerlessness. The walls were slowly toppling to the ground, stirring up heavy layers of dust; the stained-glass windows had vanished long ago. I looked around and every single person was poor. The others, the rich people, stayed away from the streets, hiding in their walled bunkers, where the air was always kept cool by whining machines. The world was no longer round; it had gone back to being flat, and the city lay at the edge. Someday, when the torrential rains tore the houses from the slopes once again, the buildings would not merely slide down into the river—they would be tossed over the outermost edge, where no bottom awaited.

On that day the city seemed to have succumbed to an invasion, not of grasshoppers but of revivalists. Everywhere, perched on walls, boxes, pallets and garbage cans, they were luring people over with their sobbing and plaintive voices, their sweaty faces and their pleading hands. Crowds gathered around them, swaying their bodies, shutting their eyes and thinking that everything would be different when they opened their eyes again. I saw people fall to the ground in convulsions, others crawl away like beaten dogs, and some who rejoiced—although the rest of us did not know why. I, who had always pictured the end of the world being played out against a backdrop of rain, racing black clouds, earthquakes and thousands of lightning bolts, started to believe that I might have been mistaken. The world was going to end in scorching sunlight. It seemed to me that all of our ancestors had gathered—there must have been millions of them—and that they had had enough of all the torments that the living were inflicting on each other. In the general apocalypse we would be united in the next world. The streets along which I was now walking would finally be only a memory in the minds of those who never quite learned to forget.

I passed a house where a crazy man suddenly began throwing his furniture out of the window. He was shouting for his brother Fernando whom he hadn't seen since the beginning of the war which the bandits had brought to our country. I caught sight of him just as he tossed out his bed. It struck the pavement, the mattress ripped open and the wooden boards splintered. Why didn't I yell at him to stop? Why did I just keep walking?

I still don't know why. The last day of Nelio's life was one long, drawn-out performance, like a dream that I can only partially remember. Something was about to end in my life. I had suddenly started to understand the real meaning of what Nelio was telling me. Maybe I was also afraid of the inevitable: that his story would end, that everything would be revealed and that he would die from the terrible wounds in his chest. I thought that for the poor, for people like Nelio and myself, death is the one thing that life gives us for nothing.

I thought about how we were forced to eat life raw. Afterward, death was waiting.

We never had the chance to prepare any joys, to polish our memories until they shone, or to meet the next day without fear.

*

Not until dusk began to fall did I go back to the bakery. Dona Esmeralda was standing outside, squabbling angrily with a man delivering flour. It was a quarrel that had already lasted a thousand years and would be repeated for the next thousand. I waited until the man had departed crestfallen and Dona Esmeralda had gone into the theater to force the actors to put on their elephant trunks and begin rehearsals in spite of the unbearable heat. Just as I stepped through the bakery door, I remembered that I had forgotten to buy herbs from Senhora Muwulene. But I didn't worry. I knew it was already too late.

I baked my bread, absentmindedly staring at Maria's lovely body visible through her thin dress. The evening brought cool air from the sea. All around me the city was sleeping, getting ready for the next day when the sun would be just as punishing.

I thought about the boy furiously lashing at the ground. I wondered whether he was still there, striking out at his own misery, or whether he had somewhere to sleep.

Right after midnight Maria went home. Surreptitiously I had stood in the dark and watched her washing herself at the same pump that I used. Her naked body glinted in the light of the inquisitive stars, and I felt suddenly indignant that I could actually resist going over and pulling her to me. Her beauty, like everything that is beautiful, was mysterious. I wished that Nelio were standing next to me, looking at her, and sharing Maria's secret. It was a memory that I wished he could have taken with him to the next world. Even though I can't explain why, I don't believe that spirits are ever naked. But maybe I'm mistaken. I don't know.

When I reached the roof, I saw that the cat was there again. It had crept up close to Nelio's face to lie down. I paused in the shadow of the door to the winding staircase and watched what seemed to be a conversation between the cat and Nelio. A chill breeze blew past my face and made me shiver. The dead had begun to gather, waiting for Nelio to join them. Who the cat was, I couldn't tell. But it must have sensed my presence since suddenly it turned its head and glared at me with cold eyes. When it blinked, I thought that it was the man with the squinty eyes, the man that Nelio had killed, and who had now found him again. I picked up a pebble lying on the roof and threw it against the side of the mattress. The cat leaped away and vanished across the rooftops. When I went over to the mattress, I could see that Nelio was very pale. I felt his forehead; he had a fever, and his eyes were glazed with that vacant look I had seen in them before. And yet he smiled at me.

"The day was so hot," he said in a low, brittle voice.

I gave him some water to drink, mixing the last of Senhora Muwulene's herbs in his cup.

Again we could hear the woman who spent the night preparing for the next day. Her pole was pounding the corn. And she was singing.

"Everything comes to an end," Nelio said. "Everything comes to an end, and everything starts over again."

He raised one hand, which was terribly thin, and pointed up at the stars, so clear and close on that night. The sky had sunk down toward the roof to make Nelio's resting place smaller.

"My father was a very wise man," he said. "He taught me to look at the stars when life was hard. When I returned my gaze to the earth, whatever had been overwhelming would seem small and simple."

I gave him some more water. Afterward I felt his pulse, which was rapid and irregular. The allotted time was coming to an end.

Nelio looked at me in silence. His story had already begun,

even though it was no more than a gleam in his weary eyes. But he still didn't seem the least bit frightened of what was coming. He was perfectly calm.

Is it possible to love death?

I never got an answer from Nelio while he was alive. But I still expect a solitary moth to alight next to me and give me the message from Nelio that I've been waiting for. That's why, in my loneliness, I sometimes dance on the roof and get drunk on *tontonto*.

I am waiting. I will always be waiting.

Nelio began to tell his story for the last time, and I knew that on that night it would be finished. He told me how they went up on to the empty stage in the glare of the spotlights. The shadows in the wings murmured, commenting on their presence. The stage breathed; every story that had been performed there over the years seemed to come alive again. The boys found themselves in the midst of a chaotic universe of plays, memorized lines, entrances and exits. It was a magic moment. Nelio gathered the others around him in the exact center of the stage. He could see that they were frightened, that they sensed the presence of all the events which had been enacted there in earlier times and which had now been resurrected. Nelio thought that they were not just a group of street kids about to perform a play for the dying Alfredo Bomba. They had also come as an audience, and they had brought the old dramas to life by disturbing them in the midst of their long night.

They started by searching the theater to see what things they might be able to use—discarded stage sets for old backdrops, costumes and wigs. Nelio gave strict instructions that nothing was to be touched unless he said so, and everything they used would have to be put back in the same place. That first night turned into one long game in which Nelio, from the spot where he was sitting in the center of the stage, watched the others appear from the wings, unrecognizable in their costumes. Occasionally he had to tell them to hush when they forgot they were in the theater illegally. He kept in mind Nascimento's warning about the armed watchmen on the street.

With the unrestrained joy of a child, Nelio watched them dressing up. Each time one of them appeared in a new costume, the whole stage would instantly change. A drama would begin, without words, without action, without any significance except that they had all been given permission to create another world from the one they normally inhabited. Pecado stepped into the light, dressed in a shimmering coat of red silk. On his feet he wore white shoes, and he moved across the stage as if prepared to defy gravity, even while waiting in the wings. A second later Nascimento appeared in the spotlight, transformed into a god, or perhaps an as yet unknown flower. He started rambling a disjointed narrative as, with great dignity, he circled around Nelio. Mandioca dressed up in various animal costumes, and also created animals that no one had ever seen before. With a crocodile's tail, a rat's legs, the breast of an insect and the head of a zebra, he crept across the stage, uttering sounds that Nelio had never heard before either.

While he watched this shifting, dreamlike parade, with one unexpected character and entrance after another, the play began taking shape in Nelio's mind. He imagined the journey, the moment when they stood by the river and glimpsed the island in the mist, the crossing and finally the arrival. He realized that it was no less than a paradise they had to try to depict. And since paradise doesn't exist, he had to conceive how it would look in Alfredo Bomba's world. He had to create a paradise that Alfredo

Bomba would feel at home in. During that first night Nelio said very little. He gazed pensively, almost dreamily, at the various costumes and props that were brought on to the stage and then removed. He made a note in his mind of what he had seen. When he sensed that dawn was near, he gathered the others around him and said that now they would have to put everything back the way it was, erasing all traces of their presence, and then leave the theater as unobtrusively as they had come.

"Tomorrow we'll start rehearsing," he told them. "For three nights we'll prepare. On the fourth night we'll make our journey with Alfredo Bomba."

When they emerged into the light of dawn and returned to the place where Tristeza was waiting with Alfredo Bomba, Nelio saw immediately that he was much worse. For a moment he worried that Alfredo wouldn't live long enough for them to show him the play. Nelio told the others to keep quiet and not to make any commotion that might disturb the sick boy. Then he sat down at Alfredo Bomba's side and talked to him for a long time.

"We're going on a journey," said he. "We're going to carry you the whole way. The trip won't take long."

"I'm scared," Alfredo murmured.

"You don't have to be scared," Nelio reassured him.

"I'm scared to have Nascimento carry me. He might drop me by mistake—or on purpose."

"I'll tell him we'll beat him with sticks if he drops you. Nascimento doesn't like being hit with sticks."

Alfredo Bomba did not seem convinced by Nelio's words, but he was too tired to make any further objections. Nelio gave him another pill from the paper cone, and then he called over Pecado and told him to massage Alfredo Bomba's feet.

"What good will that do?" asked Pecado suspiciously. "He's not cold."

"We can't let the blood collect in his feet," Nelio said firmly. "Just do as I say."

Pecado rubbed Alfredo's feet while Nelio made sure the others took turns wiping his sweaty forehead and saw to it that he always had cold water to drink. Those who weren't needed to take care of Alfredo Bomba were sent out on the street to wash cars and then buy ice and bread with the money they earned. The heat hung on, and someone was always sitting by Alfredo's head, fanning him with part of a broken umbrella. When the watchmen sat down on the steps of the theater after midnight and started playing cards, the boys again crawled in through the broken window at the back of the building.

That night they began rehearsing their play. Nelio gathered them around him onstage.

"None of us knows anything about theater," he said. "We're going to have to do this without help, but that's something we can do better than anyone else—we can survive without help."

"I want to play the monster," said Nascimento.

"You'll get to play the monster," said Nelio. "But only if you don't interrupt until I've finished talking. The key thing is that we make Alfredo Bomba forget that he's sick and forget where he is. Then we can take him wherever we want. And we'll wait until he's asleep before we bring him here. When he opens his eyes, he'll think he's dreaming."

"It'll be hard to get him through that window if he's asleep," Pecado said anxiously.

"There's a door in the back," Nelio said. "The night before we perform our play, we'll leave it unlocked."

Then they started rehearsing the journey to the island that Alfredo Bomba's mother had once told him about. They tried to create a dream that would have the same power as reality. Nelio was filled with doubt. He felt as if he were casting about in a dark room. Often he would get angry because the others didn't do as he said or made too much commotion. It was soon clear that it would be almost impossible for him to use either Nascimento or Mandioca as actors. Nascimento had found a monster head, which he refused to take off, although he never managed to grasp when he was supposed to be onstage, what he was to do, or what he was to say. Finally Nelio lost all patience and told him to wrap himself up in a piece of blue cloth and pretend to be the sea.

"What should I say?" Nascimento wanted to know.

"The sea doesn't speak," replied Nelio. "The sea is endless, it billows or it lies calm. You don't say anything, because the sea never speaks."

"That sounds like a very boring part," Nascimento protested.

"But important," replied Nelio. "If you keep on objecting, you won't play any part at all."

The one who demonstrated the most natural ability to act was Pecado. He instantly memorized everything Nelio told him, he made his entrances on cue, and he spoke the words that Nelio wanted to hear. Nelio himself was in charge of the lights, turning them off and changing colors when needed. They were all very tired, but he urged them on. Each morning when they emerged from the theater building, their faces pale and drawn, they could see that Alfredo Bomba was sinking deeper into his illness and moving swiftly toward the end. They didn't have much time.

On the third night they went through the whole performance that they had created. Except for the fact that Nascimento fell asleep in the wings, snoring inside his monster head, everything went almost the way Nelio wanted it. When he sat in the balcony and watched what was happening below him on the stage as he made the beams from the spotlights rise and fall, he sometimes even forgot where he was. The journey to the island shed its outer skin, which was the dream, and became a real journey that was being played out before his eyes.

Afterward, when they once again gathered onstage and Nelio told Nascimento that he couldn't sleep in the wings, he said that now they were ready. They couldn't make the performance any better.

"Before we leave here tonight, we'll unlock the door at the back. Then tomorrow night we're going to carry Alfredo Bomba over here so that he can be part of the play."

"Isn't he just going to watch?" wondered Mandioca.

"When he's watching he will also be part of it," replied Nelio. "That's the whole point of what we're trying to do."

"He might not understand any of it," Pecado said. "He might be so disappointed that he won't even want to watch the whole thing. He might fall asleep."

Nelio didn't have the strength to reply. Nothing would be any different. All that was left was to wait for the following night. He simply told the others to get everything ready so they could leave the theater before it was light.

That morning Nelio realized that Alfredo Bomba only had a few days to live. He had stopped eating, his skin was stretched taut over his skull, and his eyes had sunk deeper and deeper. They sat in a circle around him, silent, tired and scared. Everyone felt anxious at being so close to death.

A hard rain fell on the city before dusk. They covered Alfredo Bomba with an old tarpaulin that had been discarded behind the gas station. But he seemed not to notice; he was deep in his restless dreams.

"Old people are supposed to die," Nascimento said, wiping the rain from his face. "Old people, not children. Not even the ones who just live on the street like Alfredo Bomba."

"You're right," Nelio said. "That's something that this world should hurry up and learn."

Nascimento sat still in the rain, looking at Alfredo Bomba. "Can spirits die?" he asked. "In the same way that people do?"

Nelio shook his head. "No. Spirits can't be born and they can't die. They just are."

"I think Alfredo Bomba will be much better off than he is now," Nascimento said.

"Old people are supposed to die," Nelio said. "Not children."

"I think he'll be back with his dog," Nascimento said hesitantly. "Alfredo Bomba likes dogs, and dogs like him."

"You're probably right. But be quiet now."

Late that night the rain stopped. Alfredo Bomba was asleep. Everyone was tense. Pecado made frequent forays out to the street to keep an eye on the armed watchmen outside the theater.

"It's Armandio and Julio tonight," he said. "Armandio, the fat one, is asleep. But Julio usually stays awake."

"They won't hear a thing," Nelio said. "We'll go soon."

Earlier in the day Nelio had gone to the marketplace and borrowed two thick broomsticks from an old broom-maker that he knew from before. On his way back he caught sight of Senhor Castigo being dragged down the street between two policemen. He was battered and bloody, and his clothes were hanging in tatters, as if an enraged mob had tried to rip him to shreds. He saw Nelio too. For a brief, confused moment he tried to remember who the boy with the two broomsticks could be. But Nelio doubted that he had recognized him.

Senhor Castigo is an omen, he thought. He has been caught and beaten. In the dark cells of the police station he'll be beaten even more. Soon there will only be scraps left of what might once have been a human being. If I hadn't escaped from him, I might have ended up just like him.

By pulling two old vests over the broomsticks, they made a stretcher. At midnight, they lifted Alfredo Bomba, who was delirious, and carried him across the deserted street. They listened in the shadows before they opened the back door and slipped into the theater. While Nelio groped his way over to the light panel in the dark, the others waited behind the stage. Nelio made a faint dawn light sweep across the dark stage, a pink glow above a sea that was still asleep. He went back to the others, and they set the stretcher down, close to the footlights. Nelio sat down beside Alfredo Bomba while the others left to get ready. He didn't want to wake him yet. He could feel from Alfredo's forehead that he had a high fever.

After a while Nascimento stuck his monster-head out from the wings and whispered that they were ready. Nelio nodded. The next moment a wind started blowing. It came gusting in from the wings, from the mouths of Pecado and Mandioca and the others. Gently Nelio woke up Alfredo Bomba, coaxing him out of his deep slumber. When Alfredo Bomba opened his eyes, Nelio was bending over his face.

"Do you hear the wind?" he asked.

Alfredo Bomba listened. Then he nodded weakly.

"It's the wind from the sea," Nelio said. "We're on our way to the island that your mother told you about."

"I must have fallen asleep," Alfredo Bomba said. "Was I sleeping? Where are we?"

"On a ship," Nelio said, his torso swaying slowly. "Do you feel the swells?"

Alfredo nodded again. Nelio helped him to sit up, leaning him against the side of the stage.

Then he left Alfredo Bomba sitting there alone and went back to his light panel.

In his old age, when death had already taken root in his body, Old Alfredo Bomba made the journey that he had dreamed of and prepared for all his life. One night, when the tide was out and the water had retreated, he waded out to a little fishing boat with a lateen sail that was going to carry him along the coast to the estuary, which only those trusted by their mothers could find. On board the fishing boat was an invisible helmsman, a dog and a man with a sack of rice; a shipwrecked monster appeared occasionally at the side of the boat. They navigated by the stars and held a steady course for the second star in Pegasus. Before dawn, they were struck by a storm from the northeast; the wind tore at the sail, thunder boomed and bolts of lightning criss-crossed each other. Afterward the sea was calm again, the shipwrecked monster seemed to have perished in the waves, and the man with the rice sack stood motionless in the bow, searching for the mouth of the river. The dog was lying next to Alfredo Bomba. It had hands instead of paws, but with the wisdom of his years, Alfredo Bomba realized that journeys along unknown coasts meant traveling in the company of strange creatures that no one had ever seen before. They drew close to land in the early dawn. The coast was lined with steep cliffs. The man in the bow offered a handful of rice to the sea, and then a river broke through the cliffs. They sailed up the river, which at first was very wide. The monster returned in the shape of a crocodile. But Alfredo Bomba felt quite safe in the company of the invisible helmsman, the dog and the man with the sack of rice. On the riverbanks people were visible, and they all waved to him. Alfredo Bomba had the feeling that he recognized the people waving to him, just as he thought the dog lying at his side was a dog he had met earlier in his life. But he thought this might have been when he was quite young, still only a child. After they had been sailing for a long time, the boat scraped against an invisible sand bar in the middle of the river. The dog stood up on his human-like hind legs, picked up the sack of rice, and waded off toward an island, which lay close to the place where the boat was stranded. The man who had been standing in the bow throughout the voyage, ceaselessly scanning the waters, now turned his head for the first time. Alfredo Bomba seemed to recognize him too. It was a face that came gliding toward him out of his past. Then he remembered who it was.

"Pecado," he said. "Is it really you?"

"Pecado was my father. I am his son."

"I remember him," Alfredo Bomba said dreamily. "You look a lot like him. But he didn't have a crooked mustache under his nose."

"Here we are. Let me help you ashore."

Pecado's son helped the feeble Alfredo Bomba out of the boat. For a moment they were wrapped in the sea, which resembled a blue silk cloth. They waded a short distance before stepping ashore. The light was now quite strong, as if the sun had grown and was shining with many eyes above his head. Pecado's son set Alfredo Bomba down in a deck chair and opened a parasol over his head. The dog lay down at his side again; the boat and the crocodile had disappeared. It was very quiet.

"What happened to your father?" asked Alfredo Bomba, who felt the silence on the little sandy island carrying him back in time with dizzying speed.

"It was my son who led you here," Pecado said. "I am his father."

Alfredo Bomba looked at him in surprise. Then he noticed that the mustache under his nose was gone. It really was Pecado who was standing next to him.

"Everything seems so long ago," said Alfredo Bomba, and he felt the sea slowly beginning to seep into his body. A wave had started rippling inside his skin.

"You've grown old too," he continued, still looking at Pecado in amazement.

Pecado smiled. Then he pointed at the river. Alfredo Bomba squinted in the glare of the sunlight. He saw Nelio wading toward him with his trouser legs rolled up. At his side were Nascimento, Mandioca and Tristeza. Soon they had gathered around him. He saw that they were all old, just like him.

"I thought we would never see each other again," said Alfredo Bomba. "I no longer understand what I was always so afraid of."

"We're here," Nelio said. "Wherever friends gather, there is never room for fear."

Alfredo Bomba felt the wave inside him growing stronger and stronger. It was about to carry him away toward something unknown but not yet feared. The water was warm, and he felt pleasantly drowsy. The sunlight was dazzling, and the faces around him were slowly being erased.

"Who brought me here?" he asked. "I should thank the man who stood at the helm."

"It was your mother," said the voice that belonged to Nelio, although Alfredo could no longer see his face.

"Where is she?" asked Alfredo Bomba. "I can't see her."

"She's standing behind you," someone said, and now it was the dog lying next to him who was talking.

Alfredo Bomba didn't have the strength to turn his head. But he felt her warm breath on his neck. The wave rippled inside him, he was very tired, and he thought that it was a long time since he had had any sleep. He closed his eyes, his mother was sitting right behind him on the sand, and he now knew that he had been afraid for no reason. What had happened would keep on happening: his friends would always be with him.

Then the suns were extinguished around him, one after the other. He smiled at the thought of the strange dog that had human hands instead of paws. He must remember to tell Nelio when he woke up. A dog that had hands instead of paws . . .

*

They stood around him, watching him sleep.

"He's smiling," Nascimento said. "But he didn't applaud. I think he was afraid of the monster."

"Be quiet," Nelio said. "You talk too much, Nascimento."

Nelio looked at Alfredo Bomba's face. He wore an expression that he had never seen before. Then he understood that Alfredo Bomba was dead. He took a step back.

"He's dead," said Nelio.

At first they didn't understand what he meant. Then they saw for themselves that Alfredo Bomba was no longer breathing, and they backed away.

"Were we that bad?" said Mandioca.

"I think we did the best we could," replied Nelio, and his voice was thick with sorrow.

None of them said a word. Nascimento had turned his back and fled inside the monster's head.

A rat rustled under the stage.

Then everything happened very fast.

The doors at the back of the theater were flung open. Someone screamed. In the harsh glare of the spotlights they couldn't see who it was. Everyone except Nelio ran to the wings. Someone kept on screaming. Nelio understood that he should put up his hands, that he should surrender. He stood in front of Alfredo Bomba, who was lifeless in his deck chair, and thought that even a dead street kid deserved to be defended. Nelio walked toward the footlights to explain that nothing was going on. Two shots rang out in rapid succession. Nelio was thrown backward and lay full-length on the stage, at Alfredo Bomba's feet. He felt his vision grow hazy and he began to sink. He vaguely sensed that someone was looking down at him. Maybe it was Julio, one of the watchmen from outside the theater. But the face was blurred, and he wasn't positive that he recognized the voice either. It might also be the transparent face of death, which had come for Alfredo Bomba, but had now decided to take him too—that's what he thought.

The face that was bending over him vanished. He heard footsteps running, fading into the distance. Then it was quiet again. The light from the spotlights was dazzling. He closed his eyes. Every time he took a breath, pain sliced through him. It felt as if he had a hole all the way through his body. In spite of the pain, he tried to work out what had happened. It must have been the thunder, he thought. I should have known that the sound of someone rattling and shaking the thunder sheets would be heard out on the street. The watchmen would start to wonder, and they would think we were thieves who had broken in. And they started shooting because they were afraid of being shot themselves. If I had stood perfectly still, they might have noticed that I'm only a child.

He heard footsteps again. This time they were familiar. Thin paws were cautiously treading across the stage. The group had come back. Nelio opened his eyes and saw their terrified faces. He did his utmost to hide from them how much pain he was in.

"You have to take Alfredo Bomba away," he said. "You can't leave him lying on the street or in a ditch. You have to see to it that he has a proper burial. Take him to the morgue and give the night watchman the money we have left. Then they'll take him to the cemetery tomorrow after it gets light. But before you leave, you have to put everything back the way it was when we came."

"Are you going to stay here?" Nascimento asked him.

"I'm just going to rest," replied Nelio. "I'll come later. Now do what I say. Even though I'm bleeding a lot, it's not as serious as it looks. Hurry. Dawn is almost here."

They did as he said. They hung the costumes back in place, they lifted up Alfredo Bomba, and then they carried him away.

All was quiet around Nelio again. He tried to sense whether he was going to die soon, or whether it was going to take time. The hole in his body didn't seem to be getting bigger. It hurt terribly when he breathed, but he wasn't going to die right away. He was not yet ready to follow Alfredo Bomba.

Nelio had been talking with his eyes closed. Now and then his voice was so faint that I had great trouble understanding what he was saying. But now he opened his eyes and looked at me.

"You know the rest," he said. "I lay there on the stage, you came, and you carried me up here to the roof. How long I've been here, I don't know."

"This is the ninth night," I said.

"The ninth night, and the last. I can tell I won't be able to hold out much longer. I'm already starting to leave my body."

"I have to take you to the hospital," I said. "There are doctors who can make you well."

Nelio looked at me for a long time before he replied.

"No one can make me well. You know that."

I gave him some water. There was nothing else I could do.

Somewhere out in the darkness I could hear two drunks arguing. I put my hand on Nelio's forehead and felt that it was very hot.

"I have nothing more to tell you," Nelio said. "It feels like my life has lasted so long. I'm glad you were the one who found me and carried me up here to the roof. I also want to ask you to burn my body when I am no longer living."

He saw that I gave a start at the thought.

"How could you carry me away from here?" he said. "How could you explain that I've been lying here on the roof and died. You must burn my body in order to get rid of me."

He was right.

"It will take an hour for me to disappear," he said. "My body is so small."

When he had asked me to do this last favor for him and he understood that I would do as he wished, he asked me again for some water. Then he closed his eyes and turned away from the world. His face was very peaceful.

What were his last words? Did he say anything else?

Even a year later, I am uncertain. But I don't think he said anything else.

My body is so small.

That was the last thing he said.

The night was quiet. I sat and looked at his pale face in the glow from the flickering lamp.

I remember that for some strange reason his face reminded me of the sea. It was etched with the experience of eternity.

An errant gust of wind swept its hand across the roof and brought with it a chill. When it departed, Nelio was gone.

And the ninth night approached its dawn.

Dawn

I will never forget that morning.

When I left the bakery, I stepped out into a dawn light that I had never witnessed before. Or was it my eyes that had changed, so that they could now take in the secrets of the light, the blush of dawn, colored by Nelio's invisible spirit, which was floating free in its own space? I stood motionless on the street; the insight that Nelio had given me up there on the roof, that a human being is always at the center of the world, no matter where he finds himself, now seemed to me quite self-evident.

A rat was sitting beside a cracked manhole cover, watching me with nervous eyes.

A slight tremor passed through the earth. I had never experienced such a thing before, but I knew what it was. The old people who had survived it in Dom Joaquim's first years as governor had recounted how the earth began to shake, how the ground had opened up, and how houses had collapsed. Those who had lived so long that they could remember that time had been waiting ever since for the tremors to come back one day, and for the earth to crack open again. I knew that was why so many old people refused to set foot on stairs or to have their beds on the first or second floor of buildings in the city of stone. They wanted to live on the ground, close to the earth, even though the fissure might open up right at their feet. They would rather be swallowed up by the warm earth than be crushed under a collapsing building.

The tremors were brief, barely more than ten seconds. Flakes of cement fell from the bakery walls, a windowpane rattled. The rat disappeared underground. That was all. Then it was quiet once more. The early-morning people out on the streets—the drowsy street kids, workers and *empregados* on their way to various jobs—stopped in their tracks. It seemed as if the quake didn't really register in their bodies; it was more like a sound they seemed to hear, a feeling that something unusual was about to happen. When it was over, there was a vast silence. The city held its breath. Then a great turmoil erupted. People came rushing out of the buildings, many still in their nightclothes. Some carried small boxes containing their valuables, others seemed to have grabbed the nearest object without thinking. I saw people holding little mirrors, fans, a frying pan. The panic was palpable. Everyone stood in small, anxious groups in the middle of the street so as not to risk being struck by toppling buildings.

It was then that I noticed something quite strange. Everyone was looking up, to the sky and the sun, even though the tremors had come from below, an invisible shaking inside the earth. I still don't understand why they did that, although I've thought about it a great deal during the past year.

I must have been the only person who wasn't afraid.

Not because I'm so brave or fearless, but because I was the only one who knew what had happened. The trembling we heard or felt, as if it were some extraordinary portent, was Nelio's spirit breaking free from the last bonds that tied him to this world and, with violent force, slinging itself through the transparent barrier that forms the border to the other world, where his ancestors and those who once lived in the burned village were waiting for him. Alfredo Bomba would be there too, and this life was already a distant memory, like some mysterious dream only partly remembered. I looked at the people huddled together and thought that I ought to climb up on the roof of a car and explain what had happened. But I didn't. I simply left and went down to the shore, where I sat down in the shade of a tree with roots almost completely exposed by the shifting sand. I sat there looking out to the sea, at the small fishing boats with their triangular sails that were heading into the wide band of sunshine.

My sorrow was heavy. The dignity with which Nelio had left this world could only partially ease my pain of being left behind. At the same time I didn't know whether I could fully trust my own judgment. I was worn out after the long nights, I was exhausted in a way that I had never before experienced in all my life.

And I fell asleep sitting there next to the tree in the sand. My dreams were troubled. Nelio was alive, he had been transformed into a dog that I was trying to find as I dashed through the city. When I woke up I was soaked with sweat and extremely thirsty. From the sun I could tell that I had been asleep for hours. I walked down to the water's edge and rinsed my face. When I went back to the city, I saw that the commotion of the morning had subsided. Here and there people stood talking about the strange shaking inside the earth, but already it seemed a distant memory. They were now waiting for the next time, maybe in a hundred years, when it would happen again.

I reached the bakery and saw that the bakers were hard at work pulling the baking pans out of the ovens. Next to one of the ovens I noticed a scrap of the bandage that Nelio had worn around his chest on the last night. It must have come loose when I shoved his body into the fire. I glanced around and then snatched up the scrap of cloth and tossed it into the flames. Then I went out to the back courtyard and washed my whole body. I thought that now I ought to go back to the home I shared with my brother and his family. My life would now return to the way it was before I heard the shots fired in the deserted theater that night. Nelio was gone. But Maria was still here, with her smile, along with all the bread that we had yet to bake during the countless nights that lay ahead of us.

But it was still too early. I went up to the roof, almost expecting to find Nelio there, his face pale with fever. But there was only the mattress, hollowed by the impression of his thin body. I shook it and then leaned it against the chimney to air. I folded the blanket, which I had to return to the night watchman. There was nothing else. I stuffed the cup that had held Senhora Muwulene's herbs into my pocket. Just as I was about to leave, I noticed the cat, which had come to visit on several nights, curling up at Nelio's feet or by his head. I tried to entice it to come closer, but without success. The cat kept its wary distance. When I stood up to go, it was still sitting there, staring at me. That was the last time I saw it. During all the nights I have since spent up here on the roof, the cat has never once come back.

Sometimes I think that the cat must have followed Nelio across to the other world. Maybe cats can keep on living in the land of the dead.

When I came down from the roof, Dona Esmeralda had arrived. She had brought along a bag of money—God knows where she got it—and she sat down on her stool and paid out the wages with her thin, wizened fingers. Although she was not miserly, it always seemed hard for her to let the money go. I think I understood why. There was so much she needed to do for her theater, so many other things she would have liked to use the money for. Not for herself. Dona Esmeralda never bought anything for herself. The hat she wore was at least fifty years old, as were her clothes and the shabby shoes on her feet.

"Did you feel the earthquake?" she asked me.

"Yes," I replied. "The earth shook. Twice—like in a dream when you shudder from something unexpected."

"I remember when it happened before," she said. "It was during my father's time. The priests thought it was an omen that the world was about to end."

We said nothing more. I repaid the money I had borrowed from the girls at the bread counter and then left the bakery. The street kids were scavenging for food in the garbage cans, the Indian shopkeepers were pushing up the heavy iron gratings on their windows and doors; the air was filled with the smell of corn gruel cooking; and no one, not one person, knew that Nelio was dead.

Without knowing why, I stopped outside one of the Indian shops and walked into the dim interior. Everything was the same as always. Behind the cash register sat a fat Indian woman, keeping an eye on her black sales clerks. A very old man bowed and asked me what I wanted.

What I wanted?

"I want Nelio back," I said. "I want him to be alive again."

The old man gave me a meditative look.

"We don't have that," he said softly. "But if senhor would like to try the shop across the street. . . . They have unusual items. They import directly from those countries where people have slanting eyes."

I thanked him. Then I bought a hat. There were some hanging on the wall behind him, and I pointed to the one in the middle.

"A hat is nice in the heat," said the old man, unhooking it with a long stick that had a claw on the end.

The hat was white, with a black band around the crown. He wrote out an order, which I took to the woman at the cash register. As I was taking out my money, I realized that it cost more than half my month's wages. I picked up my new hat, set it on my head and went back out into the sunlight.

I walked to a café and had some food. My mind was empty.

In the evening I returned to the bakery. Maria was already there.

Her dress was gauzy and thin, her smile was broad.

"Did you feel the earthquake?" I asked.

"No," she said and smiled. "I was asleep." Then we began working. At midnight I followed her out to the street. I touched her arm as we parted. She smiled.

That night I did not go up to the roof. When I needed some air, I went out to the street and sat on the steps.

The following day I returned home to my brother and his family. They were very glad to see me. My sister-in-law wondered whether I was ill.

"A man who buys a new hat isn't ill," said my brother. "A man does as he pleases. He goes home if he wants to, or he stays away."

I lay awake in my bed for a long time, listening to all the sounds coming through the thin walls.

I knew that something was happening inside me, but I did not know what it was.

Not yet.

Several weeks passed. I baked my bread, touched Maria's arm, and hung my hat on the hook next to the ovens. On a few occasions when I didn't feel like going home in the morning, I crawled through the ventilation shafts and watched Dona

Esmeralda's rehearsals of the play about the revolutionary elephants. Different actors tried out for the role of Dom Joaquim, but none of them in Dona Esmeralda's eyes was suitable. The actors seemed more and more confused about the meaning of the drama. They tried playing it in various ways: as a tragedy, a comedy and a farce. But no matter what they did, the elephant trunks got in the way. One time the beautiful, young and pampered Elena started to cry onstage. It looked so odd to see her trying to wipe her tears behind the trunk. That was the only time I laughed during those days after Nelio's death. A single laugh that floated weightless in the space where I no longer felt at home.

One night I followed Maria out to the street, saw her smile and watched her leave. I went back into the bakery, shoved the baking pan into the oven, and closed the door.

I knew then that this would be the last night I worked for Dona Esmeralda.

I would finish up everything. In the morning I would wash myself at the back of the bakery; I would take my hat and leave, never to return.

I had come to the realization that I could no longer be a baker. I had a different mission for the rest of the days that were allotted to my life. I had to tell Nelio's story. The world could not get along without it. I would not allow his story to be forgotten.

After more than a year I can still remember that moment quite clearly. I didn't actually make a decision. The decision already existed inside me, but it wasn't until that moment that I knew what I had to do. I thought about how I would miss the fragrance of fresh bread. I would miss Maria and her gauzy dresses. Maybe I would even miss Dona Esmeralda and her theater.

And yet that moment was not a difficult one. I think it would be more truthful to say that it was a relief.

In the morning, after I had washed and then taken my hat from its hook, I waited for Dona Esmeralda to tell her of my decision. But she didn't come. Finally I turned to one of the enticing girls at the bread counter.

"I'm quitting today," I said, tipping my hat. "Tell Dona Esmeralda that José Antonio Maria Vaz will not be working here any more. Tell her that I've enjoyed the time I've worked here. And tell her that I will never, for as long as I live, bake bread for any other baker."

Was it Rosa I spoke to? I remember her surprised look. Who would be so stupid as to voluntarily quit working for Dona Esmeralda? With thousands of people already out of work, with no money and no food?

"You heard me right," I told her, tipping my hat again. "I'm leaving now, and I won't be back."

But that was not entirely true. I had already decided to wait for Maria that evening. I wanted to see her because I wanted to say good-bye and wish her good luck in the future. Maybe deep inside I hoped that she would come with me? I don't know. But where would she have followed me? Where was I actually going?

My answer was: I didn't know. I was carrying out an important mission, but I didn't know which way to go.

After I left the bakery on that last morning, I felt a great sense of freedom. I couldn't even see why I should grieve for Nelio.

Maybe it would be better to grieve for Alfredo Bomba, who probably would not be happy where he was now. For a long time he would no doubt be yearning for his life on the street, for the group of street kids, for the garbage cans and the cardboard boxes outside the Ministry of Justice.

That's the way it is. A person can yearn for a garbage can or for life eternal. It all depends.

I went over to the plaza where Nelio's equestrian statue stood. When I got there, I saw to my astonishment that it had fallen over. There was a great crowd in the plaza. The Indian shopkeepers had not opened their shops, but Manuel Oliveira, on the other hand, had thrown wide the doors of his church.

The equestrian statue had fallen.

I realized that the tremors of the day before had been strong enough to crack the foundation of the heavy statue. The bronze horse and rider lay on their side; the man's helmet was crushed. The last remnant of a bygone era had been toppled. Reporters from the city's newspapers scribbled notes, a photographer took pictures, and children had already started playing and jumping on Dom Joaquim's last monument.

Manuel's church was crowded with people. They were rattling off their prayers as a safeguard and incantation that the tremors would not return. Old Manuel stood under the tall black cross at the far end of the church, looking at the miracle that had occurred. He might have been crying; I was so far away that I couldn't tell for sure. I left the plaza, thinking that Nelio's spirit was hovering above my head. His suffering was over, the bullets in his body could no longer poison him. As one last salute, he had made the horse in whose belly he had lived topple to the ground. For hours I sat on a bench near the hospital, where there's a view of the whole city. From there, if I squinted, I could even see the rooftop where Nelio had lain for the nine nights he told me his story.

I had much to think about. Where would I live? What would I live on? Who would give a man who has only a story to tell the food that he needs? I sat there on the bench in the shade, growing more uneasy.

Then I thought about the children who live on the streets; I thought about Nelio, Alfredo Bomba, Pecado and the others. They found their food in garbage cans, the free meals of the poor. That food was there for me too. I could live anywhere. Like a lizard I would seek out a crack in the wall that was wide enough for me. There were cardboard boxes, rusting cars. The city was full of places to live that cost nothing.

I knew that I could no longer live with my brother and his family. That was a home that belonged to the life I had left behind. I got up from the bench feeling strangely elated. I had been worrying for no reason. I was a rich man. I had Nelio's story to tell. I needed nothing else.

That evening I waited in the dark outside the bakery for Maria. When I saw her coming, I suddenly didn't dare approach her. I tried to hide in the dark, but she had already seen me. Her dress was gauzy, and she was smiling. I stepped out of the shadows; I felt almost like an actor emerging from the wings on to the illuminated stage. I hastily ran my hand over my face to make sure there was no elephant trunk stuck to my nose. Then I tipped my hat.

"Maria," I said. "How could I ever forget a woman who sleeps so soundly that an earthquake can't wake her? What were you dreaming about?"

She laughed and tossed back her long black *tranças*.

"My dreams are my own concern," she said. "But I like your hat. It suits you."

"I bought it so that I could tip it for you," I said.

Her expression was suddenly somber. "Why are you standing out here?"

I had taken off my hat and was holding it to my chest, as if

I were at a funeral. I told her the truth. That everything was over. That I had quit.

"Why?"

"I have a story that I have to tell," I said.

To my astonishment, she seemed to understand me. She didn't seem surprised like the girl at the bread counter had been.

"You must do what you have to do," she said.

Then we parted. She hurried to the bakery. She didn't want to be late. I didn't even have time to touch her arm. That was the last time she stood so close to me.

Maria, the woman I will never forget, is close at my side. The Maria I sometimes see on the streets, from a distance, is someone else.

I watched her leave. She turned around once, waved and smiled. I took off my hat and held it in my hand until she was gone. I never put that hat on again. I didn't need it any more. I set it on top of a garbage can that was nearby. Later I thought I saw what was left of my hat on a street kid's head. It seemed to me that the hat liked being where it was.

A year has passed since Nelio died.

I watched Maria disappear, and then I walked into my new life. I started living as a beggar, looking for food in garbage cans, sleeping in the crannies of buildings and walls. And I started telling my story.

Nelio's group disbanded. I sometimes saw Nascimento, who had joined a group of the wildest kids, the ones who lived outside the central marketplace. He seemed the same as usual. He took his cardboard box with him wherever he went. I wondered whether he would ever manage to kill the monsters inside him. Although now he had a knife, which he often sat and sharpened.

I found Pecado one day when I was wandering around the rich people's district of the city. He was selling flowers on a street corner. I wondered whether he had grown them in his own pockets the way Mandioca did. He must have been doing good business, because he was wearing clean clothes with no holes in them.

Tristeza I stumbled upon one time outside one of the big cafés where tourists and *cooperantes* tend to gather. He was sleeping in the middle of the pavement, and his sneakers were gone. He was barefoot again. He was the filthiest street kid I've ever seen. He stank. He had permanent sores from fleas and scabies, and he was itching and scratching in his sleep. He was terribly skinny, and I thought that Nelio had been right. He wouldn't last long in this world, which didn't need people who were slow-witted. I left without waking him, and I never saw him again.

Mandioca was gone. For a long time I wondered whether some accident had befallen him, or whether he was dead. By chance, much later on, I found out that he had voluntarily gone to one of the big buildings where white-clad nuns give children clothing and food. He had decided to stay. And I don't think he ever did go back to the streets.

I even saw Deolinda again.

That's one of the darkest memories I have from the year that has passed since Nelio lay on the rooftop and died.

It was late one night, on one of the main streets that leads past the area where the pavement restaurants are, near the rich district of town where a lot of *cooperantes* have their houses. I don't remember where I was going, since I'm seldom on my way to anywhere except where my feet happen to take me. Girls were always standing at the intersections, offering themselves. I found it embarrassing to walk past them, and I usually fixed my gaze on the pavement or in some other direction. But on a street corner, late one night, I saw Deolinda. She was heavily made up, almost unrecognizable; she was wearing provocative clothes, and she was tapping her foot impatiently. After I had walked past, I stopped and turned. I hoped that one day Cosmos would come back from his long journey and take care of his sister.

I hoped that it wouldn't be too late.

At night, when I'm on my way to my rooftop, I sometimes stop outside a restaurant to listen to the music. Whenever I hear the monotonous but lovely notes of *timbila*, I'm drawn back in my mind to the nights that I spent with Nelio. I could stand there for hours, listening. From the music rise voices, forgotten long ago by everyone except me.

One time I went out to the big cemetery when Nelio spent a night in Senhor Castigo's tomb. I found my way over to the section reserved for the graves of the poor. Somewhere lay the remains of Alfredo Bomba's body. His bones had already become mixed with others in the earth; they lay there, packed together, one person's jawbone next to someone else's hand, and they cried out like a choir, in utter despair at their desolation. I seemed to sense the restless dance of all the spirits that cannot find peace, and as long as the spirits are not content, the war will continue to ravage this land.

My story is drawing to a close. I have told everything, and now I will start over again.

I know that I am called the Chronicler of the Winds because no one has yet made the effort to listen to what I have to say.

But I know the day will come.

It will come because it has to come.

*

A year has passed since the shots were fired.

I spend my nights on the roof of the theater.

That's where I still belong.

The baker who works during the quiet hours of the night, the man who replaced me, will never tell anyone that I'm there. Sometimes he shares his food with me.

I need the silence of the roof after the long days under the searing sun. I still have my mattress. Here I can lie and look up at the stars before I fall asleep. Here I can think about everything that Nelio told me before he died. I know that I have to keep telling his story even if only the winds from the sea listen to what I have to say. I have to keep talking about this earth, which is sinking farther and farther into unconsciousness, where people must live to forget and not to remember. I have to keep speaking so that the dreams will not grow hot with fever, then cool and finally die. It's as if Nelio wants to place his hand on the earth's forehead and mix Senhora Muwulene's herbs into the rivers and oceans of the world. The earth is sinking farther and farther, the groups of street children are more numerous and grow larger—the street children who live in the poorest of countries, the lands of street children.

My story is done, but it keeps on starting over. In the end it will hover like an invisible note, embedded in the wind that ceaselessly blows from the sea. It will exist in the raindrops falling on the parched earth, and in the end it will exist in the air we breathe. I know that it's true, what Nelio told me, that our last hope is to remember who we are, that we are human beings who will never be able to control the warm winds from the sea, but maybe one day we will understand why the winds must always continue to blow.

I, José Antonio Maria Vaz, a lonely man on a rooftop under the starry tropical sky, have a story to tell . . .

ALSO BY HENNING MANKELL

FACELESS KILLERS

It was a senselessly violent crime: on a cold night in a remote Swedish farmhouse an elderly farmer is bludgeoned to death, and his wife is left to die with a noose around her neck. And as if this didn't present enough problems for the Ystad police Inspector Kurt Wallander, the dying woman's last word is *foreign*, leaving the police the one tangible clue they have—and in the process, the match that could inflame Sweden's already smoldering anti-immigrant sentiments.

Crime Fiction/978-1-4000-3157-3

THE DOGS OF RIGA

On the Swedish coastline, two bodies, victims of grisly torture and cold execution, are discovered in a life raft. With no witnesses, no motives, and no crime scene, Wallander is frustrated and uncertain he has the ability to solve a case as mysterious as it is heinous. But after the victims are traced to the Baltic state of Latvia, a country gripped by the upheaval of Soviet disintegration, Major Liepa of the Riga police takes over the investigation. Wallander thinks his work is done, until he is called to Riga and plunged into an alien world where shadows are everywhere, everything is watched, and old regimes do anything to stay alive.

Crime Fiction/978-1-4000-3152-8

THE WHITE LIONESS

When Wallander is called in to investigate the execution-style murder of a Swedish housewife, it initially seems like a routine case. He uncovers a suspicious stalker who may have committed the murder out of brutal passion. But when the suspect's alibi turns out to be airtight, Wallander must look deeper into the case, and what he discovers is far more complex—and dangerous—than he ever imagined: he soon uncovers an assassination plot and finds himself entangled with the secret police and a KGB agent.

Crime Fiction/978-1-4000-3155-9

SIDETRACKED

A teenage girl has been loitering in a rapeseed field all day, and Wallander arrives just in time to watch her douse herself in gasoline and set herself aflame. The next day he is called to a beach where Sweden's former minister of justice has been axed to death and scalped. The murder has the obvious markings of a demented serial killer, and Wallander is frantic to find him before he strikes again. But his investigation is beset with obstacles—a distracted department, a long-distance relationship with a murdered policeman's widow, and his unshakably haunting preoccupation with the young girl who set herself on fire.

Crime Fiction/978-1-4000-3156-6

THE FIFTH WOMAN

In an African convent, four nuns and a unidentified fifth woman are brutally murdered. A year later in Sweden, Wallander is baffled and appalled by two murders. Holger Eriksson, a retired car dealer and bird-watcher, is impaled on sharpened bamboo poles in a ditch behind his secluded home, and the body of a missing florist is discovered—strangled and tied to a tree. What ensues is a case that will test Wallander's strength and patience, because in order to discover the reason behind these murders, he will also need to uncover the elusive connection between these deaths and the earlier unsolved murder in Africa of the fifth woman.

Crime Fiction/978-1-4000-3154-2

ONE STEP BEHIND

On Midsummer's Eve, three role-playing teens dressed in eighteenth-century garb are shot in a secluded Swedish meadow. When one of Inspector Wallander's most trusted colleagues—someone whose help he hoped to rely on to solve the crime—also turns up dead, he knows the murders are related. But with his only clue a picture of a woman no one in Sweden seems to know, he can't begin to imagine how. Reeling from his own father's death and facing his own deteriorating health, Wallander tracks the lethal progress of the killer.

Crime Fiction/978-1-4000-3151-1

FIREWALL

A body is found at an ATM, the apparent victim of heart attack. Then two teenage girls are arrested for the brutal murder of a cab driver. At first these two incidents seem to have nothing in common, but as Wallander delves deeper into the mystery of why the girls murdered the cab driver he begins to unravel a plot much more involved than he initially suspected. The two cases become one and lead to a conspiracy that stretches outside Sweden.

Crime Fiction/978-1-4000-3153-5

BEFORE THE FROST

Having just graduated from the police academy, Linda Wallander returns to Skåne to join the police force, and she already shows all the hallmarks of her father—the maverick approach, the flaring temper. Before she even starts work she becomes embroiled in the case of her childhood friend Anna, who has inexplicably disappeared. As the case her father is working on dovetails with her own, they soon find themselves forced to confront a group of extremists bent on punishing the world's sinners.

Crime Fiction/978-1-4000-9581-0

THE RETURN OF THE DANCING MASTER

When retired policeman Herbert Molin is found brutally slaughtered on his remote farm in the northern forests of Sweden, police find strange tracks in the snow, as if someone had been practicing the tango. Stefan Lindman, a young police officer recently diagnosed with mouth cancer, decides to investigate the murder of his former colleague, but is soon enmeshed in a mystifying case with no witnesses and no apparent motives. Terrified of the disease that could take his life, Lindman becomes more and more reckless as he unearths the chilling links between Molin's death and an underground neo-Nazi network.

Crime Fiction/978-1-4000-7695-6

ALSO BY HENNING MANKELL

"Wallander is a loveable gumshoe. . . . He is one of the most credible creations in contemporary fiction."
—The Guardian *(London)*

THE MAN WHO SMILED

After killing a man in the line of duty, Kurt Wallander resolves to quit the Ystad police. However, a bizarre case gets under his skin. A lawyer driving home at night stops to investigate an effigy sitting in a chair in the middle of the highway. The lawyer is hit over the head and dies. Within a week the lawyer's son is also killed. These deeply puzzling mysteries compel Wallander to remain on the force. The prime suspect is a powerful corporate mogul with a gleaming smile that Wallander believes hides the evil glee of a killer. Joined by Ann-Britt Höglund, Wallander begins to uncover the truth, but the same merciless individuals responsible for the murders are now closing in on him.

Crime Fiction/978-1-4000-9583-4

Forthcoming from Vintage Crime/Black Lizard in fall 2007 . . .

VINTAGE CRIME/BLACK LIZARD
Available at your local bookstore, or visit www.randomhouse.com.